REGENERATION

Infiltration Series (Book 2)

SUSANNA ROGERS

Bucher & Reid

Bucher & Reid

Cover by Amygdala Book Design

978-0-6481868-3-0

DEDICATION

To my buddy, James,
because you're the best

.

ALSO BY SUSANNA ROGERS

Infiltration (Book 1)
Validation (Book 3) – out soon
Parallax Error – out early 2018

ACKNOWLEDGMENTS

I have too many people to thank and can't possibly do this in any particular order. I'm also very nervous I may have left someone out. A big thanks to James Rogers, Louis Rogers, Chris Kunz, Michael Cain, Lotte Plumb, Josie Kelly, Sacha Pulsford, Sophia Robbins, Annie Sommer, Stephanie Swain and a special mention to Taya Lunn because I made you cry and that made me very happy.

The list goes on – thanks to Claire Boston, Lorraine Mauvais, Juanita Kees, Teena Raffa-Mulligan and Anna Jacobs. Also to my technical and medical experts Tessa Plumb, Nick Stott, Tony Rogers, Andrew Tran, Jo Taylor and Brendan Murphy.

CHAPTER ONE

The martial arts arena was my kind of place, the only spot in school that felt comfortable. For me, anyway.

Ben sat close beside me on the mat, our thighs touching while we waited for an announcement. He laughed at a joke, then gave me a friendly nudge. "Sorry if all this messing around is interrupting your training schedule."

I was about to tell him that strictly speaking this wasn't an interruption because we hadn't started the afternoon's training yet, then saw the teasing twinkle in his eye. He knew me too well. Knew I was never going to get rid of the 'old' Nicola.

Mr. Matthews, the martial arts teacher, strode into the room with the principal at his side. While we were all wearing the regulation sports shorts and tee shirts, Ms. Di Giorgio had on a pair of killer heels and a tight, tailored suit.

"Good afternoon." She stuck her chest out, the buttons on her jacket in danger of bursting open. "We are being held up as the model school for all of California and this is only the beginning. You can all be truly proud to be students at Altabena High." When she got no reaction, she added, "This is an honor and we'll need increased discipline to attain even higher standards."

Her words reminded me of where I'd come from and why I was here. I had to be on my guard because I never knew where danger might be coming from. If my superiors discovered I was still alive, they'd kill me and then it'd be all too easy for them to get to Ben.

Ms. Di Giorgio smiled. "The other thing I wanted to tell you is that we're going to be the hosts for the inaugural martial arts contest for the southern schools region. And we're going to win! You're going to win this for the school!"

She held up her clenched fist. "Make no mistake, this contest is going to be huge. Word has it that State Ruler Bartley himself will be present to watch the contest and tour the school."

Ben and I exchanged glances, then I looked around. No one else cared. Why would they?

The State Ruler would one day become Supreme Ruler Bartley, but no one else here knew that and it'd be kind of hard for me to explain it to them.

The principal said a few closing words that were meant to be inspiring, then passed us back to Mr. Matthews who told us to get back to our training, which was fine by me.

Ben nuzzled closer to me and snuck in a quick kiss on the cheek. "Catch you later, Nic."

He joined his grappling buddies while I headed to the back of the room for my warm up, a combination of squats, lunges, sit ups, pushups and burpees, repeated until I was ready to drop. I was only half way through my third round when a tall girl about my age strode in to talk to Mr.

Matthews at the front of the mat.

Every head in the room turned. And stayed there. The mouth of every male in the room dropped open – every male, that is, except Mr. Matthews. I had to give him credit there. Meanwhile, I could swear some of the guys were drooling.

What a way to make an entrance.

The girl was a six-feet tall Nordic beauty, her blond hair tied back into a ponytail to better reveal high cheekbones, pale eyes and full lips. I wasn't sure what she was doing here when she could've been off making a killing as a supermodel. I pushed back some stray strands of hair behind my ears as I squatted. Suddenly 'brown' felt boring.

"What's the matter?" Mr. Matthews yelled. "Haven't you seen a girl before? Get back to work, the lot of you."

Yeah, what were they staring at? And why was Ben still looking at her?

Mr. Matthews waved to me, which was strange enough since I wasn't exactly his favorite student, then headed my way with the girl in tow.

He was grinning, also very unusual for him. "Nicola, I'd like you meet Dominique Savage."

Great. She had the exotic looks and the name to go with it while I was plain old Nicola Gray. She shook my hand but the smile on her face didn't reach her eyes. Then again, probably neither did mine.

"Dominique is our secret weapon," the teacher said.

I raised my eyebrows. "Sorry?"

"She's the secret weapon who's going to help us win the martial arts contest in front of State Ruler Bartley. Dominique is a judo expert. She trains every morning at the Sports Institute. In another couple of years, she'll be on the Olympic team, for sure."

As if I hadn't been through enough changes in the past months since coming here. As if I didn't find it hard enough to fit in even with Ben at my side. Now this.

"We can only put forward one competitor in the female division," Mr. Matthews said. "And that'll be Dominique."

My eyes widened. "Excuse me?"

"We'll have a bout between the two of you first to determine the winner, of course."

And he assumed Dominique would win? My blood was boiling.

The teacher turned to the girl. "Let's start you off with some grappling."

The two of them walked across the mat to meet the puppy dogs – sorry, grapplers – who were waiting with their mouths gaping, Ben included.

I kept an eye on the grapplers while I slammed into the bag, though apparently I wouldn't provide enough of a challenge for Dominique. One of the guys held the pads for me, only to complain because my kicks were so hard the reverberations were running through his forearms.

I used to be a secret weapon. I used to be on a mission. When had that changed?

After one of the hardest and yet least satisfying workouts of my martial arts career, I saw Moose heading toward Dominique. Mr. Matthews had left. This was typical Moose.

Hands on his hips, he was doing some serious macho posturing which made me assume he was trying to impress her. Then he said, "All due respect and everything but I just don't think a girl your size is any match for me."

Suddenly I was on her side. Dominique looked up at him from the floor where she was wrestling, though thankfully not with my boyfriend. Surely Moose couldn't be that stupid or maybe he just wanted to be manhandled by the new babe.

She raised one perfectly arched eyebrow. "You think so?"

He spread his arms. "It's just the way it is. Men are more muscular and are built for this sort of thing whereas you're built for…cooking and housework."

I hoped she cleaned him up.

Dominique stood slowly, brushing down the front of those lithe legs. Arms out, Moose lunged toward her but she was quicker. One arm around him, she had him behind her, knees bent, butt out. She flipped him over, both of them in the air for a split second before she landed on top. At least there was plenty to cushion her fall.

Dominique got to her feet while Moose moaned on the floor that his ribs had been broken. I doubted it.

Clapping and cheering brought a smile to her face. Made her giggle, in fact. A couple of girls high-fived her and the boys congratulated her. Behind me, I heard some kids mumbling about 'The Dominator'.

Moose moaned again so she placed one foot on his chest, her hand on one knee as she leaned over in a victory stance.

"I didn't quite catch that," she said.

He held his hands out. "I said I'm sorry!"

The others moved away, everyone relaxed and smiling, everyone except me. And maybe Moose. I actually felt sorry for him. How had that happened?

Dominique chatted to a small group, then made her way to the front of the room. The guys continued talking and training but it wasn't hard to tell they were all checking her out from behind. How shallow. Ben was still grinning, a couple of the guys slapping him on the back and joking around with him.

At the front of the room, Dominique was talking to Daniel, a scrawny Chinese guy, and his equally scrawny friend, Lorenzo. Normally the two of them were vying for academic excellence whereas now they appeared to be vying for female attention.

Dominique straightened, her body language telling me something wasn't right. I headed across the mat to join them.

She shoved Daniel in the shoulder, his eyes going wide with shock.

I stepped between them. "Hey, he didn't do anything."

Dominique's eyes narrowed. "Yes he did. He and his little friend were telling me about the video they took and how they were going to post it online."

"What's wrong with that?" I asked.

"Without my permission?"

"Just ask them to get rid of it. What's the big deal?"

She glared at Daniel first, then Lorenzo, both of them saying in unison, "We'll delete it."

Daniel turned the camera around, allowing her to watch while he pressed the delete button. "Sorry, we only use our skills for the forces of good, not evil."

Dominique shot them a look more devastating than any physical blow, then left.

"Are you guys okay?" I asked them.

Daniel looked more confused than scared. "Sure."

I glanced back at the mat, where no one seemed to have noticed what had gone on, then followed Dominique into the hallway.

"Hey," I yelled. "They didn't mean anything."

"Neither did I." She stopped and turned, hands on her hips.

"And they didn't deserve to be treated like that."

"Their problem, not mine."

Something didn't sit right with me. A lot didn't sit right. If she was here to get to Ben, he'd be caught completely unaware.

"Where did you say you were from?" I asked.

"I didn't say."

Reece headed toward the door, then slowed down. He was hard to miss with his fuzzy bleached hair and the regrowth from hell, and he was always hanging around, slipping into the martial arts arena, following me around though never speaking to me.

Dominique's upper lip curled in disgust. "What are you staring at?"

Carefully eyeing up the situation, he put his hands out and stepped back to leave without a word.

"What was with the hard ass routine with Daniel and Lorenzo?" I asked her.

She did the lifting-one-eyebrow-thing and held my gaze but I was pretty good when it came to a stare-down too.

Eventually she said, "There are really strict rules when it comes to the Olympics. They won't accept bad sportsmanship, and the martial arts judges are dead set against any sort of showboating."

"Why didn't you just say so?" I shrugged, tried to act

nonchalant. "Well, then there's no problem."

"Glad to hear it."

Dominique ducked inside the girls' locker room and I headed back toward the martial arts arena, only to be intercepted by Ben.

"Are you okay?" he asked. "What's up?"

I breathed a sigh of relief. He was trying to keep an eye on me, which was sweet even if it should've been the other way around.

"I'm fine," I said. "It's just–"

"Because I thought I saw Dominique head out here too."

I grabbed Ben's arm and started walking. "Let's get some fresh air."

The air outside was indeed fresh against our sweaty bodies though it never got freezing cold in Altabena even in the evening.

Leaning against a wall, I took one of Ben's hands in both of mine. "You have to be careful. We both do."

"What's brought this on all of a sudden?"

"There's nothing sudden about it."

"It's taken a long time but you've been a lot more relaxed lately," he said.

"Well, I shouldn't be."

He pulled his hand away. "This again?"

My heart sank. I'd been through this with him so many times before that I didn't know where to start. I came from the future, the year 2120. My superior officers in New Nation wanted Ben dead because one day he was going to develop a virus that would kill millions of people. That's what they said, but the Ben I knew was smart and serious and funny and would never do something like that.

One other thing I knew for sure – I was never going back to New Nation, not for anything, and I'd made sure my return would never be possible.

"The easiest way for them to get to you is to get rid of me first," I said. "That'd make you an easy target."

He raked a hand through the dark, wavy hair that looked good even when he was sweaty. "It's been months, Nicola. They think you're dead. They don't have a clue you're here any more."

I didn't know that. Not for sure.

"It's that new girl," I said. "There's something about her I don't like."

"Because she's good looking?"

"No, because she's highly skilled. She's from out of town and she's a ring-in. We don't know why she's here."

"To win the martial arts contest."

"What if she's like me? What if she's been sent here from the future?"

Ben waved his hands for me to stop. "Whoa, take it easy. She's not a spy or an assassin. Nicola, sometimes you need to chill."

Chill? I didn't do 'chilled'. I was intense and uptight and lots of other things including crazy in love with Ben. Without love, life wasn't worth living and there was nothing I wouldn't do for him – but I couldn't become chilled or cool or other descriptions involving the colder end of the spectrum.

I stared at him. "You're not listening."

"If she's out to get you, why didn't she just finish you off?"

"She might be gathering information first, like I was. She might be clearing the way for an army or waiting for clearance from her superiors."

He shook his head. "I don't believe it."

"What?"

"You're jealous."

My mouth fell open. That was the most ridiculous thing I'd ever heard. I'd been raised in the military and we suppressed all emotion, so I often had a hard time identifying them, not to mention dealing with them. But I was not jealous.

"Something about Dominique isn't right," I said.

"You're worried about nothing. Look, I've got other things going on in my life too, other than just…this."

"Ben, you can't let yourself become complacent. We've been through this before. You don't know what we might be up against or what strategy they might have next time."

At that moment, he switched off. I saw it in his eyes. A wave of anger swelled inside me.

"You can't see it," I said.

"You think so? Because sometimes you can't see what's right under your nose."

What was he talking about? Didn't he know how dangerous complacency could be? His life was on the line but because someone wasn't standing in front of him with a gun, he figured it wasn't a problem.

"I'll catch you later." He left.

I turned and hammer fisted the wall.

Ben wasn't like me. He hadn't been brought up by the military, hadn't been trained and drilled into submission, hadn't been stripped of all humanity.

He couldn't see we were never going to be completely safe. I had a pretty good idea what my superiors in New

Nation were capable of. Unfortunately I didn't know exactly what they would do, only that they would do something, and that was my biggest problem.

How could I fight something if I didn't know what was coming?

CHAPTER TWO

Tonight I was going to show Ben that I could be just as chilled as the next person and if that didn't work, I was going to do the next best thing and pretend. I was going to be Party Girl or my version of it.

He held my hand as he led me down the path at the side of the house, the music and shouting getting louder with each step.

When we reached the edge of the building, I squeezed his hand. We were in a small courtyard dominated by a huge maple that towered over the house.

Ben opened his mouth as if to say something, then pulled me protectively behind him as he headed into the yard where the party was in full swing. French doors led back into the house and I'd have to check the other exits. There was a lap pool jammed in along one side of the fence, a few kids were lounging around on a trampoline and there was even a red punching bag hanging up under the patio. Must be a family of exercise freaks. My kind of people. Why they had a bathtub in the back yard, I didn't know.

Ben let go of my hand and stared at me. "What?"

"Nothing."

I was hardly about to confirm I was in bodyguard mode checking out my surroundings.

"Got any beer?" I asked.

He grinned and swung his backpack off his shoulder. "Sure do."

I saw a flash of blonde and red through the corner of my eye and knew exactly what was coming. Or who.

Dominique could not have been more stunning in a long-sleeved, red jersey dress that looked like liquid poured over her body. Suddenly my jeans and my favorite baseball tee didn't seem good enough.

A hand on Ben's shoulder, she greeted him with a kiss on the cheek which he returned. I wished he didn't seem so pleased and that it didn't make me feel so lousy.

Dominique checked me out with a condescending look, then deigned to say hello. This was going to be a long night.

"Hi," I said.

"I've got to take care of the beers." Ben headed for the ice and suddenly the giant tub made a lot of sense.

He didn't make it far before Daniel and Lorenzo grabbed him.

"Just the man we wanted to see," Lorenzo said.

Daniel nodded. "Remember the other day we were talking about how an EMP could be used as a terrorist weapon by disabling electronic devices and leaving a city in chaos?" Ben looked at him blankly so he added, "An electro magnetic pulse."

"I remember, guys," Ben said. "But right now, beer is more important."

Daniel nudged Lorenzo and grinned. "I get it. Beer."

The two of them walked off, oblivious.

Dominique looked down her nose at Daniel. "Is that the dweeb who nearly ruined my chances with the Olympics?"

"He's a friend," I said. "Give him a break."

"I was thinking of breaking his leg."

I couldn't believe how self-centered one person could be. "Wow."

"Wow, what?"

"'Bye."

Maybe I'd misjudged her and she wasn't a soldier sent from the future. She was just a girl, albeit a not-very-ordinary and a not-very-nice one.

Ben was standing by the bathtub, a Pabst in his hand.

I walked across. "Is it okay if I have one?"

"Sure." He knocked back his beer and grabbed two more from the tub, passing one to me. "Unusual for you to drink."

It was all part of my plan for being chilled. "Just trying to get into the party mood."

His green eyes twinkled with a teasing look. "Wow, a whole beer." He drummed his fingers on the can, then took another slug. "I'm getting in the mood too. I'm going to get shit-faced."

That didn't sound like him but since I was 'chilled' I wasn't going to argue.

Lauren joined us and I'd never been so glad to see her. I hadn't seen nearly enough of her lately. Since my arrival in Altabena, I'd learnt that relationships were complex and needed tending. A bit like a garden. Not that I was any good at gardening either.

"Your hair looks gorgeous," I said.

She had blond foils in the brown hair that brushed the top of her shoulders in blow-dried perfection.

Her eyes went wide. "My God, Nicola. Is that a beer in your hand?"

I shrugged. "Sure."

She smiled. "But you're allergic. How will you cope?"

"Allergic to alcohol?" Will said. "What a bummer."

They'd been seeing each other for about a month. Will was the sort of guy Lauren wouldn't have noticed before because she wasn't looking. She was a little more open minded now.

"Lauren's kidding," I said. "It's kind of an in-joke. I won't break out into a rash or have a fit or anything."

"She also won't get drunk," Lauren said, a hint of disapproval in her voice.

"Why would I want to do that?" I asked.

Lauren smiled. "See!"

Will pulled her close and nuzzled into her neck, making her giggle. He was also one of the reasons I hadn't spent so much time with Lauren lately.

Ben wasn't far from us, drinking beer and laughing with some other guys.

One more job to do and then I'd relax. I excused myself to go to the bathroom and made my way toward the French doors.

Inside, a few people were draped over the sofas and others were chatting in the kitchen. The living room opened out from a central hallway that went down to the front door which was closed. I strode to the front to check it was properly secured.

Back in the yard, I chatted to Lauren and Will while Ben took a couple of shooters that were being passed around. Simone and Taylor, who were firmly part of the 'cool' crowd, stopped to talk. Last year Lauren worked out how mean they could be so she now preferred to ignore them, yet somehow that only made them want to talk to her more. I was never going to work some people out.

After a while, I checked out the side path again and popped back into the rear living area where I saw Daniel and Lorenzo playing table tennis through a set of glass doors.

I wandered in and watched for a bit. I'd never been allowed to play games when I was growing up because they were pointless. Which was their whole purpose.

Daniel saw me grinning. "You want to have a go?"

"Sure."

He very kindly explained the rules and gave me a few tips. I lost the first two games which made him smile but I had a feeling he knew what was coming. We played round after round with Lorenzo and Daniel alternating when one of them got tired.

I wasn't sure how much time passed before the sound of a wolf whistle from the next room cut through the air.

Daniel looked to the doorway. "Wonder what's going on."

So did I. A bad feeling in the pit of my stomach, I dropped my paddle on the table and headed for the door. The living room had been cleared and everyone was in the yard facing the back of the house, their heads tilted up, gawking at something.

I pushed past, then looked up. Ben was staggering on the roof, a Pabst in one hand while playing air guitar with the other and singing a truly terrible rendition of a song which, apparently, was called *Bad to the Bone*.

He was right about one thing. This was bad. I should never have let this happen and now my heart was pounding for all the wrong reasons.

"Ben," I yelled but he didn't hear me.

More shouting. "Another song! Sing us another song."

I pushed to the front, waving my arms. "Ben!"

Now I had his attention.

"Nicola!" Ben threw his hands up. "Damn, I spilt my beer. Can someone throw me up another one?"

Not far from me, one of the guys had an unopened can of beer and was taking aim, ready to toss it onto the roof.

I shoved two people out of the way and glared at the guy. He lowered the can.

"Come up here, Nicola," Ben yelled.

People around me cheered.

"It's a b-beautiful night. Come and dance with me." He held one arm out around an imaginary person and started wiggling his hips. More cheers.

Suddenly Lauren was beside me calling Ben's name and telling him to get off the roof. "The window's right behind you. Just climb back inside."

"You and Will make such a cute couple," Ben said. "Don't they make a cute couple?"

He had center stage and everyone around us thought this was hilarious even though he was staggering way too close to the edge of the roof for my liking.

"Keep him talking," I said to Lauren.

I steamrolled my way through the crowd to the tree at the side of the house and hoisted myself up, suddenly very grateful for my jeans and Converse sneakers. As I made it up onto the roof, the dormer window was open to my right and Ben was to my left.

I motioned toward him. "Come on, Ben. Let's go back inside."

"No, *you* come here."

Everything he said and did elicited a cheer. What was wrong with these people?

He held his hand out and I stepped closer and took it, then he threw his arms around me, mumbling my name over and over.

I held him at arm's length. "Let's go, Ben."

"A dance! You have to dance with me!"

His empty beer can clattered as he tossed it onto the other side of the roof and spun me around. His hand on my upper back, he dipped me like a professional tango dancer. My heart swam and sank. I wanted to be close to Ben but most of all I wanted him off the roof.

I stepped back. "Come on, Ben."

There was a huge round of applause so he turned and bowed to the crowd. He was leaning over the edge, teetering, suddenly swiping his arms through the air in an effort to stay upright.

It happened in slow motion. He tried to get his balance. I reached for his arm. I grabbed a piece of his shirt. Too late. He was already on his way over. I crouched down to lower my center of gravity so I didn't go over the edge too. All at once, I felt the pull of his weight, a force too great for me to handle, and a second later Ben was dangling over the edge of the roof. I had him by the hand. Only just.

He looked up at me, his eyes saying sorry, but that wasn't enough to keep me holding on forever.

"Get the trampoline!" I yelled. Though my eyes were

on Ben and his pitiful expression, I saw movement from the corner of my eye and desperately hoped the others were shifting the trampoline.

Slipping, slipping, gone…

As he slid from my grasp I felt a sense of hopelessness. So much was out of my control. I wanted to keep him safe forever and I couldn't. If anything happened to Ben, my heart would break into a thousand pieces.

I watched him fall backwards onto the trampoline in slow motion, then a cheer rose from the crowd and the world went back to regular time. Glad that was over, I turned to the dormer window behind me and crawled inside because it was so much more dignified than using the tree.

This could've been worse. Ben could've been hurt.

Ben…what was going on with him? I hadn't seen this coming, so how would I see what other threats lay ahead?

I found him in the back yard, one arm draped over Lauren, the other over Will who seemed to be holding him up.

"S-sorry, Nicola," he said.

I reached up and cradled his jaw in my hand briefly. He looked exhausted. Even his smile sagged. Maybe I should've been angry. Instead I was relieved.

"We've got to get you home," I said.

Ben kept repeating that he was sorry. The jingle of keys made me turn. It was hard to miss Reece, who stood out thanks to his mocha skin, bleached Afro hair and seemingly permanent regrowth. Now he was standing in front of us shaking a set of car keys.

I breathed a sigh of relief. "We'd love a lift home. Are you right to drive?"

"I haven't been drinking." And that was all he said for the entire trip back to Ben's house even though I thanked him repeatedly and said how much we both appreciated the ride home.

Ben managed to get out of the car on his own and Reece drove off. He was a strange one, always hanging around and watching, yet now when we needed him he was quite gracious in not making a big deal out of this.

I sat on the steps outside the front of Ben's house and he joined me, his head in his hands.

I wasn't even sure where to start. "What were you thinking, Ben?"

He didn't answer right away. "I'm sick of always doing the right thing."

"What's that supposed to mean?"

"I'm so pissed off with the whole world that I don't know why I bother." His head was still in his hands. "What's the point of getting good grades and being a good person? It doesn't stop me feeling like crap."

"What are you going on about?"

"I only wanted to get drunk. To forget."

"Getting drunk is one thing. Climbing onto the roof is another."

I hated saying it. I felt like somebody's mother.

He turned to stare at me, his face full of despair. "You think you're so smart."

I didn't like where this was headed. "Ben..."

"I saw you when we got to the party, checking out your surroundings, making note of the exits. It was a party, Nicola, not a military operation. We were supposed to have fun, hang out with friends, have a few drinks. Then you had a beer. No, I bet you didn't even have a whole beer."

My lips tight, I didn't say anything, didn't tell him it was just as well one of us was sober tonight.

"Dominique comes along and you think she's some sort of spy or assassin. Talk about ridiculous. You always think someone's out to get us." He stood and extended his arm as if addressing a crowd. "Hey, if anyone wants to kill me, I'm free now. If anyone wants to kill Nicola, she's here too. Come and get us."

He slumped back down onto the step beside me. "You don't even know what day this is."

I had no idea what was going on. "What…what day is it?"

He shrugged and gave me a look that was completely hopeless. "The anniversary of my mom's death."

Suddenly all the pieces fit. My poor, beautiful Ben.

"I'm sorry." I put my arm around him and held him close because I didn't know what else to do.

It was a while before he spoke again. "Every year for my mom's birthday, Dad bakes a cake. Actually bakes it himself, then forces us to have a slice in memory of my mom. I didn't have any of the damn cake."

I squeezed Ben a little tighter. He might not have wanted to talk before but now the words came tumbling out.

"Dad has the gall to tell me I should visit her grave, but I'm not going. Haven't been since the funeral. He'd rather send me to a therapist than talk to me about how it felt when I found her body. He flat out refuses talk about it. No one wants to talk about it. My friends think that because it happened years ago I should be over it. And I am over it. Mostly. I just have trouble this one day of the year but no one wants to talk to me because it's too hard. Well, sometimes it's too hard for me too."

"I'll talk to you, Ben," I said.

"But you don't listen. You're always looking out for danger and then you don't even see what's right in front of you."

Was I really that bad? My mouth fell open.

He threw his arms around me. "I'm sorry. I didn't mean it."

But it was true.

He'd tried to talk to me the other day after Dominique turned up at school and I hadn't picked up on it then either. I should've been more sensitive and now I felt terrible. I'd failed him.

Problem was I'd been raised to deny my emotions because they got in the way of my role as a soldier. The two things didn't go together. I couldn't be hardened bodyguard and compassionate girlfriend at the same time.

I had to protect Ben. Because he was going to do great things. Because forces from the future would try to kill him, just as they had before. Because I loved him.

There was one thing I hadn't figured on earlier, though.

I had to protect Ben from himself.

CHAPTER THREE

School again. I found this much easier than a party environment, especially since the weekend's gathering hadn't gone so well. Ben had spent the rest of that night vomiting and all of Sunday hung over. I was driving him to school today and was looking forward to seeing his non-vomitous, non-hung over face.

At home, I'd made coffee for my parents and was shoveling cereal into my mouth.

"Good news." Sitting opposite me, Mom lifted a mug to her lips. "Grandma and Pop are coming."

I coughed, my food stuck half way down my throat. "Here?"

"Of course. Where else would they stay?" She patted my back. "Are you okay?"

I nodded. "Sure. Fine."

I was so not fine. I had never been less fine in my life. Even when Ben was dancing on the roof, I knew things would be okay. But grandparents coming to stay – that was not okay.

Before I'd been transported to Altabena, my superiors had implanted my new parents Jan and Philip Gray with computer chips to give them the memory of seventeen wonderful years with their daughter. Me. They'd just moved to a new town and to help things along, they'd always wanted a child but couldn't have one.

No one else had been implanted with a memory chip, not as far as I knew. There'd been no need because I was never supposed to be here this long. Now, suddenly, this nice old couple was about to find out they had a seventeen-year-old granddaughter.

How was I going to get out of this one?

"I thought they were living in the south of France," I said.

"They were. I mean, they are. Gran had been thinking about us, then snapped up a couple of cheap airfares."

"Why don't they go straight home instead? You know, to Miami. All that sunshine."

If only they'd stay on the other side of the country. I didn't wish they were dead like Dad's parents – though there was a time I'd been that heartless – but I still wished these people would stay far away.

"Gran said she wanted to see us." Mom covered my hand with hers. "I don't want you to stress too much, but things aren't quite right with them."

Mom had her worried face, which was reason enough for concern. "What's not right?"

"Grandma might be going senile."

I sipped my coffee. "Really?"

"She was very confused when I was speaking to her. I've never known her that way before." Mom cleared her throat. "She acted as if she didn't know who you were. She even said 'what daughter'?"

I choked and spluttered, afraid I might spit out my

coffee. Eventually I swallowed.

Mom said, "I'm sorry, honey. It was as though you didn't exist. I don't even like telling you this but if they're coming, you need to be prepared. I'm finding this whole deal about old age and senility really hard too. I knew it might happen one day, but I'd hoped that time would be far off."

Then it came to me. "Surely it's too dangerous for her to travel. She's old and frail and anything could happen."

Mom raised her eyebrows. "There's no stopping her when her mind is made up. You know what she's like."

No, I didn't. I had absolutely no idea what she was like. That part I could cope with. But she didn't even know who I was. That was the hard part.

"What about Grandpa?" I asked.

Mom's lips went thin. "He hasn't been himself for a long time."

What was that supposed to mean? I had to get rid of them, but how? If they came here, it'd be the future and the present colliding with tragic consequences – for me.

Dad strode into the kitchen and gave Mom a kiss. "I've got to get to the office, honey. The boss just called and they want me there right away."

"But you haven't had breakfast," Mom said.

"I'll grab something later."

"Hold on." I stood, grabbed a travel mug from the cupboard, tipped his coffee into it and secured the lid.

"You're a star." He kissed me too.

What would I do without these people? I knew what it was like to be on my own and never wanted to go through that again. This news about my so-called grandparents made me feel vulnerable.

An image of Ben's sister Celia building a house of cards flashed in my mind. She'd placed a couple of extra cards at the top to finish off her construction and the whole lot had come tumbling down.

I threw my arms around my dad and held him tight. I didn't want to lose him.

He placed his hands gently on my back. "Whoa, what brought that on?"

There was a time I hadn't let my feelings show. I'd barely had any feelings, and now look at me.

"Coffee to go!" I handed him the travel mug and he left.

Still wondering what the hell I was going to do, I finished off the remains of my breakfast while Mom took her empty plate to the sink.

I looked up at her. "I'll do the cleaning up."

She frowned. "Has an alien taken over our daughter?"

I didn't answer. Not wishing to get into this whole hug-business, I gave her a quick kiss and wished her a good day at work.

Five minutes later, Mom left for work while I finished tidying the kitchen, then grabbed my keys and bag. Outside, I headed for the car my parents had bought me several months ago, a nice sensible used Honda. I already had a driver's license because my superiors had sent that down along with the other documents I needed to live legitimately in Altabena.

Unfortunately I'd never had any actual driving lessons. We still had cars in New Nation but I'd never driven one when computer controlled pods were far more efficient. So before my parents bought the trusty Honda, I'd carefully watched what others did, emulated their actions and taught myself how to drive. After a shaky start, I was doing pretty well.

Ben's front door opened as soon as I pulled up outside his house. I preferred to wait on the street as it avoided using the driveway and then having to reverse. I was an excellent driver, as long as I was going forward.

He leaned across to kiss me as he got in the car. It amazed me he could look this handsome even in his school uniform of navy shorts and a white shirt. In the not too distant future, uniforms would be the norm and we'd all conform.

"Feeling better today?" I asked.

"Heaps." Ben secured his seatbelt, something I'd noticed he always did right away, when I was driving anyway.

As I came to a screeching halt at the next intersection, Ben gave me a dirty look.

"What?" I said. "There's a stop sign so I stopped."

He nodded. "Sorry about the other night."

I checked for cars. "No need to be."

The car jerked forward as I took off, then jerked again when I changed into the next gear. My next gear change into third was fractionally smoother though the engine seemed to be struggling.

"Damn stick shift," I muttered.

Through the corner of my eye, I saw Ben open his mouth to speak, then stop himself.

"What?" I asked.

He waited until I pulled up inside the student parking lot. "It just amazes me that you're such a perfectionist with everything else and then you're such a…"

I turned to look at him. "Such a what?"

Ben's brow furrowed. "Such a lousy driver. Sometimes I wonder how you got your license."

"Because I'm a woman?"

"No, because you're so bad."

I got out of the car, slammed the door shut and stormed off. There was such a thing as too much honesty.

Ben caught up with me. "I'm sorry, Nicola."

I stopped and took a deep breath. "Don't worry about it."

"Women are very good and safe drivers."

"Great, so other females are good drivers, just not me! It was better five minutes ago when I thought you were a sexist pig."

He threw his hands up. "Okay, I'll be a sexist pig if that makes you happy."

I gave him a quick kiss on the lips, smiled so he knew everything was okay, and left. He really did make me happy and I could probably ignore the stupid comments about my driving.

The hall was crowded as I walked toward my locker but I could've sworn Reece was in front of it, fiddling with the lock. His fingers were on the handle as I approached.

I tapped him on the shoulder. "Need a hand?"

He turned. Didn't say anything, but then he never said much.

"That's my locker," I said.

His expression was blank. "Oh, I thought it was Haley's."

He turned to leave but I grabbed his arm. "Thanks for the ride home the other night." He shrugged so I added, "Your timing was perfect."

I watched him walk off. Perhaps I was being paranoid

but there were a few times recently when I could've sworn someone had been in my locker. That didn't explain why Reece would snoop around when there was nothing for him to find inside. Maybe he was going to plant something.

Or maybe I had this all wrong. If I suspected everybody all the time, I wouldn't notice genuine danger when it appeared. Something was coming even if I didn't know what or when.

At recess, I knew where to find Lauren but I didn't expect to find Reece with her. He looked distinctly guilty as if I'd caught him out.

"Here she is." Lauren was beaming. "Reece was just asking about you."

He didn't say anything.

I gave him a pointed stare. "I seem to be bumping into you all the time – at my locker, at recess, at the arena."

He shrugged. "I was thinking of joining the martial arts program."

"Is that why you hang around there so much?"

Another shrug.

Lauren rolled her eyes. "Or maybe you've got a crush on Dominique like every other guy here."

He shook his head, rather too vehemently. "Not me."

Will joined us, which took all of Lauren's attention, and Reece turned to leave.

I reached for his arm. "You're already professionally trained."

"Sorry?" he said.

"Last year I saw you in action during the riot at the anti-curfew party. I know you're well trained."

He gave me the blank expression again. I didn't go for

35

the strong and silent routine.

"Is there anything you want to talk about?" I asked. "Anything you want to tell me?"

He shook his head.

The bell rang so he left. It wasn't that I thought Reece posed any danger to either Ben or me, but there was something odd about the way he was always hanging around. I didn't have him pegged as an assassin sent by my superior officers. I didn't have him pegged as anything at all and that was what bothered me.

The day sped by. After school, Ben caught up with me in the hallway next to my locker, which didn't look as if anyone had rifled through it. I checked, of course.

"You ready?" he asked.

I slammed my locker door shut. "Always."

Ben ambled away slowly whereas usually he raced off to training after school. We both did. His shoulders were slumped and he didn't seem himself. It had been better that morning when he was telling me what a terrible driver I was.

"Has something happened?" I asked.

"I was just thinking about Celia."

"She's okay, isn't she?"

"Sure."

I didn't know if *sure* meant *sure* and *okay* meant *okay*. And I didn't want to take any chances, not after Saturday night.

"We don't have to go to training right away," I said. "We can just sit somewhere."

Ben didn't say anything as we headed for the martial arts arena. Then he kept shuffling past the arena and I shuffled along with him, all of which meant I was getting better at relationships and reading people. This was actual progress.

He stopped in a small deserted courtyard that was surrounded by empty classrooms and a high brick wall so we were effectively in a cul-de-sac. Though not a pretty part of the school, it was quiet. He slumped down onto a bench and I sat beside him.

I felt extremely uncomfortable because as much as I wanted Ben to talk to me, I wasn't used to this sort of situation, not to mention which I had a very limited understanding of families and little sisters. If that's what the problem was.

Still, I had to start somewhere. "What's up with the cutest little girl in the world?"

"On Sunday, she told me not to be so sad," he said.

"When you were hung over?"

"I was grumpy as all hell, but not around her. She came up to my room when I was studying and said I shouldn't be sad because Mom was dead. Celia's eight. I thought she was too young to cotton on but she's got the dates memorized – Mom's birthday, wedding anniversary and the date of her death. She knew exactly what day it was on Saturday."

Whereas I hadn't had a clue.

Ben looked down at his hands. "I worry about her. She shouldn't have to deal with this shit."

"Neither should you," I added.

He held my gaze. "You shouldn't have to either for that matter, but I've got to unload or I'll go crazy."

One thing was for sure. Life had been a lot more straightforward when I didn't have to contend with all these damn emotions – Ben's grief, his fears for Celia, my own feelings.

I took Ben's hands into my own. "I'm glad you're talking to me. This is a lot better than when you were insulting my driving."

That brought a half-hearted smile to his face.

"You take good care of Celia," I said. "But you can only do so much."

His hands felt large in mine, and it struck me that being physically strong didn't mean you held up better in situations like this. I wished I could do more for him.

The sound of footsteps slamming on the pavement made us both look up. Reece was racing toward us. His pale eyes were panicked and stark against his dark skin. His hair was going crazy as always, his brow covered in sweat.

"You've got to go." He grabbed my arm. "You're in danger. She's here. Looking for you."

She? Surely he didn't mean Dominique. "Who's looking for me?"

"Nicola…" Reece dragged me back but I yanked my arm away. Ben took to his feet, probably ready to stand up for me.

I nudged him back gently with my hand. "I'll handle this."

Reece bent over, panting. "She's after you."

"Who?"

He straightened, more composed, though still rushing. "She went to the martial arts arena first, stood at the front of the room and looked around. Moose went up to her and she backhanded him, knocked him right over. She's strong and she's after you. I know she is."

I'd never heard Reece talk this much. "You've got to slow down. Who's after me?"

He drew a breath. "Not *who*. *IT'S* after you."

The back of my neck prickled. No one else was around. The classrooms were locked. We were in a courtyard with only one way in and one way out. Some sort of threat was nearby and the danger wasn't emanating from Reece.

Ben walked across to lean casually against a tree. He thought I had this under control. And he was wrong.

Reece was pleading with his eyes. "It's coming!"

I stared at him. "You're not making sense."

"Nicola, it's a drone sent to eliminate you!"

My mouth fell open. "A drone…"

How did he even know that word? In an instant, I knew.

"Ben!" I yelled.

I looked behind Reece and saw her. *It.*

Not Dominique. Not at all.

Slower than a human but stealthy. I hadn't even heard it coming. I should've known it would happen this way.

Tall and strong, this thing was too perfect right down to the empty eyes and the face that barely moved. The drone existed for one reason only. She'd been programmed to complete a mission – to kill me first, which would leave her free to get to Ben.

Her movements robotic, the creature stepped closer and stood with her legs apart. Even in a black tee shirt and pants, she looked like a soldier but she wasn't human. She was something else.

She took in Reece first. Nothing. Then shifted her gaze to me.

And all the time, not a word.

The drone turned to Ben. She reached for something

behind her back, then lifted the laser pistol in her hand.
And pointed it straight at him.

CHAPTER FOUR

Reece was closer to the drone than me. He leapt across the courtyard. Threw himself against her raised arm. She fired. There was a flash and the whooshing sound of the beam being released.

He'd knocked her to the ground. Knocked the pistol out of her hand too. He slid along the pavement, his head hitting the wall with a thump, then didn't move.

"Run, Ben!" I yelled though it was useless. He'd have to get past the drone first and there was only one way out of here.

"Get the gun." The next best thing.

I ran toward her. The drone stood, her black clothes covered in dirt, and kicked Reece in the gut while he lay immobile on the ground.

"Over here, bitch!" I shouted.

She turned. I landed a punch in the middle of her face. She stumbled back. I slammed a kick into her thigh, then another and two precision punches that landed on her jaw. Her leg buckled. Her head got knocked around.

But her expression remained the same. She didn't groan. Didn't feel pain because she wasn't human.

I saw Ben through the corner of my eye. He had the pistol. The drone slammed a fist into the side of my head. I covered, too late. Pain reverberated through my skull. The drone might not be able to feel anything but I sure as hell could.

Ben pistol-whipped her in the face.

"Shoot her!" Reece yelled, groaning on the ground.

The drone punched Ben on the chin, lowered her gaze to the gun in his hand and knocked me back.

No way could I let that thing win. I jumped on her back and took her to the ground. My legs were wrapped around hers so she couldn't move, my arms over her neck in a rear naked choke. She tried to pull me off. Damn, she was powerful but no creature was strong without air, not even a drone.

I held on for dear life – for mine, Ben's and even Reece's.

"Shoot her." Reece again.

Ben pointed the pistol at the drone.

"No, you'll get me too."

I got the words out quickly, held on tight and squeezed. Suddenly, she went limp in my arms. Unconscious. I held on a little longer to be sure, then pushed her off and stood.

Bent over, I sucked in deep breaths. That had taken it out of me. A life and death situation will do that to a girl.

I looked up at Ben. "You've got to shoot."

His eyes were wide, his mouth open. His face was filled with fear but not enough of it. Not adequate despair, not ample desperation, not what he needed to get the job done.

He wouldn't shoot her. He probably thought she was

human.

The drone's eyes flicked open. Reece and I were yelling at Ben to shoot, for all the good it would do. He was horrified, mumbling something. There was so much noise in my head I couldn't think straight. This couldn't be happening.

The creature sat up, ready to stand. She would kill him. That's what she was programmed to do — kill Ben and anyone else who got in her way.

"NOOO." A scream. My own.

I ripped the pistol from Ben's hand, and took aim. The first beam went straight through her chest, the second through her head. The drone dropped to the ground.

"You killed her," Ben said, a tremor in his voice.

I should feel happy or at least relieved. I'd saved Ben. The drone was going to kill him and would've gladly killed all of us. Instead I felt like shit.

"Nicola..." Ben's voice tapered off. "Is she...? Was she an assassin?"

"She's not human, Ben," I said. "You know that, don't you?"

The look on his face told me he didn't.

Reece said, "It's a drone, a living creature cloned from a human, programmed for a particular function. To kill."

"It's not cloned." I corrected him. "The first ones trialed a couple of years ago were cloned but they couldn't make them function properly so now they use newly dead bodies."

A couple of years ago. I was talking about what was going on during the year 2120 but I think Reece already knew that. He knew a hell of a lot more than I'd have given him credit for only an hour ago.

"But she looks so real." Ben's eyes narrowed. "How do you know all this, Reece?"

He didn't say anything. The quiet-and-mysterious-thing he had going earlier wasn't going to work for him any more, not when his secret was out.

Reece was from the same place as me. The future.

"How long have you been here?" I asked him.

He pushed his hair back only for it to spring back to exactly the same position. "I got here about a year before you did."

"He's from…?" Ben muttered.

I squeezed my boyfriend's hand.

"I was a scout," Reece said. "Sent here to survey the area, collate information and send it back but the communications weren't functioning properly."

I could well imagine. "What was your mission?"

He shrugged. "That was it. Information gathering. Everything else was strictly on a need-to-know basis. What about you?"

I didn't want to tell him my role because I'd never been a simple scout. I'd been something much worse.

"How long have you known about me?" I asked.

"I suspected for a while. You were like me when I first arrived. Inept. Struggling to fit in. Emotionless. Almost like a robot."

"Gee, thanks."

"But I never knew for sure. Until today, that is. I saw the drone and thought I was a goner but it looked right through me. Then I thought it must be coming for you."

"So did I."

But it had been programmed to kill Ben. That meant my superior officers thought I was dead because if they suspected I was still alive, they'd have arranged for my death as well. Two for the price of one.

His eyes narrowed. "I saw what was going on. It was after Ben."

"Yes."

"Why him?" Reece covered his mouth with his hand, then let it fall. "Shit, I was better off on my own. I should've stayed away. Kept my mouth shut."

"In which case Ben and I would probably both be dead now," I said.

"Yeah, there is that, I guess."

I spread my hands. "I'm trying to say thank you."

"I only came here to warn you. I didn't want to get involved." He brushed down the front of his jeans. "Damn it, Ben. Why didn't you just shoot that thing? That would've been a hell of a lot easier."

For Reece maybe, not for Ben.

I stared at the drone's lifeless body. I was going to have to get over this too. That thing wasn't a person but it had been alive and it looked so damn human it was confronting. I felt sick to my stomach. Too many feelings. Too much stress. Too much to handle.

Ben pointed to the drone. "What are we going to do now? We've got what looks like a dead body on our hands."

A click cut through the air, followed by a gentle whirring sound, and that was when it hit me. Must be the self-destruct program setting in.

"We've got to get out of here." I grabbed my backpack. Ben grabbed his. "It's gonna blow. Run!"

The three of us ran out of the courtyard. Behind us, a loud bang. I turned to look. The buildings were still standing, dust and fine debris flying everywhere, the air filled with the unnatural stink of ozone. It was one of the byproducts of a molecular explosion – in this case, a compact explosion designed to obliterate the drone to mere molecules. No identifiable remains.

"Wow, that stinks." Reece reached for my arm. "We have to go."

We ran to the student parking lot, knowing the explosion would have attracted attention and someone would be on the way.

The three of us stopped in front of my silver Honda and I realized Reece knew this was my car, whereas I didn't know very much about him at all.

Ben shook his head. "There one minute and gone the next. How did that thing get here in the first place?"

"Same way I did," I said.

"But how? In what?"

Reece sucked in his cheeks. "What were you expecting? A time travel vehicle, a Delorean perhaps?"

A joke about *Back to The Future*. At a time like this. Really?

"That's not helping." I glared at him, then turned to Ben. "I don't know exactly how time travel works but you don't need a vehicle. You need wormholes. You know more about that stuff than I do."

"I'm out of here." Reece turned to leave.

"Wait," I said. "The authorities in New Nation, do they know you're still alive?"

He shook his head. That meant no one would be after him. For now.

Reece's haircut – or lack thereof – said he was young and reckless and didn't care, but his expression said something else. He was every bit as worried as I was.

"If they sent one drone, they can send another," he said.

There was a lot more the authorities from the future could do. They could rethink their plans, work out the most effective approach, refine the programming. They could send several drones or several hundred. They could come up with a something completely different altogether, something we wouldn't see coming.

Reece came out with the words I didn't want to say: "They can do whatever the hell they want and all we can do is react."

Police sirens in the distance. Time to go.

"We got this far," I said. "So did you. And none of us is on our own now."

I squeezed Ben's hand. Wished I could keep him safe.

The authorities in New Nation were a powerful force.

And whatever they had planned, they wouldn't stop here.

CHAPTER FIVE

His half-black, half bleached hair made Reece hard to miss as he headed for the cafeteria where Ben and I had just been.

"Hey." He stopped beside a wall to allow others to pass by.

"How are you doing today?" I asked.

He shrugged and did the man-of-few-words thing.

I smiled wanly. "Are we still on for this afternoon?"

Reece nodded.

"Catch you later." I stepped away.

He grabbed Ben's arm. "I always liked you. But I don't know who you are any more."

Ben pulled away. "What's that supposed to mean?"

"It means I'd like to know what was going on yesterday and why that thing was after you."

"Hey." I stepped between them. "Ben's a regular guy. I'm the one from New Nation. So are you."

"Do you really think I can forget?"

"Later, Reece."

He stepped back. "Yeah, later."

Ben and I snuck away to eat lunch on a small patch of

grass at the side of one of the school buildings, which was what we'd planned in the first place. Some younger kids were hanging out nearby but they were too preoccupied to bother with us.

We ate in silence, not the comfortable sort between people who know each other well, but the edgy sort between two people who wanted things to go back to the way they'd been before

Ben placed his empty wrapper on the grass and leaned back on his hands. "When were you going to tell me you were catching up with Reece later today?"

"Now or maybe later. I don't know."

"You two are in the traveling-from-the-future-club." He made quotation marks with his fingers.

"No, we're not in a club."

"You're very chummy, though," he said. "All of a sudden, you're in this together."

"This is stupid, Ben."

His lips went thin. "As stupid as you getting jealous about Dominique?"

I threw my hands up. "Why are we having this argument?"

"Because I don't trust him. I didn't like the way he turned up two minutes before the drone."

"He warned us. Threw himself in front of that thing. An armed drone."

Ben bit his lower lip. "I didn't like the way he was accusing me of something earlier on."

"I don't like it either but it doesn't matter what I like."

"I liked it better before yesterday." The accusatory tone disappeared from his voice, replaced with wistfulness.

I looked down at my knees. "So did I."

"Back then it was just you and me."

That was exactly what I'd liked about it too. "I'm worried, Ben."

"The drone's gone," he said. "You killed it. That thing's not coming back."

"That's the whole problem. We don't know what they might send next."

He gave me a look that said 'this again?' I'd talked through some things with him late yesterday afternoon but it was a lot for him to take in so I'd gone easy.

"There's one thing I agree with Mr. Matthews about," I said. "He says your number one tool in self-defense is awareness. You've got to be aware of your surroundings, think about potential dangers, anticipate what's coming. We have to be able to think like the enemy to be able to stand up to them. It's our only chance."

"Wow," Ben said. "You agree with Mr. Matthews about something."

"If they sent one drone, they can send another."

Ben shot me a stern look. "Now you're quoting Reece."

My mind was ticking over. "They could plant a computer chip in someone's brain and make them turn on you. Mr. Matthews would be the perfect choice. He's already a good martial artist. He's got the skills."

Ben looked bored. "They could plant a chip in *your* brain if they know you're here."

My big sore point. I had to hope like hell that the drone hadn't delivered information to the future on my whereabouts. I was safer if the authorities in New Nation thought I was dead. We all were.

"My superior officers don't give a shit about you or me

or anyone else here." I had to make him see sense. "They could blow up your house with your whole family in it. If they knew where you lived."

Ben got to his feet, brushing off his jeans. "You're freaking me out, Nicola. I don't need this."

I'd gone too far, touched a nerve. Ben loved his family, his dad, his little sister, Celia.

I stood up. "They don't know where you live. They don't have that information."

Because I'd made sure my superior officers didn't have Ben's exact location. I had plans too – of erasing his records as he progressed through school and college to make sure he was untraceable in the future.

Shoulders back, Ben glared. "You've got through to me now. There's danger everywhere and nothing we can do. We're screwed. The whole world's screwed."

The kids hanging out on the grass nearby stared at him as if he were an idiot, then got back to their conversation.

I sidled up beside him. "No, we're not. We just have to be careful. Maybe we should go away, just the two of us. Maybe you were right the first time."

It was something we'd talked about before, a romantic idea Ben had come up with. We could run away to San Francisco or perhaps one of the bigger towns around here, but it wasn't as simple as it sounded. We'd have to change our identities, leave the past behind us completely, and make sure no one could ever locate the old Ben and Nicola.

"I can't do that to my dad," Ben said. "Or Celia. She's so little and she needs me. Josh is away at college and I couldn't do it to him either, even though he's a pain in the neck."

Truth was I couldn't do that to my family either. Besides, hiding out like criminals didn't sound like much of a life and I had a horrible feeling my superior officers would still know Ben was alive somewhere and try to track him down.

I rubbed my hand along his jaw and felt the scrape of stubble. "You didn't shave."

His expression softened. "You like it when I don't."

It was true. I did. Closing my eyes briefly, I pressed a kiss against his lips.

"I'm not so good with the pressure, Nic," he said. "It's too much for me. I like *this* a hell of a lot better."

My heart beat a little faster. "I do too."

"I need you to be *you*," he said. "Not a soldier, not a bodyguard."

He wrapped his arms around me and pulled me close. The citrus from his shampoo wafted to my nose and the rest of him smelled like nothing in particular and like everything. This was where I belonged.

"We need time for the two of us," he whispered.

I held him at arms' length. "I'm working on that, really I am."

Ben wanted to get closer to me in every way and I wasn't sure I could go there. I wasn't sure this was the right time for physical intimacy either, though it would only annoy him even more if I said that.

My lips curled to a self-conscious smile and he put his arm around me as we walked away. I wanted to put that sparkling grin back on his face. I longed to be the person he wanted me to be.

But I had to be something else.

I had to make sure we both stayed alive.

CHAPTER SIX

After school, I pulled the Honda up behind Reece's car in his driveway, the two of us stepping out of our cars at the same time.

"Wow," I gazed at the manicured grass and the porch swing at the front of the house. I had no idea what I thought Reece's house might look like but this wasn't it. "This looks so…suburban."

Reece laughed, something I hadn't seen much of lately. "I know. Ain't it great?"

I followed him inside. "Yeah, I guess it is."

Several portraits lined the hallway – of a married couple with a blond child on their knee, the same kid as a teenager with long hair, followed by a formal portrait of him as a handsome young man holding a college degree. The framed photo at the end of the hallway of Reece with his crazy hair couldn't have been more out of place, besides which the others in the photos were distinctly white and Reece was mixed race.

In the kitchen at the back of the house, a woman looked up from the vegetables she was chopping. With a fitted black outfit and cropped silver hair that was striking against her olive skin, she looked as far from domestic as you could get.

Reece introduced me to Connie.

"Lovely to meet you, Nicola," she said. "I'd like to say Reece has told me all about you but he doesn't talk much."

I liked her casual smile, her Jersey accent that seemed so out of place, and the way she didn't look like a typical parent. She was way too old for a start.

"No, he doesn't," I said. "I saw the pictures in the hall. Your other son's very handsome.

"Thank you," she said. "He passed away eight years ago. I like looking at his handsome face every day, and now I've got another handsome young face to look at. Can I offer you a snack or drink?"

Reece grabbed two Cokes from the fridge. "No, we're good. Just on our way upstairs."

When we reached his room, he dropped down onto the bed while I sat on a chair by his desk. The carpet was pale gray, the dark walls covered in posters which told me Reece was into mixed martial arts, heavy metal and babes in bikinis. Such a teenage male cliché.

"You don't look like military," I said. "Why'd you grow your hair like that?"

"Because I could."

A good enough reason as any.

Reece leaned forward resting his forearms on his thighs. "I always wondered. How'd you do it?"

"Do what?" I asked.

"I've seen where you live. Nice house. You've got two parents who seem like actual, real parents and you registered in school and got a driver's license and did all those normal things, so how'd you do it?"

I shrugged. "It was all set up for me."

"The authorities from New Nation did all that for you?" he asked.

"Sure. Didn't they do the same for you?"

A curt shake of his head. "I got dumped here with nothing, no ID or documents, no home, no idea how I was going to get by."

Reece had been sent here before me. Perhaps the authorities had learnt from their mistakes with him or perhaps they'd thought Reece was expendable. More expendable than me.

"How'd you manage?" I asked.

"I was living on the streets. Connie used to see me every day when she passed by. She took me in."

"But what about your official documents? You can't register in school without them. You can't do anything."

A smug smile took over his face. "Connie arranged it. She's officially my guardian."

"But how?"

The smile broadened. "She's connected."

"To what?" I asked.

"*Connected.* As in connected to the mafia. She arranged everything with her old contacts in New York."

I screwed up my face. "Is that even possible?"

Reece gave a slow confident nod. "Her husband was some sort of mafia bigwig. Their son died. Overdosed. The husband went on a rampage and got shot, so Connie left it all behind and moved west. She knows people. People who owe her."

The story made me like Connie even more.

Reece held my gaze. "What was your mission?"

"Same as yours. I was a scout."

"Your superior officers sure went to a lot of trouble for a scout." His eyes told me he didn't believe me.

"Yeah, they did. So when I started at Altabena High, that's the first you'd heard of me?"

"Any reason I should?"

"No, I never saw you at military college, that's all."

I didn't need to tell him I was a hero back in New Nation. I'd saved a room full of school children from two armed gunmen holding them hostage. I'd gone to the school to speak to the kids about the benefits of military college with my sergeant as part of the regular promotional program and had ended up at the wrong place at the wrong time. Or maybe it was the right time. My superior officer had frozen under pressure whereas I hadn't. I'd done exactly what I needed to do.

It had been big news when it happened – and one of the main reasons I was chosen for this mission – so if Reece had no inkling, he must've been here a while.

"Why was the drone after Ben?" Reece asked. "Why him?"

"Ben is going to do great things one day."

"Like what?"

"He's going to find a cure for cancer."

A grin on his face, Reece whacked his knee. "Shit, you're kidding me! He's the one who does that?"

"I am neither shitting you nor kidding you."

"Then why does someone from New Nation who knows what's going to happen want to kill him? Why does anyone?"

"I don't know."

I wasn't game to tell him the killer virus was created as a byproduct of the cancer cure. Reece already knew about

56

how the virus swept across the country, obliterating the population. We all did. The things we depended on – public transport, electricity, running water, medical services, bread, food supplies – became intermittent because there weren't enough healthy people to run vital services.

Then the Bartley government initiated martial law. Because nothing was more important than feeding the population. The government provided basic food and services to the people, introduced disciplinary measures necessary for survival, and took away everything else.

That was before my time but then, so was *this*.

Reece might not be so impressed if he knew how the virus enabled Bartley to take control and might even try to get rid of Ben himself. Reece didn't act or look like a soldier now but I'd bet there was still a soldier inside him. Like there was a soldier inside me.

"One more thing," Reece said. "How come you're still here?"

I was going to ask him the same thing. Our superior officers had been able to keep tabs on everyone no matter where we were, which place or which time, thanks to advanced GPS technology.

"You mean the geopositrons?" I asked.

I probably still had some geopositrons in my blood but the microscopic molecules needed to reach a critical mass to work together and I'd got rid of as many as I could – because I was never going back to New Nation. Ever.

One thing I knew for sure, if the authorities from the future could still trace me, they'd eliminate me without a second thought.

"They went down the drain," I said. "And you? How'd

you do it?"

Reece's expression clouded over, his expression serious. "I got rid of them too but I made a mistake."

My mouth fell open. "Don't tell me they can still locate you."

"That's not it. I thought the geopositrons might contaminate the water supply or the sewerage, so I collected them along with my blood in a container and dumped it at the local hospital. They have huge incinerators for medical waste. I thought they'd burn everything off."

"But they didn't?"

Reece stood and reached for a piece of paper from his desk. "There's heaps of scientific stuff online about it but this sums it up better."

He handed me the newspaper clipping.

Sci-Fi Find Puts Altabena on Map

Before I started reading I knew exactly what that 'sci-fi find' was going to be. Scientists had discovered GPS functionality in microscopic artificial molecules and were investigating the way they interacted. Researchers had no idea where they had come from or how they'd been created.

This was in the *Altabena Times*. Common knowledge.

"I don't know how the geopositrons got from the hospital to the research facility," Reece said, his tone apologetic.

"Doesn't really matter." I pointed to the screen. "Geochemical Global has them now. The question is, what are we going to about it?"

Reece didn't say anything. Maybe he didn't know what to say. If the researchers worked out how to replicate the geopositrons, they might reach the critical mass of interaction and the New Nation authorities would probably then assume Reece was still alive.

If he was in danger, that would pose a threat to me and Ben too.

"What about your PR device?" I asked.

That was what we used for communications.

"I put it on a plane," Reece said. "Far as I know, it's traveling the world."

Normally that would've made me laugh.

But I didn't have a lot to laugh about right now.

CHAPTER SEVEN

I walked into the kitchen as Mom was hanging up the phone. She turned to the sink and started banging some mugs around.

"Everything okay?" I stood beside her.

"Sure, honey." Her eyes were glazed in contrast with the brilliant smile on her face.

"You look tired."

"I started work at 7.30 today so I could finish early," she said. "Of course I'm worn out."

She'd been tired last year, tired like she'd never been before. That was one of the things I remembered about her cancer diagnosis, cancer that had been treated successfully. Still, that was no reason for me to overreact.

"Who was that on the phone?" I asked

"Just a friend." Mom seemed to be back to her usual cheery self again. "I spoke to Grandma earlier on. They'll be here next week."

Okay, now I was ready to overreact. "So soon?"

"I told you about it ages ago."

I'd been in denial, hoping this particular problem would go away.

"I'll pick them up from the airport," I blurted out.

"It might be better if I came with you, honey. Grandma was a bit strange when I mentioned you."

I tried not to sound as if I were panicking. "No, it'll be better if it's just me."

If I was dealing with my so-called grandparents on my own, I could prime them, even though I had no idea what story I could come up with. Certainly not the truth.

She gave me that concerned Mom look. "Are you sure?"

"Sure I'm sure. It'll be a good chance to get to know them…better, I mean. You know, it's been a long time."

"Fine, I'll leave it in your capable hands."

Mom's smile didn't reach her eyes and that tired look overtook her face again. I didn't feel very capable.

"How about if I stay home tonight and keep you company?" I asked.

"Don't be silly. You said Ben's cooking, didn't you? You can't miss that. Besides, Dad will be home for dinner so I'll hardly be on my own."

"You sure you're okay?"

She whacked me on the shoulder. "I've got my own mother turning up soon. I don't need two mothers! You've been a bit…sensitive yourself, honey. You sure nothing's wrong?"

"Nope," I said.

Nothing at all.

*   *   *

I had two big problems at the moment – Ben and Reece. Okay, maybe there were more problems that that.

The sound of chairs scraping, laptops being slammed shut and feet shuffling on the floor filled the air as soon as the bell rang and Mr. Rodriguez waved for us to leave the class.

"You still want me to come over tonight?" I asked Ben.

He rubbed my knee. "Absolutely."

"Ben…" I began but he headed straight for the teacher's desk at the front of the room.

By the time I caught up, he'd already launched into a question. "Remember last year, we had that discussion about time travel."

The science teacher nodded. He was always changing his facial hair and currently sported a goatee that added an edge to his exotic Eurasian looks. It suited him.

"Of course I remember," he said.

Ben continued. "I've been reading up on it. Stephen Hawking says all physical objects exist in three dimensions and as well as that, there's a fourth dimension. Time."

"That's the theory, yes."

"Okay, so if you were traveling through time, wouldn't you need a time travel machine of some sort?"

The teacher grinned. "What? You want to jump in a Delorean?"

The *Back to The Future* joke again. Ben didn't laugh.

Mr. Rodriguez continued. "Who's to say you'd need an actual vehicle? The wormholes would do all the work but they're tiny, remember. Smaller than molecules or atoms. They're like little wrinkles that constantly form and disappear, then reform. And they link two separate places and two different times. The hard part would be enlarging them to a size where they'd be workable."

"You're saying the wormhole itself would be the machine?" Ben asked.

"Possibly. We don't really know for sure."

Ben nodded while I tried to look like I understood. I was a lot of things, but a great scientific mind, I was not.

The teacher packed up his things. "Anyway, don't you have martial arts classes now or something?"

"Later," Ben said.

Mr. Rodriguez nodded. "Me too."

Ben looked as surprised as I felt. "Really? What do you do?"

The teacher shadowed the sweeping moves of Filipino Kali. The martial art involved unarmed combat training, as well as knife and weapons based training.

"Very smooth," I said.

"I hope so," he replied. "I've been training for a long time. I don't talk about it much though, not to students. By the way, next week's excursion has fallen through."

"Why's that?" I asked.

"It's a government lab, and the relevant government authority issued an instruction banning visitors. They're clamping down but on what, I don't know."

On everything. The aim was total control and that started in small ways with minor infringements on our liberty and the introduction of rules that didn't make sense unless you looked at the big picture. Still, this might be an opportunity of sorts.

"What about Geochemical Global?" I asked. "They're not government."

"I'm surprised you've even heard of them," the teacher said.

"Ben read about them." I nudged him.

Mr. Rodriguez stared at me first, then Ben. "You two are coming up with some strange things today."

I threw my hands up. "We have young, inquisitive minds and understand the value of a well-rounded education."

Which sounded dorky even to me.

"I'll see what I can do," the teacher said.

Outside, Ben pulled me over to the side of the hallway "So what was that all about?"

I told him about Reece's geopositrons and Ben shot me a look that made me wonder how he could switch from regular to enraged so quickly.

"Then that's *his* problem."

"Look, I'm not even sure it's a problem," I said.

"Everything about him is a problem."

Ben turned and walked away.

When did the lovely guy I started dating last year get replaced with this moody monster?

CHAPTER EIGHT

Make or break time. I remember how nervous I'd been when I was first sent to Altabena and how weird everything was, the feeling that I didn't fit in, that I was never going to fit. Those same feelings were coming back to me now.

I was standing in the waiting area of Altabena Airport holding a sign bearing the names of my 'grandparents' so they knew who the hell was picking them up.

An older couple headed my way. My 'grandfather' looked just like the photos I'd seen. Meanwhile, I looked at 'Grandma' and saw my mom in thirty years' time. A light brown bob showed off striking cheekbones and sharp blue eyes that seemed familiar, only these eyes were staring at me in an expression that was Mom-meets-Hannibal-Lector.

If I could handle this woman, I could handle anything.

I shook April's hand and, to be fair, she returned the greeting. She also didn't stop with the evil glare.

"Lovely to meet you." I shook her husband's hand too. "I'm Nicola."

At least he was smiling. "I guess you already know

we're Michael and April. You know, like the names on the sign."

I turned to April. "I can see where Mom gets her looks from."

"Don't try to flatter me." She added a sneer to the deadly expression. "It won't work."

"Just as well Jan didn't get her looks from me!" Michael said, trying to lighten things up.

His wife glared.

"Well, it wouldn't be very good if Mom ended up bald but otherwise you look good for your age." The words slipped out of my mouth before I could stop myself.

He ran a hand across the top of his head. "You noticed, eh?"

"Sorry." I reached across for April's suitcase. "Let me take your bag."

She shoved a large carry bag into my hands and pointed to her suitcase. "The wheel's broken."

"No problem."

Michael took the sign from my hands and tossed it in the bin while I carried the bag and broken suitcase, and April sauntered ahead unencumbered.

When we reached the car, I picked up his suitcase. "Please, allow me."

"Don't forget," he said. "I'm pretty good *for my age*."

"Still, you're my guest."

I slung the cases into the trunk and opened the passenger's door for him. April pushed ahead and took the front seat, probably so she could better glare at me. She sat tightlipped until we were on the highway.

"For the record," she said. "Michael and I are family, not guests."

"That's even more reason for me to take good care of you," I said.

"*You* are the guest."

"Believe me, I don't take my new home for granted."

"Well, Nicola," Michael said from the back seat. "Sounds like you must have been very well raised to have such excellent manners and maturity."

"Thank you."

I'd had a lot to catch up on. In New Nation, I'd been disciplined and slapped into shape until I was exactly what my superior officers wanted me to be. Respect and obedience were different from compassion and relationship skills.

April cleared her throat. "I'll be frank. I think you've been manipulating Jan because she now believes you're her daughter and won't listen to reason. I think you owe us an explanation."

The car screeched around the corner as I turned off the highway.

"It's kind of like an adoption," I said.

"*Kind of like?* You'll have to do better than that."

I'd learnt a lot about lying while I'd been here. Stick as closely to the truth as you can, that was the secret.

"I've been with them about five months," I said. "It's all legal, a guardianship or something."

"If that's the case, then where were you before?"

"An institution, but not the sort of place you'd want any kid to grow up. I have a proper home now and they think of me as the child they never had."

"That's why it's so painful," April said. "Because they always wanted a child. I wanted a grandchild too, not a stranger, not someone who has forced their way into Jan's home. This whole pretense…it's sick."

Time for those excellent manners. "I'm sorry you feel that way. We decided that the healthiest way to deal with the situation was for all of us to pretend I'd always been there."

"Says who?"

"The counselor."

"This is madness! I won't have it."

Michael leaned forward and rubbed his wife's shoulder. "Maybe you should listen to the girl, April. If Jan says Nicola is part of the family—"

She threw his hand off. "You didn't speak to her, Michael. *I did*. She's been completely brainwashed…as if she really believes she has a daughter of her own."

That was a pretty good description of the way the chip implants worked. Grandma was on the ball.

"Look," I said. "I'm being open with you about this now but as soon as we get home, we're all going to pretend I'm their daughter. That's how we handle things and that's not going to change."

"It's warped." April spat the words out.

"I know it's weird. A lot of things have been weird, especially since Mom's sickness last year."

"Sickness?"

"When she got cancer."

"She had…cancer?"

I must have serious foot-in-the-mouth disease. Why had I mentioned anything at all?

"Is she okay?" Michael asked. "Please tell us she's okay."

"They got rid of the cancer with one simple procedure," I said. "Not even any follow-up treatment.

She's fine."

"Seems like there's a lot she hasn't told us," April said quietly.

"Sorry, I thought you knew."

April placed a hand on her chest. "I'm her mother. She should've told me. I can't believe she kept this from me. It's too terrible for words."

"Probably because she knew you'd kick up a huge fuss," Michael said.

"So it's my fault?" Outrage in her voice. "Right, that's it! Stop the car."

I came to a screeching halt that made April lurch forward in her seat.

She fumbled with the seatbelt. "I've had enough."

Michael shouted, "For God's sake, don't do this again! You didn't like Phil because he wasn't good enough, and you did everything you could to stop the marriage going ahead. Haven't you moved on since then?"

This woman had tried to stop Mom and Dad getting married? Really? Mom had said her mother was controlling but I didn't think she'd meant anything quite that bad.

April turned to look at her husband. "You can't...I don't..." She folded her arms, her lips tight. "Please drive."

So I did.

I'd been through some intense training in my time but had never felt like I was stuck in the middle of a soap opera before.

As soon as I pulled up outside the house, I shot out of the car to get their bags from the trunk. "Not sure if Dad'll be home yet but Mom's waiting for us."

April put her hands on her hips. "Can you refrain from

calling them Mom and Dad?"

"No," I said. "I can't."

She looked ready to explode. "Fine. Just don't try calling me Grandma!"

Michael rolled his eyes. "I don't think you need to worry about that."

I covered my mouth to hide my snigger while April stormed up the front path, then looked over her shoulder and added, "By the way, you're a terrible driver, young lady."

So I'd been told before.

This was going to be interesting to say the least. I wasn't sure exactly what was going to happen when we got inside, only that it'd be good.

CHAPTER NINE

Staying out of April's hair while I was at home had become a full-time occupation, so I jumped at the chance when Ben invited me over for dinner. Even better, his Dad was away overnight on business which meant we'd have time to ourselves later.

I got on well with Ben's father as long as I didn't probe into anything too deeply. I'd been there once when Ben had tried to talk about his mom's death, only for him to be cut off. Maybe it was too hard for his Dad but it was hard for Ben too.

Celia and I sat at the kitchen table playing cards while he cooked dinner for the three of us. I'd decided to teach her a new game so I'd looked up the rules for gin earlier to be prepared. We didn't play games where I came from.

"This is a lot harder than snap or old maid." Celia bit her lower lip. "Ben, can you help?"

He stirred the pot of pasta. "Not right now."

I coached Celia until eventually she had a winning set of cards. She brushed her blond hair from her face. "Gin!"

"Good work." I glanced down to admire her hand. "High five."

She slapped my palm with hers.

"Can you guys please set the table," Ben asked.

Celia took care of the cards while I got up.

Ben turned to face me. "Nic, it's really nice watching you with Celia. So good to relax and do normal things. This is so much better than talking about end of the world scenarios."

I grabbed the glasses and turned to the fridge to pour water into them. We were safe here in Ben's house but 'safe' was a relative word.

"Celia's bedtime is eight o'clock," Ben said. "Then we can have some me-and-you time."

Ben insisted the spaghetti bolognaise he'd prepared wasn't fine dining but it was a lot better than anything I'd ever made. Since arriving in Altabena, I'd learnt to cook, just not very well.

After dinner, Ben insisted on cleaning up while I kept Celia company. The two of us sat cross-legged on the living room floor building a house of cards.

Ben's announcement that it was bedtime garnered some complaints before Celia agreed to go if I read her a story. Brushing her teeth and preparing for bed seemed to take an eternity but by the time Celia got to her room, she was happy to snuggle up in bed.

"I'll pretend you're a mommy." She tucked her hands under her cheek on the pillow.

We were heading into dangerous territory. "I'd rather just be Nicola. Is that okay?"

"But you'll be a mommy one day."

Would I? There'd been a time when that had not been even a possibility, and now I wasn't able to look that far ahead.

I picked up the book on the nightstand and started reading. Eventually, I noticed Celia's eyes had closed, her breathing rhythmic. Ben was leaning in the doorway with his arms crossed, watching as I pressed a kiss to her cheek and then tiptoed out.

Outside the room, he cupped my jaw in his hands and pressed me up against the wall. Made me feel special. Wanted.

He took my hand, led me to his bedroom. Candles lined the windowsill and his desk, the flickering flames providing a gentle light. He'd laid a red checkered rug on the floor along with a bottle of chilled wine in an ice bucket and two long-stemmed glasses.

"It's beautiful," I said.

He nuzzled soft kisses to my neck. "Like you."

Taking his hand, I sat on the rug, where Ben poured two glasses of white wine and handed me one. I was going to finish the whole glass, enjoy myself and make sure I didn't ruin the evening.

He clinked his glass against mine. "To us."

The first mouthful tasted alcoholic so I tried to concentrate on the fruitiness of the wine instead. Soon I started to feel more 'chilled'.

Ben motioned toward a small bowl of strawberries. "I only had chardonnay. Strawberries are really meant to go with champagne."

I took another sip. "It's better than beer."

"Beer wouldn't be very romantic."

I picked up a strawberry, held it to Ben's lips and popped it inside when he opened his mouth. Was this romantic? Was this what he wanted?

We sat in silence. I wanted this to last forever. Didn't

want anything to interfere with our time together. Didn't want to move forward or backward or anywhere else.

Ben took the empty glass from my hand and put it aside. He ran his fingers through my hair and pressed a kiss to my lips. A first kiss. A chaste kiss. The next kiss was more passionate and set my nerve endings alive. Warmth settled deep in my belly. Maybe it was more than warmth. Maybe I wanted more too.

He reclined me onto the rug so we were lying on our sides, our bodies pressed against each other as we kissed. His arms were strong and I felt petite when he held me, slid his hands along my back, my butt, my thighs.

I unbuttoned his shirt slowly and slipped my hands over his chest. I lay back to admire his bare chest while I ran my fingers over the layers of muscle.

I knew what would be coming next. Lately Ben would dive into action, his hands all over me, and it'd make my whole body sizzle. That was the problem. I liked it. Too much.

"There's something I need to ask you," I said.

He pulled back, resting on one elbow. "I should've known."

I sat up. "The other day with the drone, it was life and death. So how can you even think about…*this*?"

"Because I'm a guy. Because I'm human. Because I want you."

"I want you too, Ben."

"Do you?"

The even tone of his voice told he me wasn't angry. I didn't answer because we'd had this conversation before. Ben was ready to take our relationship a step further and I wasn't.

"I don't care about drones and that other crap." He sat up, held my gaze. "I care about you. *You're* important to me."

I rubbed the back of his hand. "You mean so much to me too, Ben."

More than he could know. Love was like that.

"I want to be with you, Nic," he said. "Is that so bad?"

He had deep feelings for me and that was enough. So why did I feel this dreadful tugging in my chest, this yearning for more, this feeling that life wasn't complete?

"I like being with you, Ben," I said. "I love everything about it, but this is still all so new to me. I think about it all the time. About us. Being with you."

"That's part of the problem." He enveloped my hand between his. "You think too much. You can never just go with the flow."

Because if I did, I might be putting both of us at risk. One of us had to be alert and aware at all times. Having a glass of wine tonight was about as much as I could do to 'let go'.

"I can look after you too," he said. "I can make sure no one hurts you, if only you'd trust me more."

I did trust Ben. Trusted him more than I'd trusted anyone in my life.

Wasn't that enough?

CHAPTER TEN

"This'll be riveting." Lauren rolled her eyes as we got off the school bus outside Geochemical Global. That was sarcasm, something I'd been able to identify with ease for some time now.

"Could be worse." I reached for her arm. "At least, we're out into the fresh air."

"What fresh air? We were on the smelly bus and now we're headed into some smelly laboratory."

She had a point, whereas I had a vested interest. I was on a mission to get rid of the remaining geopositrons – or GPS molecules as they'd been called – and it felt good to be on a mission again.

Lorenzo bumped into Lauren, then apologized and started talking to her. I wasn't sure how well that particular conversation would go because he was studious and excited about the excursion, whereas Lauren wasn't.

Meanwhile Ben sidled up beside me. "Heard from Reece today?"

"Yeah."

"Shouldn't *he* be the one doing this? *His* mess is the reason we're here, after all."

We'd been through this before. Reece wasn't in our science class and could hardly invite himself along.

"He's not even at school today," I said.

"Sick?"

I shook my head. "Cutting class. He sent me a message earlier to wish us luck."

"Like he cares."

I didn't have time for this argument. "Ben, I need you more than ever today."

"I'm always with you. You know that."

"Go right in with the others." I pointed toward the main entrance. "I'll be there in a sec."

I hung to the back of the crowd, then crouched down to fiddle with the shoelace on my much-loved Converse. I looked up at the single camera perched over the main doors. No security guards. The sliding doors – regular doors with swipe card access mounted on the wall to the right – were wide open while the other students filed through.

Mr. Rodriguez motioned for me to get a move on, so I strode inside to join the others. He went to the counter to speak to the receptionist who was wearing way too much make-up and had hair that was too long and too blond. Leaning back in her chair, she had a hand on her chest as she giggled breathlessly, her eyes glued to my boyfriend.

"Thanks, Ben," the teacher said. "I can take over now."

After I caught up with them, another set of doors opened and we were ushered through. The blond receptionist kept her eyes on Ben the whole time.

"What was that all about?" I asked.

He shrugged, oblivious. "What?"

"Nothing."

Sometimes 'oblivious' was good.

Half an hour into the tour of the laboratory, I nudged Ben. "We can't wait any longer."

Alexander Wong, the chemist in charge of the tour, reminded me a lot of Lorenzo and Daniel. Like this guy, they were both quiet, though extremely animated when talking about computers and the subjects they were passionate about.

As soon as he had a chance, Ben asked, "Can you tell us about the GPS molecules that are here?"

The question sounded nerdy but we were in nerd territory at a chemical laboratory, so perhaps it wouldn't stand out too much.

"Have you been reading the papers, young man?" Alexander asked.

Ben nodded. "There's lots of information online too."

The chemist's eyes lit up. "I'm very glad someone has brought the subject up. The molecules are incredibly interesting – unlike anything we've come across before. Since you've shown an interest, I might show you where they're kept."

My lucky day. If we got close enough, perhaps I could find some way of disposing of them. He led us down a wide corridor and stopped in front of a large window that looked into a separate laboratory.

And that was where we stayed. In the corridor.

"You can see the GPS molecules from here," he said. "On the far bench suspended in plasma that was specially developed as a neutral environment for them."

Ben and I had no problem getting a view into the lab. Two vials of straw-colored liquid sat on opposite ends of a pristine white bench. So close and yet so far away.

"The amazing thing is that the molecules are artificial," our guide said.

"You mean they're man-made?" Lorenzo asked. I could kiss him for asking questions and taking the pressure off Ben.

Alexander Wong nodded. "We keep them in two separate vials because the molecules seem to get 'excited' when the two quantities are in close contact."

He had a good understanding of the technology. Too good.

Beside me, a man in a white lab coat swiped his security card and pushed the door into the lab open. I could race in after him and swipe the vials, but my chances of being caught were too great. Not such a good idea.

"So who made the GPS molecules?" Lorenzo asked. "Where did they come from?"

Alexander threw his hands up. "If we knew that, we'd probably have other answers too. At the moment, we've got lots of questions and that's what makes it so exciting."

Lorenzo nodded. Then Mr. Rodriguez told us it was time to get going and herded us toward the foyer. I was running out of time. Having the location of the geopositrons was one thing. Being able to get back into the building was another.

I sidled up beside Ben. "We need to get hold of a security swipe card. Fast."

The blond receptionist was at the front counter, an array of plastic cards to her left. As soon as she saw Ben, her lips curled to a sultry smile.

"You distract her," I said quietly. "Just smile."

Ben grinned that dashing grin of his and leaned over

the front counter. The receptionist touched her hair, looking about as distracted as any woman I'd ever seen.

"Excuse me." I held a screwed up tissue in the air. "Do you have a waste paper basket back there?"

Glancing at the tissue with distaste, she pointed behind her, then kept her gaze riveted to Ben's.

"I was just wondering," Ben said. "Why you'd choose this line of work instead of, say, modeling?"

Lame? Obvious? Not to her. I could've gagged, meanwhile the blond woman giggled and touched Ben's arm. If I wasn't mistaken there was some serious eyelash fluttering going on.

I swiped a security card from the edge of her desk and tossed a perfectly clean tissue in the trash. As I made my way to the other side of the counter, the noise levels were going down since the others were on their way out of the door.

"I've had all sorts of other jobs," the receptionist said. "I'm just doing this to fill in for a while."

Ben nodded. He didn't look as if he was about to leave so I placed my hand on his shoulder and said his name. Loudly.

The receptionist lowered her gaze and looked at him through mascara-clad eyelashes. "Looks like your little friends are leaving."

Ben stumbled backwards. "Okay, sure. Bye."

More eyelash fluttering. "Bye."

"About time," Mr. Rodriguez said when we got to the bus.

The only seats vacant were at the front. Lauren stood up at the back and waved, motioning to me to join her, though Ben and I wouldn't be able to sit together if we did that. I shrugged and sat down at the front.

Ben slid down beside me. "Did you get it?"

I nodded, still slightly disturbed by that receptionist. Ben took my hand into his and held it. Sometimes he knew exactly the right thing to do and also exactly the right thing to say, which was nothing.

It was impossible to tell what the authorities from the future would think when the two vials of geopositrons were close enough to react and the molecules became 'excited' as our guide had told us. I had to get rid of them – for Reece, for Ben, for all of us.

The driver slowed down as we neared the school. He peered to his right at the overcrowded teachers' parking lot and crawled past. Buses often had trouble getting in and out of there.

We drove past the school and someone yelled, "Just keep going!" which earned a laugh.

The driver parked further down the street, raising a collective moan from the kids as soon as he pulled up.

Mr. Rodriguez stood at the front of the bus. "Come on, you can walk. It won't kill you."

Another moan. Ben and I were first off the bus, the others following closely behind as we ambled up the street toward school on the opposite side of the road. Except for the fact I was planning on breaking into a laboratory to steal the geopositrons, things felt remarkably normal and that was exactly the way I liked it. 'Normal' was good.

A bright yellow muscle car passed in front of us, two guys with long hair hanging out of the window yelling, so we waited by the side of the road. The air was suddenly still, while below my feet I felt a low rumble in the ground.

The hair on the back of my neck stood on end. Ben

took my hand.

And that was when we saw it.

An explosion. A giant roar ripped through the air, a horrible sound that reverberated through my head. I covered my ears, wished this wasn't happening, hoped I was wrong on all counts.

The explosion started in the center of the school grounds. A huge ball of matter rose into the air, then cascaded outwards like fireworks around the center point, obliterating everything in its path.

The school had just been blown up.

Along with everyone in it.

CHAPTER ELEVEN

Devastation. Now I knew the meaning of the word. Knew exactly what it looked like.

The huge cloud of dust settled around us while we stood in shock. Where the roof of the tallest school building had once stood, there now appeared to be…nothing. That same dust rained down all around us.

School wasn't merely a collection of buildings. Structures could be rebuilt. There were students and teachers in there, friends, kids I saw in the corridors, people who'd never have the chance to grow up. Human lives lost.

I tried to swallow but couldn't, my throat suddenly dry and filled with dust. The dust was so fine, the stench of ozone in the air, that it told me what had caused the explosion – a bomb that obliterated matter to its molecular level. Many years ago, long after September 11, bomb experts had learnt from the effectiveness of that explosion how to create a charge that would annihilate its target with the same resounding success.

I looked across at Ben. Alive. Looked back at the others. Lauren. Alive. Couldn't begin to think of those who weren't here, who would never be here again.

Ben held my gaze. Didn't speak. Probably couldn't.

"Stay together," Mr. Rodriguez yelled. "Nobody move from this spot."

He was so loud I could hear him clearly despite the ringing in my ears. Then he started issuing instructions. Asked who had a phone which, of course, was everybody. Singled out one person to call the police and another to call for ambulances. Told them exactly what to say. Gave concise instructions.

I had to hand it to Mr. Rodriguez. He was good in a crisis.

So was I. I stepped away.

Ben reached for me, panic in his eyes. "Nicola, no."

"I'll be back."

Survivors. I had to look for survivors.

I ran across the road, then trudged around the edges of the school. Or what remained of it. My eyes stung. I could barely see in front of me through the dust. I pulled my tee shirt up to cover my mouth. Tried to get in some clean air but there was no such thing.

"Is anyone there?" I yelled.

I called out even though I knew…

This wasn't an earthquake. There were no large beams left under which someone might be pinned, waiting to be rescued. There was no steel structure left standing. I was surrounded by the finest rubble, nothing I could recognize as part of a building. Total obliteration.

"Hello? Can you hear me?"

Rescue crews would no doubt dig through the fragments and remains looking for survivors, not that it would do any good. A molecular bomb would leave nothing here that resembled a human being.

Still, I looked around, called out, desperately hoped I was wrong.

Who'd been at school today? Not Reece. He probably had no idea that cutting class would save his life. Who else was there? Taylor and Simone who'd been mean to me when I first arrived in Altabena. I didn't wish this on them or Moose or anyone else. Dominique would've been at her morning training session so she'd be fine. Then there were the teachers. They had lives too, families who'd be reeling after this, children who'd grow up without a parent.

I bent over, my hands on my knees as I dry retched. There was nothing I could do. Less than nothing.

And I was supposed to be a soldier. Not any more.

My eyes were on Ben as I headed back to the others. I trudged along at first, then felt a stabbing through my heart that made me run. I did what I should've done in the first place and hugged Ben. If the world was going to end right now, there was nowhere I'd rather be than in his arms. My body shook so he gripped me tightly. Eventually he let me go and brushed my cheek to wipe away the tears but there were none. I couldn't cry. The moisture had been sucked from inside me.

Lauren staggered toward us, her face streaked with tears, her arms outstretched. We hugged, the three of us, my two best friends. I'd never had friends before I arrived in Altabena and now I was selfish. Thankful I still had them. Grateful we hadn't been at school.

Sirens in the distance cut across the sobs and moans that filled the air. I tried to suck in some air. Inhaled only dust.

I took the phone from my pocket and dialed Mom,

spluttering as soon as she answered.

"Nicola, are you okay?" It was so good to hear her voice but I had trouble getting actual words out of my mouth.

I looked up to see Ben was on his phone too, Lauren hanging off his arm.

"What's wrong?" Mom asked.

"I'm okay. I'm in one piece."

I told her what had happened.

"I'm coming right now," she said.

"Not here. You won't be able to get close. At home. I'll meet you at home later. I love you, Mom. And tell Dad. Tell him I love him too."

I motioned to Ben and Lauren that I'd be right back.

Like the rest of us, Mr. Rodriguez was covered in falling debris, his light brown complexion now pale thanks to a layer of dust.

I tugged at his arm. "You should tell everyone to call their parents and let them know they're alive."

The instruction would be better coming from him. Besides, I didn't think I had much of a voice left for shouting.

He nodded. "Of course, of course."

I was right. He was good at yelling instructions.

And I went back to where I belonged. With my friends. Ben had one arm around me, the other around Lauren who was a sobbing mess whereas I was a shaken mess, and Ben couldn't be a mess even if he tried. He was shell-shocked, though. We all were.

I'd never been in the middle of a war zone, only training drills, and there was only so much that training could prepare you for. Training wasn't life-and-death. I'd had that experience once before as a soldier. Calm and capable, I'd taken control and done what I had to do to save the lives of schoolchildren. Here, the lives were already gone.

This was no accident, no act of nature, no freak accident. It didn't take a genius to work that out, but I knew what the others around me didn't. My superior officers from New Nation didn't care about the devastation they'd caused, the lives lost, families ruined, an entire community in agony.

The bomb that blew up the school had been sent from the future because it was a surefire way to eliminate Ben.

Blow up the whole school with him in it. What could be easier?

Except it hadn't worked.

*   *   *

Funny how I'd been brought up being taught to be strong, denying I had feelings, and indoctrinated into believing that serving my country was the only thing that mattered. Now all I wanted to do was hug and hold the people I loved. I was so overwhelmed with emotion that I didn't know what to do with all these feelings.

Students from science class had been tended to by paramedics though none of us were physically hurt. Police officers had asked us questions and taken down our names. We'd hung around long enough for that, then been told to leave the scene. Because that's what it was. It used to be a school. Now it was a crime scene. I'd spoken to Mom on the phone several times and she'd even tried to drive to school to get me, but road blocks had been set up around the area.

Eventually, I'd walked home. Wanted to walk, in fact.

Ben and I had stumbled off together, neither of us speaking. I'd told myself the exercise was good for me and that it didn't matter that my car was gone. And it didn't.

Mom and Dad ran up to me before I'd even made it to the front path. She hugged me and Dad threw his arms around both of us while we stood on the pavement. A passing car slowed to watch. A couple of neighbors had come out to wave, solemn expressions on their faces as they kept their distance. I guess word had got out.

My face suddenly wet, I tried to work out where the tears had come from, then realized Mom was crying. I wiped the tears from her face.

"I'm okay, Mom," I said.

It only made her cry more. Dad put his arm around her. Did his best to console her.

"You didn't try to be a hero, did you?" he asked me.

I shook my head. "Didn't get the chance."

There'd been no warning, nothing anyone could do. If only I'd known my superior officers might try something like this, then maybe I could've done something. If only I'd had some idea *when* they might set the explosion off, we could've evacuated the school. Still, I imagined it – a world where the school had been blown up but everyone was safe.

We were never going to be safe again.

"You look like a wreck." Dad smiled grimly. "The most beautiful wreck I've ever seen."

I glanced down at my crumpled clothes cloaked in dust and my arms covered in grime, which gave me a pretty good idea what my face and hair must look like. Probably a lot like what Lauren and my other friends had looked like.

Mom's parents were waiting for us in the living room,

April perched on the edge of the sofa while Michael paced the floor. He raced up to me, then hugged me stiffly and held me at arms' length.

"You're alive." He appeared to consider this. "That's good."

I nodded. "I think so too."

Shaking his head, he took a step back. "A tragedy, such a huge tragedy."

April got up and brushed the dust from his arms, then looked at me. "Oh my gosh, you're filthy."

"Yes, I am."

As if that was the worst thing I could be at a time like this.

She reached across to shake my hand, then wiped her fingers on her pants when she thought no one was looking. At least she was being civil. I could hardly expect her to be grandmotherly.

Mom put her arm around me. "Sit down, honey, and tell us what happened."

April put her hand out. "She'll dirty the sofa."

Mom glared at her and mumbled to me how terrible this was, how glad she was I was okay, how sorry she was. She needed to talk and that was okay. I opened my mouth to speak but the words wouldn't come out.

"I'll get you some water." Michael raced to the kitchen, then came back with a glass. I could tell it was water because it wet my throat, but it tasted like dust. A big chunk of my world had just turned to dust.

I tried to explain to them what had happened, the order of events, the devastation, the feeling that the world would never be the same again. I was aware I sounded robotic, as if I was reading out a statement or repeating what had happened to someone else on the other side of the globe. I was in shock. It couldn't be any other way.

"Everything changed in an instant," I said. "One minute everything was fine and the next the school was obliterated. All those people. All those lives lost. Now there's nothing."

The full magnitude of events hadn't hit me yet. Maybe it was impossible to comprehend all at once.

April sat on the edge of her seat on the opposite side of the room, her arms wrapped around herself as she stared at me. "How can you be so calm? Why aren't you crying? We haven't even seen you shed a tear."

Mom stood. "Don't you dare question my daughter, not after what she's been through."

"She's not your—"

Venom in her voice. "You might be my mother but if you say one more word, I'll kick you out of this house. I'm sick of your complaining and grumbling and your sour attitude. Nicola has been through something devastating. It's bad enough for us and we weren't even there. I am so damn grateful to have her here with me, so grateful she's alive, and you will *not* give her a hard time about this or anything else. Is that clear?"

Wow, I didn't think moms were allowed to tell off their own mothers like that. Meanwhile, the look on April's face told me Mom had never spoken to her that way before. The older woman appeared about as shell-shocked as anyone I'd seen today.

"It's okay, Mom," I said. "April is right. I'm not crying. Maybe that's not normal. I don't know. None of this is normal. None of it is right."

Mom dropped back down on the sofa and threw her

arms around me, which seemed to be her answer to pretty much everything, while I wondered what I was doing sticking up for April anyway. My life would be easier if the two of them just left. Mom's life wouldn't be easier, though. Despite their disagreements, she loved having her mother around and it wasn't my place to come between them.

I wasn't exactly sure what happened after that. I remember Mom coming into the bathroom to take away my filthy clothes while I soaked in the tub. Later, Dad tried to talk to me, though I couldn't tell what the conversation was about or even if it was a proper communication. What stuck with me was the feeling that he wanted to be close to me. It made me feel more human.

At some stage, we had dinner or, rather 'dinner happened' like everything else that kept happening around me. I constantly had that strange feeling as if I was looking down on myself and watching events unfold from above. I was there and at the same time, I wasn't.

That evening, my parents and I huddled on the sofa watching the news broadcasts. We'd already scoured the internet for updates. I'd logged onto PeoplePlace but social media was a bad place to be when a big chunk of your society had just been annihilated. It felt empty and meaningless and not somewhere I wanted to be.

The old folks had joined us in the living room, watching, not saying much. They were never going to be my grandparents, not in the way Mom and Dad were my parents. My folks believed I was their daughter.

More than that, they truly believed in me. I'd become part of their lives. I was their daughter in every way that mattered and I loved them.

State Ruler Bartley came onto the television, no surprises there. He was head of the state of California. For now. He wasn't Supreme Ruler of the whole country yet and hadn't handed over the reigns of leadership to his son who would rule for decades, only to be followed by his son after that. This hadn't become a dictatorship, though it would. The United States hadn't crumbled to be replaced with New Nation. Yet.

Bartley was speaking at a press conference. He didn't look like a future dictator. He looked like a man in a suit.

"This was an act of terrorism against the families of Altabena. What has happened is completely unforgiveable. Numbers are still being confirmed but it is believed fifteen hundred students and teachers lost their lives today in a random act of extreme violence. No warning was given. No other threats have been made. No terrorist group has claimed responsibility for what happened."

He waited. Took a meaningful pause while cameras clicked and reporters rustled in their seats. His mouth thin, Bartley shook his fist in the air.

"We will fight this to the end. We will band together. We will find the terrorists who did this. Rest assured, they will be punished."

I thought the chances of that were pretty slim but didn't say anything. I'd have helped the criminal investigation if I could, really I would, but there was nothing I could tell them that they would believe.

Besides, I had a job to do. I had to look after Ben and my own family. I might not be able to save the world but I could look after my corner of it. After all, I was only one person. I wasn't a huge organization or an army or a government. I couldn't save the world, could I?

Bartley's speech continued.

"Anyone who knows or has seen anything is encouraged to call this number." A phone number was shown on the screen. "If you've seen anything suspicious, whether it was a neighbor or a friend or anyone else, you must come forward to the authorities. No matter is too small to report, not when the safety of a country is at stake. The culprits will be held accountable for what they've done. I guarantee you. They will pay."

That was one of the things created by the Bartley government in the future – a culture of suspicion and secrecy where people were encouraged to spy on each other and report back to the authorities. It had worked for the Stasi in East Germany and the KGB in Russia in the twentieth century. It worked the same way in New Nation as well.

"He's right," April said. "Low standards and loose morals have got us where we are. Young people need more discipline. They need to show more respect."

"Shush." Mom waved her hand and kept watching the screen.

Meanwhile, Bartley went through some of the old clichés like 'no stone unturned' and repeated that our thoughts and prayers were with those who'd lost their lives today and their families.

Was he genuinely shocked and disgusted? Probably. That didn't change the fact he was still going to take over the country one day using any means possible. Then he went on to explain how the surviving students of Altabena High would receive a couple of days off school, after which they would be expected to attend Hamilton High School where arrangements would be made to cater for them. How generous. As if school was the first thing on our minds.

April nodded. "That's an excellent idea. Then you can get back into a normal routine."

I stared at her. "What's normal? Are we supposed to act like nothing happened? Will they give us time off for all the funerals?"

Michael, my supposed grandfather, stood. "I'm sorry, Nicola, for your friends, for everything." He took his wife's hand. "Let's leave them alone now, dear."

Mom had her head in her hands and looked like she needed another hug, so I obliged. Time was moving in strange ways, where big chunks of it seemed to disappear yet during other moments, the weight in my gut was huge and time dragged.

Later, I brushed my teeth because that was what I always did. I watched in the mirror as enormous tears slid down my cheeks. I didn't know where they'd come from or how they'd got there. I started to gag, so I tossed my toothbrush in the basin and sobbed and tried to spit and attempted to clean myself up. My knees weak, I leaned on the counter top and sucked in deep breaths, told myself I only had to make it as far as the bedroom.

I could do this. I was one of the lucky ones. I was alive.

My body was racked with sobs as I collapsed into bed. I muffled my cries because I didn't want to disturb anyone, partly because they deserved some peace and partly because I felt alone and wanted to stay that way.

Faces flashed before my eyes, kids I knew, kids I didn't know, people who were dead. I was swimming in an ocean of dead bodies, bloated faces floating toward me, while I tried desperately to reach them. Dreaming or delirious? I had no idea which.

Suddenly wide awake, I saw Ms. Swann, my English teacher. The sight of her friendly face made me cry out so I slapped a hand over my mouth, held it in. I was back in English class and she was quoting Tennyson.

'Tis better to have loved and lost than never to have loved at all.

It brought back my pain from last year, the decisions I'd had to make, my love for the people around me. Made me realize how fragile life is, how things can change in a heartbeat, how sometimes there's no answer and no turning back.

Lying in the fetal position, the tears streamed down my face onto a pillow that was already soggy.

I'd heard people talk about crying themselves to sleep.

I had no idea that was something that could actually happen.

CHAPTER TWELVE

The gentle background sounds of my parents getting up in the morning, the patter of footsteps and the hushed voices woke me. Which meant I must've been asleep.

Maybe I could stay in bed for the rest of the day, for as long as I wanted, for the rest of my life. My head was heavy on the pillow and my face felt like it was full of mucous, which was remarkable given the number of times I'd blown my nose through the night.

I rolled onto my back. Found I could get out of the fetal position after all. Eyes wide open, I thought of the people who'd survived, people I could still help, people whose lives I still shared.

And I had a reason to get out of bed. I'd run ten-mile marathons while carrying a weighted backpack and they were all easier than getting out of bed now. My limbs felt like concrete blocks. At least they could move. At least I had limbs and a mind of my own and a life.

Normally I raced through the house. This morning I took it slowly and ambled toward the kitchen, toward the sound of mumbled voices.

"We can't tell her now." Dad's voice. "Not after what

happened yesterday."

I stopped outside the door, glancing inside to see the two of them sitting at the table, shoulders hunched, expressions serious. I stepped back where they couldn't see me and thought about leaving. I thought about staying too.

"I know you want to protect her," Mom said quietly. "I do too."

"Let's just leave it a week, that's all I'm saying."

"A week is okay."

"Well, we can't leave it much longer than that," Dad said.

A pause. "I could change the date of my—"

"No, you can't."

The hushed tones, the grave expressions, the way Mom had been tired so often again lately – it all made sense now. Her cancer had come back. That's what they were talking about.

No, no, not again. My legs suddenly weak, I leant against the doorframe to steady myself. My chest seized up, my throat constricting, my life falling apart all over again.

I took a few moments. I had to think about Mom. She didn't need me to be a mess. She needed me to be strong. So I forced myself to find the soldier inside me and walk into the room. I forced myself to be someone else.

"When are you booked in for surgery, Mom?"

Her mouth fell open. "Two weeks."

"You need a hug."

That seemed to be my standard answer for everything so I wrapped my arms around her, then gave Dad a quick kiss on the cheek and sat on a chair opposite them as though it was a day just like any other.

Eventually, Mom said, "I'm not worried about the surgery. They'll be removing some tumors from my chest. It's the chemo I'm dreading. Five days a week for eight weeks, and that's just the first round."

"I can drive you." Then I remembered my old Honda had been obliterated in the student parking lot. "You know, in your car. I can help take care of the house and Dad. I can do lots of things."

Dad covered my hand with his. "We appreciate that, honey, honestly we do."

Mom lowered her gaze, her lower lip trembling as she opened her mouth to speak, presumably to say something, but couldn't get the words out. And I knew there was only one thing she wouldn't be able to say.

"This is much more serious than before, isn't it?" I asked.

Head still down, she nodded. "The cancer has spread. The treatment needs to be highly aggressive because this is a fast-growing cancer."

I nodded, calm on the outside, while my heart lurched in my chest.

The cancer cure that would be created in another twenty years was much more sophisticated than any drugs they had now. The antidote targeted cancer cells, zoned in on them, and annihilated them. Unlike current cancer therapies, it didn't affect healthy cells, only cancerous ones. There were short-term side effects and initial flu-like symptoms but the main side effect was that generally people kept living. There were rare cases where the cancer wasn't caught in time, something which didn't happen very often. In 2120, that was.

I tried to be strong but I wasn't. Tears tumbled down

my cheek like an enormous waterfall.

The sounds of feet scraping on the mat and banging outside the back door grabbed our attention. It was my 'grandparents' returning from their morning walk.

There was a round of good mornings from everyone and some questions about coffee and breakfast. I wiped the tears from my cheeks, composing myself in order to put the kettle on.

April stepped closer, her eyebrows raised. "They told you?"

She already knew and that was okay.

I nodded. Poured hot water over the coffee grounds in the stainless steel coffee press.

"I didn't think you could cry," she said quietly.

It was true I hadn't been able to cry yesterday when she'd been there. That was after the bomb when I'd been relieved I was still alive, along with my few remaining friends. Today was a different story.

"I love my mom and dad," I said. "No matter what you may think."

I poured the coffee and April carried the mugs to the table, a smile plastered to her face. Maybe that wasn't such a bad idea. Maybe Mom did need a smile.

Sitting here made me feel as if I didn't know what I was doing after all. The four of them were talking and I felt like an outsider. I wanted to be alone again. I wanted to be with Ben too. I wanted everything and nothing.

"You don't have to stay home if you don't want to, Mom," I said. "Not for me, anyway. You should go to work if that's what you want. Do what's best for you."

Mom looked up. "It's my day off, honey."

April laughed. "Trying to get rid of her?"

I suppose that was her idea of a joke. Also my cue to leave. Unfortunately April wasn't far behind and caught up at the foot of the stairs.

Fed up, I decided to get in first. "I helped take care of Mom last year when she got sick. I did as much as I could. You weren't here to see me take care of her but that doesn't mean it didn't happen."

She straightened. "She didn't tell me about her illness last year. If I'd known, I would've flown straight over. There's no need to rub it in."

"That's not what I'm doing. This isn't a competition."

"*I'm* here to take care of her now." She placed a hand on her chest for emphasis.

"I'm not going anywhere, April, so get used to it."

As if I didn't have enough to deal with, now I had the equivalent of a bomb blast in the middle of my home.

I deserved better than this but we didn't always get what we deserved.

*   *   *

"Pleased to meet you," Lauren said as she shook hands with April and Michael.

Lauren always seemed to know the right thing to say in social situations and to people's parents and other adults. She'd already given my mom a big hug and was following up with a suitable level of enthusiasm for my new grandparents.

April held Lauren's hand in both of her own. "We're sorry about what happened yesterday. I'm glad you're safe."

Lauren managed to extract her hand. "I'm still in shock. We all are. You must've been relieved to find out Nicola was okay yesterday."

April blinked. Didn't say anything.

"Of course, we were," Mom said.

After some polite chat, Lauren and I said it was time to leave. I did the hug-thing with Mom again though she cut the embrace short to answer the phone, her back to us while she spoke. I gave Michael a friendly wave, hoping that might be the right thing to do. The smile on his face told me I'd done okay.

April leaned closer to shake my hand, which surprised me.

"I can't believe you have friends," she said to me quietly.

Lauren grabbed my arm and said rather too loudly, "Lovely meeting you both."

When we were out of the front door, she asked, "Did she just say what I thought she said?"

"Yep."

"Wow."

She had that right.

The two of us got in Lauren's car. She'd already told me on the phone how grateful she was that I'd given her a ride to school yesterday while her car had sat safely outside her house.

She turned to me as she started the engine. "Your gran is really weird. She's not like your mom at all. I hope you don't mind me saying this, but how can she even be part of your family?"

"Good question."

A nervous giggle escaped my lips. Yep, because clearly April was the odd one out, the one who didn't belong, the intruder.

My giggles turned to full-blown laughter. I couldn't

remember the last time I'd heard something so funny or the last time I'd laughed so hard. Every time I stopped laughing, I'd remember how serious Lauren's expression had been when she said that and it set me off again.

By the time we got to Ben's house, I'd composed myself.

"It wasn't that funny," Lauren said.

She had no idea.

Ben ushered us into the living room where the television was blaring.

"Just a minute," he said.

It was the end of a news bulletin about the bomb blast. The reporter was explaining how the explosion was like nothing ever seen before. Forensic scientists who were starting the long process of examining the fragments and remains had never seen this level of destruction and claimed to have no idea what sort of explosive device could have caused the disaster. Building matter had been obliterated so that all that remained was dust. The reporter even said it was as if the buildings had been reduced to the molecular level.

Did he know? No, he couldn't.

In some ways, the rest of the news report was quite predicable. A mammoth clean up was in progress. Heavy machinery had been brought in to help the armed forces who'd arrived last night. Rescue teams were searching for human remains. Outside the cordoned off area, families of the dead huddled together in hope or grief or both.

Bartley came back on the television and introduced the President who'd flown in from Washington overnight. My parents had voted for her. I probably would have too if I'd been old enough. That didn't change the fact I didn't want to hear what she had to say.

I switched off the television. Ben stared at me but didn't complain. With perfect timing, Lauren threw her arms around the two of us and we did the big-hug-thing all over again.

"I have to get going now," she said.

"But you just got here," Ben said.

"Gotta get back to my mom. Since yesterday, she's barely taken her eyes off me. Last night she even slept on the floor next to my bed. Snored like crazy too. I told her that's not happening again. The only way I could get away from her today was because I gave her a sob story about how your car had been blown up and you needed a lift."

I raised my eyebrows. "And that worked?"

"Sort of," she said. "I'm going to put my foot down with my mom. After today."

Ben pressed a kiss to Lauren's forehead. "Here's to tomorrow."

"I'll be fine," Lauren said. "Nicola's the one who needs our support. I thought my mom was bad but she's nothing compared to the granny from hell."

I nodded. "April's a handful."

Lauren raised her eyebrows. "You call her by her first name?"

"It's better than some of the names she calls me." I smiled to show I wasn't hurt, and I wasn't. I had bigger things to worry about.

She shrugged. "Oh well, I just wanted to make sure you two were still okay. Now I'll head back home and remind my mom I'm still alive too."

After Lauren left, Ben and I went outside and sat on the lounge chairs by the pool. The sun was shining, which somehow didn't feel right when the school had been blown up and Mom's cancer had come back with a vengeance.

I told Ben everything – about how April wanted me out of the house and Mom had put her foot down, which seemed to have pissed the older woman off even more. And I told him about Mom's prognosis.

Ben slid onto the banana lounge beside me and I rested my head against his shoulder. He didn't say much. After all, what could he say that would make me feel better? Instead he stroked my hair and held me.

"I'm sorry, Nic," he said.

"Me too. I'm glad we're safe though, you, me, Lauren, those of us who made it."

"Interesting that Reece wasn't at school yesterday."

"It's just as well."

"That's not what I meant."

Surely he didn't think…

He added, "Quite a coincidence Reece chose yesterday of all days to cut class."

I sat up straight on the edge of the chair beside him. "It's not like that. Reece didn't plant the bomb. He couldn't have."

Ben's eyes narrowed. "Well, someone did."

"The bomb came from the future."

He appeared to consider this. "How can you know that?"

"You saw the news broadcasts."

I explained how the molecular bomb reduced matter to its smallest constituents which was exactly what the school explosion had done. It was hardly surprising that forensic scientists were already questioning what sort of device could have done this, since that device hadn't been invented yet.

"Why blow up the whole school?" Ben asked. "It's the sort of thing kids make jokes about but no one wants it to actually happen."

"My superior officers don't have your exact location but they do know where you go to school."

Ben's face dropped. "So they blew up the whole school…to get to me. That's what you're saying?"

I nodded.

His expression clouded over even more than before. "If that's true, maybe it would've been better if they'd just killed me first and left everyone else alone."

"Don't blame yourself."

"I'm not. I'm just saying that one life versus fifteen hundred lives…it isn't fair."

"None of this is fair, and none of it's down to you. They wanted to get rid of you and clearly they didn't care who else they took down with them."

He looked down at his hands. Didn't say anything for a while. "They won't stop."

"No, they won't."

"Then why don't they send another assassin or a drone or blow up all of Altabena?"

I shrugged. "We don't know what they might do next. They might not be in a hurry. They could try to eliminate you in five years, ten years, whenever suits them."

He pressed his eyes shut. "You know how you didn't want me to be complacent? You don't have to worry about that any more."

I squeezed his hand. "Ben, I need you. The world needs you. You're going to go on to create a cure for cancer."

"That's not much help to you now."

It would be if I could simply pop back to the future long enough to grab a vial of the cure and then miraculously come back. Maybe if I hadn't rid myself of my geopositrons, my superior officers would know I was still here and bring me back to New Nation. Then what? They'd execute me for treason. Maybe that wasn't such a good idea after all.

The deadly virus was also the byproduct of the cancer cure, and my superior officers blamed Ben for that. I didn't believe them, though. No one was going to convince me that was down to Ben.

The virus had caused deformities and created mutants who were segregated in the Badlands. These people had blackened eyes and the telepathic ability to transmit emotions, though I now had my doubts about some of these 'truths' we'd been told in New Nation.

Bartley probably loved the virus because it was what had allowed him to consolidate his power. Meanwhile my superior officers had rebelled and come up with a plan to get rid of him, and it involved getting rid of Ben in the process.

"There's always a way, Ben," I said. "We'll work something out."

"Like what?"

"That's the bit I haven't worked out yet."

I squeezed his hand tighter. At least we had each other.

CHAPTER THIRTEEN

It was strange how life went on when you weren't one of the ones who'd died.

I sat on the bed, my ear to the phone.

"Alto's is a really nice restaurant," Ben said. "The tables are candlelit. There are real tablecloths and no burgers on the menu. You can dress up a bit. Doesn't have to be in an actual dress. Anyway, you look good to me no matter what you wear." He added with a chuckle. "Or don't wear."

Best to get the conversation back onto the restaurant. "Well then, isn't it lucky I like pasta and risotto as well as burgers?"

"We deserve a night out, just the two of us. It'll be a date."

My lips spread to a smile. "A proper date. I've heard of those."

"A candlelit dinner."

"So romantic. I wouldn't miss it, Ben. See you at seven."

As I hung up, I saw April had stopped in the doorway of my room, a judgmental look on her face. That seemed to be the only expression she had.

"Everything okay?" I asked.

She walked away.

Ben and I had a few more days until we'd have to go back to school on the other side of town and that meant we had time on our hands, which wasn't necessarily a good thing. I was actually looking forward to going back to school, any school, and having days with structure. If I had structure I'd have less time to think, to feel bad, to worry about the future.

A candlelit dinner wasn't exactly structure. It was better.

For the first time in days, I felt a lightness in my step as I wandered into the kitchen where Mom stood, her back to me as she wiped the counter top.

"Mom, have you and Dad ever been to Alto's?" I asked.

"Hmm," she said without turning.

"I won't be home for dinner tonight. I hope you don't mind too much. At least your folks are here to keep you company."

Dad had gone away overnight on business. Mom had insisted he go, in fact. Had insisted she was fine.

Leaning over the bench, her hair hung over her face, her posture telling me something was wrong.

I put my arm around her. "Are you okay?"

"It's just…" she began. "All of a sudden…"

Her legs gave way but I managed to keep her upright for a few moments until she gathered her strength.

"Mom?"

"I feel a bit queasy, honey."

She never complained about anything, which told me

this was bad. My arm still around her, I led her to the living room and helped her slouch onto the sofa in a semi-reclined position.

"That's better," she said.

"What's the matter?" April appeared out of nowhere, a habit of hers.

"Just a dizzy spell," Mom said. "I'm much better already."

She didn't look better. She looked like she'd gone 'splat' on the sofa, unable to move.

April called out for Michael and kept rambling about how Mom was doing too much and needed to rest and should never have gone to work which, apparently, was all my fault.

Perhaps the nagging shocked Mom into a state of improved health because she sat up, suddenly more coherent, and announced she felt much better.

Michael walked into the room, while April commandeered the conversation, refusing to let him get a word in.

Mom stared at her mother. "All this talking is giving me a headache."

"You should definitely take it easy," I said. "I'll cook tonight."

Mom smiled. "But will we be able to eat it?"

"I can do pasta. Anyone can cook pasta."

In my case, badly, though I'd progressed to the stage where my cooking was edible. Dinner wasn't the problem. I wasn't sure I should go out tonight and leave Mom alone with her mother, especially when Dad wasn't home. I had a bad feeling about it, even if I couldn't articulate exactly what would go wrong. Since arriving in Altabena, I'd learnt to trust my instincts, which was exactly what I had to do now.

"What about a girls' night in?" I suggested. "A nice dinner. Well, a dinner I've cooked, followed by some girly movies, maybe chips and soda."

"And what about me?" April asked, her hands on her hips.

"Of course, you're invited." I turned to Michael. "You're welcome to join us too as long as you can stand watching back-to-back romantic comedies."

"Thanks but I'll pass," he said.

"Honey, don't you have plans?" Mom asked.

My stomach dropped at the thought of missing out on a romantic, sophisticated dinner with Ben at a fancy restaurant. It wasn't just the dinner. I longed to see Ben. Couldn't get enough of him.

I composed myself. "Nothing that can't wait."

Glancing around the room, I noticed April was glaring at me. What had I done wrong now?

"I'll run you a bath, Mom," I said. "Would that be a good idea?"

Relief in her eyes. "That'd be wonderful, honey."

Also a great excuse for me to leave the room and escape the wrath of April. I raced up the stairs to run the bath, then realized I didn't need to hurry. I tipped in some bubble bath, not too much, just a little. It was kind of dark in Mom and Dad's bathroom, so I decided some candles might be a good idea or maybe I just had candlelight on the brain. I searched the kitchen for two enormous candles and lit them, which set the mood perfectly.

After the bath was full, I went back downstairs to let Mom know everything was ready.

"Let me help you," April said.

She tried to take Mom's arm, except she shook her off. "Honestly, I feel much better now."

Mom must've decided it was easier to let April keep fussing because eventually she let her come upstairs with her. I watched the two of them go, then told Michael I was heading for the kitchen.

The thought of phoning Ben and letting him know I couldn't make it tonight left a hole in the pit of my stomach. I was finally starting to feel a bit 'up' and now this was dragging me down. I slumped on a chair at the kitchen table, sitting there like a zombie.

Sensing movement through the corner of my eye, I looked up to see April leaning in the doorway, her arms crossed.

"I saw what you did up there," she said. "The bath, the candles."

"Yes," I said.

"What about your date tonight?"

I stood up. She'd overheard my conversation with Ben earlier and it probably didn't take a genius to work out how I felt and where I'd rather be tonight. Even April could work that out.

She glared at me as if accusing me of something terrible. She'd had a lot of practice glaring at people whereas I wasn't used to being at the receiving end and wasn't sure what to say. Turns out I didn't need to worry.

April turned and left while I stood there with my mouth open and told myself I wasn't doing this for her. I didn't need to be congratulated.

I didn't need her at all.

CHAPTER FOURTEEN

Too many funerals, too many lives lost, too many places to be. And I couldn't face any of them. Ben had forced me to face this, though, the official state ceremony to commemorate the lives lost in the school bombing.

We'd piled into the Altabena Football Stadium, the only local venue that could accommodate the crowd. It seemed disrespectful somehow, but we were here. Everyone was here. My parents understood my need to be with my friends, so they'd arrived with Mom's folks and sat elsewhere with other parents from the school, while I sat with Ben, Lauren, Dominique and Reece. Lauren was looking out for her boyfriend, Will, who was here with his school group but she had no chance of finding him in this crowd.

The sun was shining on the podium at the center of the playing field, though not on us at the back of the third tier of the stadium. The hard seats and concrete surrounds made it feel colder than it was. We stood for the national anthem, which only seemed to exacerbate how steep the seats were, so it was a relief to sit down again.

We were supposed to be in awe because State Ruler

Bartley was speaking first, closely followed by the President, with a short closing speech by the Principal of Hamilton High School where we were headed tomorrow.

"Our hearts go out to those who lost their lives and to their families," Bartley said from the podium. "An unprovoked attack of this magnitude on innocent school children is unprecedented in the history of the United States. We will show the perpetrators of this hideous terrorist act that we are strong, that we can get through this together as a community, that we can overcome."

He continued in this vein for a while and I just sat there, numb, staring in front of me without seeing or hearing or even wondering about my friends who sat beside me. Ben took my hand and squeezed it, reminding me he was here and alive.

How was I supposed to grieve with so many thousands of people around me? How could I even breathe?

"We must stick together." Bartley raised a fist in the air. "This is not a time for weakness. This is a time to band together, to raise our standards, to refuse to accept anything less than the best. We deserve a community that is safe. That's the very least we deserve. And that is why we're tightening up in many ways, starting with the curfew for teenagers – for their safety, for the safety of the community."

"Screw the curfew," Lauren muttered.

"Screw Bartley," Reece said, somewhat louder.

Concerned, I looked around to see several people staring in our direction. Dominique had folded her arms and seemed fed up, the same way Ben looked.

Apparently a state ceremony was not the place for the

voices of students who'd survived or parents of those who hadn't or anyone else who'd had personal experience with the disaster. The ceremony and speeches weren't intended for us. I wasn't interested in Bartley's posturing and grand statements about how we would overcome. Easy for him to say.

This ceremony should've been personal. It should've been about the kids who died. Instead it felt fake.

Ben nudged me. "Let's go."

He motioned to the others and we left amid stares from the people around us as we headed down the steps toward the exit. I didn't appreciate being judged like this. We'd been through a lot and deserved to grieve in our own way. None of us spoke as we headed along the stadium's concrete corridors and made our escape.

Outside, we heard the ceremony continuing but were far enough away to ignore the words. Reece suggested his place and we all agreed.

His basement had been turned into a teenage hangout complete with an old sofa, several beanbags, a giant rug and a flat screen television that looked strangely out of place next to the other ageing furniture.

Lauren and Dominique took the sofa while the rest of us sank into the beanbags. Reece grabbed some beers from a bar fridge in the corner and handed them around. It seemed as good an idea as any.

"I had to get out of there," Ben said.

"I know what you mean," Lauren said.

It made me feel better to know the others felt the same way I did. I didn't like being told how to act and grieve and what was appropriate behavior at a time like this. Just because we were sitting around drinking beer didn't mean we didn't feel it on the inside. We all did.

Eventually Dominique spoke up. "I feel like a fake. I haven't been here very long and I barely knew those kids and now they're gone."

"You're still one of us," Lauren said.

"That's it, though. They're gone and I'm not."

Lauren nodded. "Yeah, I'm the same. I think, why was I one of the lucky ones? Why them and not me? And if I was so lucky, why do I feel so damn bad all the time?"

These were the things that weren't being said at the state ceremony, the things we were supposed to say to each other, the things that helped us share the load. Maybe they weren't grand statements or truths and maybe they didn't need to be.

"I feel kind of guilty too," Reece said. "It's like I'm the only kid in the world who got rewarded for cutting school."

I wasn't sure why we should feel guilty either. But we did.

There was a glint in Lauren's eyes. "Do you think that's something State Ruler Bartley will mention in his speech?"

Reece threw his hands up. "Sure, and they might add an item to the school syllabus on how cutting class can save your life."

"Except if you'd cut class, then you wouldn't have attended that class in the first place." Lauren appeared to be on a roll. "Ah, the irony."

"I have no idea what you just said." Reece stood up. "You know what we need? More liquor."

"I'll drink to that." Lauren took another slug of beer.

I did too, though beer would not have been my first

choice of beverage. Or my second. But that wasn't what this was about.

Reece headed up the stairs, closely followed by Ben, only I had a feeling he had something else on his mind so I joined them. In the kitchen, Reece handed Ben a bottle of vodka.

"Funny how you weren't at school that day," Ben said.

Reece opened a cupboard door, looking for something. "Yep, it was hilarious that I didn't get pulverized."

Ben stared at him. "That's not exactly how I'd put it."

Reece put his hands on his hips. "If you've got something to say, why don't you come out with it?"

I stepped between them. "This is ridiculous."

"Nicola insists the bomb came from the future." Ben stared at Reece. "Same place you come from."

"I'm not the one—" Reece began.

"That's enough!" I said. "The only people we can blame are the ones who planted the bomb. Not you, Ben." I turned to Reece. "And not you either."

I carried my own grief and had my own doubts too. Lately I'd been wondering if Ben would've been better off if I'd never been sent to Altabena. Well, I was here now.

"So why is he pointing the finger at me?" Reece asked.

"You two need to pull yourselves together," I said. "We'll never make it if we can't rely on each other. Other people don't understand. No one else would even believe the truth."

Ben held my gaze. "Does that mean you have a plan?"

I shrugged. "All I know is that we've got to be ready."

"I've got a plan." Reece reached for a stack of shot glasses from the cupboard behind him. "We drink."

That brought a smile to Ben's face. "I like the sound of that."

Tomorrow we had school. Today we had friends. And vodka.

I'd never been drunk before and wasn't interested in starting now. But I could keep my friends company.

CHAPTER FIFTEEN

Government officials had kindly arranged for the remaining Altabena students to be bussed to Hamilton High. Luckily, Lauren hated taking the bus as much as I did, so she'd offered to drive me and Ben on our first day.

Mom was still insisting she was fine and I was still insisting on making coffee and breakfast and cleaning up in the morning. All part of our little routine.

Dad pressed a kiss to my forehead as I wiped the counter top. "I know you're nervous, honey."

"No, I'm not," I said.

"It's your first day at a new school. Doesn't seem that long ago that you started at Altabena High."

It wasn't. And it was. I'd been a completely different person back then – different values and standards, different everything. I'd also been clueless, and that was the last thing I needed him to point out at a time like this.

"You were worried about making friends," he said. "Didn't take you long though, did it? After a short time, you were invited to sleepovers and going to parties and fitting in just fine."

I wasn't the only one who was clueless.

Dad hadn't finished yet. "It'll take time. You've got to be patient."

"I get the message," I said.

He got up and placed a hand on my shoulder. "We don't expect you to just get over what happened and the friends you've lost, but you know as well as we do that you've got to get on with things."

His good intentions didn't stop me feeling annoyed. "Isn't that what I'm doing?"

"Have a good day, honey. Gotta run."

Great, now he'd done the concerned-dad-thing, he was leaving.

Mom sipped her coffee at the table. "He worries about you."

"He worries about you too." I threw my hands up. "And I worry about you, so we have this circle of worry."

April and Michael came in from their morning walk, and suddenly the kitchen became the center of non-stop chatter as April gave us the run-down on what they'd seen while they were out. She continued to fuss over Mom while I made a second pot of coffee, loaded the dishwasher and did things that were actually useful.

Mom stood and looked at me. "I really appreciate that, honey. I've got to get ready for work."

This elicited more comments from April on how she didn't understand why Mom was going to work when she should be resting. I could think of at least one good reason.

I left the room to sit at the foot of the steps in the front hall and wait for Lauren. Funny how Dad could be so right about some things and so wrong about others. I was anxious about a lot of things – the lives that had been lost, the future ahead, the threats still to come – but not about school.

The bomb had changed so many elements of my life. I was increasingly aware of how quickly things could change, of the frailty of human life, of how vulnerable we all were. Also aware how lucky I was. Somewhere along the line, the meaning of the word 'lucky' had changed to mean 'alive' or 'survivor'. It didn't mean we *felt* lucky.

Lauren was late, not that it mattered. I very much doubted we'd be reprimanded for tardiness, not under the circumstances.

I stood and picked up a framed photo from the sideboard. Mom had taken a selfie of the three of us last year after Dad and I had finished a fun run. Dad and I were sweaty and pink in the face while Mom was a picture of health. Pictures could be deceiving. Dad was the one who was out of shape but he was in a hell of a lot better state than Mom was.

What would I do without her? How would I cope?

I had biological parents in New Nation and a brother, a soldier with the dangerous job of patrolling the Badlands, but I'd never had a family until I got here. All I'd had was seventeen years of training on how to be self-sufficient, independent, obedient and loyal. I'd been in Altabena for five months and all of that had all gone out the door. Now I needed my family more desperately than ever.

Out of nowhere, my eyes welled with tears that tumbled down my cheeks. I hated that there was nothing I could do to help my mom. I despised that disease. And I hated feeling so vulnerable all the time. Hated the weight on my shoulders and the knot in my gut and the constant feeling that everything could fall apart in a heartbeat and there was nothing I could do.

April stepped into the front hall, presumably on her way upstairs. I felt her staring at me so I put the photo back and wiped the tears from my cheeks while my back was to her. I didn't need her in my life and certainly didn't want her to see me like this.

Still, she lingered and asked, "What were you looking at?"

I pointed. "Just a photo."

"The three of you look so happy in that picture."

"Yes."

"The two of them were happy before you came on the scene too, you know."

I turned to face her. "Were they?"

She stared right back at me, looking into my eyes that were probably still red from crying. For the first time, I had the feeling she was actually seeing a real person.

Eventually she said, "You don't have to keep proving yourself to me by looking after your mother and cleaning up and helping all the time."

"You really don't get it."

"You're onto a good thing here."

"Yeah, I am. Mom and Dad are good people. The best. And I don't want to lose them."

It was pretty damn obvious why I did the things I did. I loved my parents. Didn't take a genius to work that out but I didn't want to sully the word by saying it in front of this woman.

April tilted her head. "You're like the river that flowed through the Grand Canyon, the water that slowly eroded the rock."

She'd lost me. "What?"

"I'm just saying that the small things add up. Sometimes it's the little stuff that combines to make a difference."

I screwed up my face. "Is that meant to be...a compliment?"

"I'm not saying I like you."

In my wildest dreams I didn't think she was. Stunned, I stood there.

She continued. "But your mother cares for you – a lot – and as long as you're good to her, I'll tolerate you."

This was so ridiculous I tried my hardest not to burst out laughing. "Wow, you'll tolerate me."

April raised her eyebrows, less sure of herself than before. "That's what I said."

I stretched my arm out. "Can we shake on it?"

"Certainly."

"Can we smile about it?" I asked.

"Certainly not."

She turned and walked up the stairs, hiding a smile. I wasn't quite sure what had just happened or where I stood with April but it seemed like progress.

Wow, I was *tolerated*. Must be careful not to get a swollen head.

A car horn tooted outside. Lauren, no doubt.

Shaking my head, I grabbed my backpack. After this, school was going to be a doddle.

* * *

In fact, school was exactly that – it was school. The new students had been welcomed at a morning gathering, given our new timetables and quickly integrated into existing classes.

I had to hand it to the other kids at Hamilton.

Normally, it was dog-eat-dog at high school whereas here the other students were being warm and helpful, or as warm as other teenagers could be. We were being treated with kid gloves, something that wouldn't last, and that was fine too.

Even during the after school rush in the hallway, I could've sworn other students were making way for me and Lauren. Or maybe we just felt conspicuous.

I pointed in the distance. "Is that Dominique over there?"

"Not sure." Lauren shrugged. "She said she was going to the gym after school."

"I wanted to catch up with her," I said. "To check she's okay."

Dominique had missed out on the warm welcome, arriving at lunch because she had her official training sessions at the institute in the mornings. She'd shoveled down some food, then headed for class and hadn't seemed quite herself, which wasn't that unusual because no one was themselves anymore.

Still, I was worried. She wasn't one of us. I'd been in Altabena five months whereas she'd only been here for five minutes.

Lauren sighed. "It's been a long day. I just want to get home. How about if Ben and I wait for you by the car?"

"Sure. I won't be long."

I headed straight to the gym and found Dominique in the locker room taking off her sweater. I dropped my backpack, leaning against the bench in front of the lockers.

"How'd you go today?" I asked.

"Great." She rolled her eyes. "I'm the new kid again."

"I know the feeling."

She gave me a dirty look as if she didn't believe me, then shuffled around in her locker. "I need to get ready. I need to focus."

"You don't need to dive straight in to training," I said. "You could take it easy for a change."

She pointed in the direction of the gym. "Or I could go in there and show them what I'm made of."

Which would be a repeat of her first days at Altabena High where her greatest success was in alienating half the student population. It was only after the bomb that we'd got to know Dominique a little better and discovered she wasn't so bad. She might not be my favorite person but I still didn't want to abandon her.

"Do you want to make friends here?" I asked.

"Sure."

"Or do you want to go in there and kick everyone's butt?"

"What's wrong with that? You've kicked your fair share of butt from what I can gather."

"I'm not saying it's wrong, only that it might not be the best way to get on with people."

She held my gaze. "It's who I am. Who am I if I'm not the champion?"

"You're Dominique," I said. "You don't have to be The Dominator."

Her eyes widened. "Is that what they call me?"

She was single-minded, trained hard and was good at what she did. I could understand her drive and determination better than she knew because I'd been there. I was still there, always striving, working toward my goals, doing my best in a bad situation.

"I don't have anything else." She threw her hands up.

"This is the only thing I'm good at."

"That's not true."

"Really? Name one thing I'm good at."

"You were pretty good at drinking beer and vodka at Reece's place the other day."

She smiled wanly. "Seemed like a good idea at the time. Until I had to go to training the next day hung over."

"Look, you don't need to prove anything to the people who are waiting for you at the gym."

"You don't understand. My mom was an elite athlete. She trained for years and got into the Olympic team. She had dreams like I've got dreams."

I shrugged. "Nothing wrong with that."

Dominique continued. "Then she got pregnant and couldn't go. I *have* to do this."

Wow, did everyone have issues with their parents? I had my own problems at home and, if I was going to get pedantic about it, they weren't even my biological parents.

"You're not the only one who's in pain," I said. "This is hard for all of us. It's hard to come to school and pretend everything is okay when we know damn well what happened to everyone else at school. We're all hurting. There's no crime in that."

Dominique pulled her tee shirt over her head. "I have to get ready."

I nodded. "Sure."

Talking to Dominique was like stepping back in time. I wished I could do exactly that – step back to a time before the school had been blown up, before our friends had passed away, before we'd had to face a pain no one should have to live through.

Still, there were worse places I could be stuck. We'd

get through this one way or another.

CHAPTER SIXTEEN

Ben stood in my kitchen, lifted the white plastic lid with a flourish and motioned toward the amazing concoction on the table – chocolate cake with chocolate frosting, topped with M&Ms because clearly there wasn't already enough chocolate.

Mom's face lit up. "For me?"

"Celia and I made it," Ben said. "Well, technically I made the cake and Celia was in charge of decoration."

Mom pressed a hand to her chest. "That's so kind of you, Ben, but it's not my birthday."

"It doesn't have to be."

So smooth. I had to hand it to him.

Mom kissed him on the cheek, not something she would normally do, not something she'd ever done as far as I could remember. Ben threw his arms around her in a warm embrace, which made me wonder if the hugging that had become so prolific would ever end.

April leaned over to admire the cake. "Such a lovely gesture. Shows you've been well raised."

I'd forgotten she was there. Almost.

Always polite, Ben nodded in appreciation. Stepping

away from her, he put his arm around me as if to say he knew where his loyalties lay. April smiled, oblivious that Ben might not think as highly of her as she did of him.

"Time for us to get going," he said.

"Where are we off to?" I asked.

"It's a surprise," he said.

Mom's lips curled to a sly smile. "Ben's full of surprises this evening."

I glanced from her to Ben. "Did he tell you where we're going?"

"My lips are sealed."

"Not fair." I whacked him gently on the chest and he pretended to be hurt.

We headed off in Ben's car or, more accurately, Ben's father's car. He was trying to make up for our missed date the other night and had said we should save dinner at Alto's for another time when we both felt up to it. He'd told me to dress in normal clothes – which meant jeans, Converse sneakers and a tee shirt – and to make sure I was warm. They were the only clues as to where we were going.

"So we're heading into town?" I asked two minutes into the drive.

Ben switched on his indicator and cut a sharp left. "Not exactly."

"Why are we backtracking?"

"All part of my ploy," he said with the greatest confidence.

We drove around for some time while I kept guessing where we might be going. Eventually we pulled up at the lake.

I looked across at Ben in the driver's seat. "I thought

you said we were having dinner."

He came around and opened my door for me. "I hope you're hungry."

Taking my arm, he led me to the swings. "You have to wait here. And you're not allowed to look. Okay?"

I kissed him on the lips and sat on the swing. "Okay."

Staring out at the lake, I heard the trunk open and lots of shuffling sounds from the grassed area behind me.

Ben came up behind me and pressed a kiss to the back of my neck. "You have to cover your eyes."

I was nothing if not obedient as I allowed Ben to lead me to a secluded area close by. A full moon shone overhead. Ben had spread a red-checkered rug on the grass. A wicker basket filled with picnic food sat at one end, along with an ice bucket, a bottle of champagne and two pink plastic glasses.

He sat on his knees and started unpacking the basket. "We've got little sandwiches and crackers and cheese."

"Did Celia help you with this too?" I asked.

He passed a delicately wrapped chicken sandwich to me. "No, if she had her way, dinner would be MacDonald's with extra fries."

I sat down on the rug, feeling more relaxed than I had in a long time. "Healthy *and* delicious. Good for building up the muscles."

"Exactly. I made the sandwiches myself with only the finest ingredients."

I pointed my pinky in the air to appear posh. "Exquisite."

"It's not exactly Alto's," he said.

"Who needs a fancy restaurant when we've got moonlight?" I leaned across and kissed him.

Meanwhile Ben leaned across for the bottle. "And champagne."

That was something we definitely wouldn't have been able to have at Alto's or any other restaurant. I wasn't sure how he'd got hold of it and didn't ask.

Ben ripped the foil from the bottle and eased off the cork, which flew into the air before he was expecting it. Concentration on his face, he shoved the bottle into my hand, looked up, his eye on the cork as he dived across the rug to catch it in his fingertips.

"Great catch!" I said.

Ben proudly held up the cork. "There are some advantages to being an ex-football player."

As he reached behind me for the glasses, I stole another kiss and insisted on pouring the champagne, made a big deal of it, in fact, which wasn't hard since it kept fizzing up. A few drops poured over the edge but most of the liquid made its way into the glasses.

He handed a glass across. "To me and you."

I had a few sips and felt even more relaxed than before. This was the two of us, spending time together, doing things our way. What could be better?

"It's such a transformation," I said.

"What is?"

"Right now you're like a renegade teenager who has illegally got your hands on some alcohol."

Ben raised his eyebrows, a quizzical look on his face. "A renegade?"

I nodded. "Meanwhile back at my place you were doing your best impersonation of a model citizen. You made a good impression on April, and Mom loves you."

"Maybe she loves chocolate cake."

"Me too. Don't take this the wrong way. I'm not complaining. I loved the decorations too. Very mature."

"Yep, mature. That's how I'd describe Celia."

I cut small slices of runny camembert to go with the crackers on my plate. "So why are you trying to get into my mom's good books?"

Ben took a generous sip of champagne. "The cake was for you too, you know."

"Because I need more chocolate in my life?"

He looked down. "Because your mom's sick. Because you look after her. Because there's not much else I can do."

Ben knew what it was like to grow up without a mom and he knew what it was like when his mom had been alive too. He didn't want me to go through that.

I kissed him lightly on the mouth. "So you said it with cake. That's a language I understand."

"There are other languages too."

He pushed the hair back from my face and gazed at me. Only seconds earlier, his face had clouded over and he couldn't face me, whereas now his eyes were gleaming with satisfaction. He pressed his mouth against mine, parted my lips and rolled his tongue against mine. It was starting to get a bit chilly so my skin felt cool, meanwhile I was burning up on the inside.

We finished eating and lounged around on the rug, sipping champagne. I loved these moments together when it was just the two of us and we could pretend, if only for a while, that nothing else mattered.

I zipped up my windbreaker and rubbed my hands together. "It's getting cold."

"I've got just the answer." Ben got up and when he

came back, he was shaking out a sleeping bag. A double sleeping bag.

I climbed inside with him. He held me close and kissed me. I unbuttoned his shirt and pressed my hands on his chest. I liked seeing his bare chest. Liked touching it. Liked touching him.

Ben nuzzled up against my neck and peppered little kisses to my throat. He made me feel special. Made me want more. Made me feel alive. He slipped his hand under my tee shirt onto the bare skin of my waist. A tingle shot up my spine. Not so long ago, I'd had no idea I could feel this way.

I was overheating so I sat up and got rid of the windbreaker. Ben slipped the tee shirt over my head too. I stared at him, not sure I could do this, not sure if I should put my shirt back on. The cold air hit my back so I slipped into the sleeping bag again, grateful for my bra, the only thing that could come between us.

It wasn't nudity I had a problem with. Not at all, in fact. It was the combination of being naked and around Ben that was hard to handle. And the way it made me feel. That was the real problem.

Ben kissed the tip of my shoulders and slid off the strap of my bra. I slipped it back up. I wasn't sure where this was headed – or maybe I knew the exact direction and that's what made me back off.

"I'm sorry," I said. "It doesn't feel right."

"That's okay." He pulled me close again. "I get it. It's never going to feel right."

"That's not true."

Ben stared into my eyes. "Isn't it? I have such strong feelings for you. I want to be with you in every way I can. I want you, Nic. I want you more than you want me."

"I'd do anything for you, Ben. I'd give up my life for you."

It was true. I would. I couldn't bear for him not to have a place in the world, to stop breathing, to not have the life he deserved. It didn't mean I was better than him or more generous or more anything. It's just the way I was, the way I'd been raised, and that was a hard thing to shake.

"But you won't give yourself to me," he said. "Not really. Not your innermost self. Not where it counts."

There was no malice in his voice or recrimination. He was simply stating the facts.

"Don't you know how I feel about you?" I said. "I can't get enough of you. I long for you. Sometimes I feel like I'm going to explode with emotion."

"I know it's hard for you. That you were brought up in a loveless place. But things are different here."

"You're right about one thing. Sometimes it was easier being a soldier. I didn't have to think. Didn't have to feel."

"That was then and this is now." He threw his hands up, impatience in his voice. "You have to get over it."

I'd seen this happen before. He wanted something. Me. And normally-patient-Ben could very quickly switch to persuasive-pushy-Ben.

Maybe he didn't know how it felt to be stuck between two worlds, the present and the future. I wanted Ben and couldn't get enough of him and at the same time I was scared. Of caring too much. Of the unknown.

He sat up and dropped his head into his hands. "It's hard for me too, Nic."

"You're much better than me at this stuff," I said. "You've had so much more practice.

"I don't truly have you, not yet, and I have this horrible feeling one day you're going to slip through my fingers."

I didn't need to be able to see his face to know this wasn't pushy-Ben. This was someone else.

Sitting up, I rubbed his neck. "I'm here, Ben. I'm not going anywhere."

He reached across to hand my clothes to me. I pulled on my tee shirt and windbreaker, and Ben put his arm around me. Right now, I needed his warmth in more ways than one and maybe he needed me as well.

"I've got my own problems too," he said. "At home. At school. Out of school. I don't tell my family I love them. I can't say it, not to Dad or even to Celia. I can tell her she's special but I can't tell her what she truly means to me."

"I'm sure she knows," I said.

"But I can't tell her. Just like there are things I can't say to you."

I gazed into his green eyes. Waited.

"I'm afraid," he said, "that if I tell you exactly how I feel about you, you'll go away."

"I'm not going anywhere, Ben."

"Like my mom went away. I loved her. She was my mom. And one day she ended it all and left us."

His voice cracked. Pain glimmered in his eyes. It was bad enough that Ben's mother had committed suicide when he was twelve years old. It was worse that he was the one who found her body.

She'd never left him though, not completely. The scars were too deep. Part of her was always with him. That was the part that hurt.

"You'll leave me, Nic," he said. "Just like she did. Not because you're mean or because you don't care, but because that's the way it is. You could disappear at any moment. Those superior officers you're always talking about – they could find out where you are and drag you back to where you came from."

"It won't happen. I got rid of the geopositrons. You were there."

"Do you really want to remind me about that?"

I'd done what I had to do. The only thing I could do. He was right, though – we didn't need to talk about that again.

"We're together," I said. "We've got to make the most of it."

"For how long? How many weeks or months or years do we have before something happens and you disappear?"

I wanted to tell him it wouldn't happen.

I wished I could.

CHAPTER SEVENTEEN

"I've only been here two days and already they're going to expel me." Lauren looked stunned, horrified more like it.

I raised my eyebrows. "What?"

"I just got called to the principal's office," she said.

We were sitting at a lunch table in the cafeteria with Ben and Reece. Dominique was due to join us as soon as she arrived from her morning training at the institute. Will would be joining us later too. We were sticking together, no matter what.

"This isn't something to do with the article you wrote, is it?" I asked.

She'd written an opinion piece for the *Altabena Times*, stating her objections to the teenage curfew Bartley had instituted. Everyone was talking about it, or everyone at school was. Her English teacher had congratulated her and all day people had been coming up to her.

Lauren nodded slowly. "They want me to take back what I said."

"Hang on," Ben said. "Who's 'they'?"

"Some dudes from the government."

"How can you?" he said. "It's printed in the

newspaper, not online where you can take a blog post down."

"They want me to submit another piece to the newspaper where I retract my statements and admit I was trying to be sensationalist."

Ben's dark hair fell over his eyes so he pushed it away. "Who's going to believe that?"

"Principal Smythe told me I'd better make it convincing. I thought Ms. Di Giorgio was bad but honestly she was a pushover compared to this woman."

Different school, different principal, same power structure. And no doubt the 'dudes' from the government weren't going to change their minds.

"My mom is going to freak," Lauren said.

"Wouldn't she stick up for you?" Reece asked.

"That's the whole problem. She'll be outraged and kick up a huge fuss and insist on taking this right to the top."

Reece stared at her. "To the top of what? This already goes to the top. State Ruler Bartley has always wanted a teenage curfew. Now he's finally got his chance he isn't going to back down."

"Neither is my mom. She'll think of something, start petitions, organize a protest march."

"Maybe that's not such a bad idea," Reece said. "A protest. It wouldn't be the first time we ever protested."

No one said anything.

"We stick together," Reece added. "They might be able to push around one person but they can't push all of us around. Like last year after the riot. Then Lorenzo and Daniel helped get the information out online to tell everyone what was going on."

Reece's face clouded over as soon as he realized what

he'd said. Daniel wasn't here any more. He'd been at school when the bomb had gone off.

"Shit, this is bad." Reece rubbed his eyes. "We can't give up. We can't let Lauren get trodden on. We could refuse to go to classes, hold a strike at school, or a sit in. It'd get publicity. We'd get our point across."

Reece might want publicity but I certainly didn't. Ben had to stay under the radar and keep a low profile or it'd make it too easy for people from the future to find him. A protest might be a good idea for him, but not for Ben.

Lauren motioned to the other tables in the cafeteria. "And all these people would stick up for us?"

"They might," he said.

"We're strangers here. These students don't know us."

"So we shouldn't even try? Is that what you're saying? That you should roll over and do exactly what you're told and stop having an opinion and stop voicing it?"

"No, that's not what I'm saying."

Dominique pulled up a chair beside us. "Wow, what's going on?"

The bell rang and I heaved a sigh of relief for the explanation I didn't want to give and the argument I didn't want to have. As we got up from the table, I wasn't sure which of us looked the grumpiest.

"See you at science class," I said to Ben, then sped up to catch Reece.

"What's up with you?" I asked as we walked.

"Whaddya mean?" He gave me a strange look and suddenly looked exactly like the guy with curly bleached hair and bad regrowth that I'd always known.

I'd have thought my question was self-explanatory. Since I'd known him, he'd been very low-key and hadn't wanted to get involved. Now he was Mr.-Let's-Organize-A-Protest.

"Suddenly you've become all militant," I said.

"So it's okay for you to get forceful whenever you need to but it's not okay for me? I'm sick of getting pushed around."

I grabbed his arm. "That's not it."

He stopped and stared at me. "Of all people you should know better. You remember what things were like in New Nation, how oppressive, how we weren't allowed to think for ourselves. That's where things are headed now."

He was right. The Bartley government was using the school bombing as an excuse to tighten the reigns and institute changes designed to control us. They'd tried it before the bombing but it hadn't worked. Then.

"I don't want to go back to that," Reece said.

Neither did I.

*　　*　　*

We could almost pretend life was back to normal. Mr. Rodriguez was sitting at a desk at the front of the class while we had our heads down finishing off a short essay. He looked the same as always, except for the facial hair he was always changing. Still, he'd stuck with the goatee for a while now.

The setting was the same but different too – new school, a different classroom, same science teacher. At the start of class, Mr. Rodriguez had introduced himself to the other students and said he'd be taking over some classes. He didn't say he was the only surviving teacher from Altabena High. Everyone already knew.

The teacher glanced at his watch, then wandered to the

back of the class where Ben and I were seated.

Placing a hand on Ben's shoulder, he leaned over. "Would you please see me at the end of the lesson?"

Ben nodded and kept writing. The teacher glanced at me so I smiled, only to see him staring right through me, one eye twitching uncontrollably. He pulled his hand back and walked to the front of the room. I guessed he was as damaged by the school bombing as the rest of us.

I felt a sense of relief when the bell went. We'd done it, got through another day, and that meant we could do it the next day and the day after that. Before, I hadn't needed constant reassurance that life would go on. I did now.

Along with the other students, I packed up my gear, then slung my bag nearer the front of the room. Ben had already made his way to the teacher's desk.

"You can get going, Nicola," Mr. Rodriguez shouted over the din as the other students were leaving.

I lifted my hand in a small wave. "I'm waiting for Ben."

Lauren had been in the next class and was waiting outside the door, so I pulled her inside. She started telling me how she was already overloaded with homework when the teacher interrupted.

"It would be better if you left."

The room was quiet now the others had gone, so Mr. Rodriguez's words cut through the air. Not so long ago, I'd been extremely obedient whereas now being told to leave only made me want to stay.

"We won't disturb you." I pulled Lauren further toward the back of the class in case we were making more noise than we thought. Mr. Rodriguez and Ben had discussed weird scientific concepts in the past and I'd always been there so I didn't know what was so different now. They'd never needed privacy before.

Lauren was talking to me in a low tone. My eyes were glued to the front of the room where Ben was slouching against the teacher's desk while Mr. Rodriguez stood in front of him, his eye still twitching. The teacher seemed different somehow. Then again, we'd all been different since the bombing.

"Are you even listening?" Lauren asked.

"No, I…"

She whacked me gently on the arm. Through the corner of my eye, I saw her turn to look at the front. Then Mr. Rodriguez reached down to his shoe and I caught a glimpse of silver.

"What's…?" Lauren couldn't finish.

I knew what it was. A knife. In Mr. Rodriguez's hand.

Tunnel vision. There was nothing else in the room, only me and the two of them at the front.

I knocked over a chair. "Ben, move!"

It happened in slow motion. A perfectly placed slash of the knife across Ben's forearm. Diagonal. To cause the most damage.

Horror in his eyes, Ben looked down at the rivulet of red on his arm.

I ran between the desks. "Nooo!"

Mr. Rodriguez was good with a knife. He'd said he did Filipino Kali. Hadn't mentioned he was a master.

One more smooth movement and he slashed Ben's throat. I heard the horrible sound as the knife ripped through skin and slid through his larynx. So quick. So devastating.

Ben…

"Nooo!"

I knocked Mr. Rodriguez off him. No resistance. The knife clattered to the floor.

Ben grasped his neck. A horrible gurgling sound escaped his throat as he crumpled to the floor, his back to the desk.

Too late. How can I be too late?

A scream cut through the air. Lauren perhaps. I would've screamed if I could. I was screaming on the inside.

I glanced down at the knife, put my foot on it and kicked it between the desks to the back of the room along the linoleum floor.

My eyes met Mr. Rodriguez's. No more twitching. Fear in his face, he looked mortified, as if he had no idea what he'd done. His hands held out, he was backing off slowly.

I should hit him. I should kill him.

But Ben needed me more. The teacher turned and ran. I let him.

One look at my beautiful Ben and my knees gave way as I dropped to the floor beside him. Blood, so much blood.

"Ben, Ben…"

I wanted to hold him. Didn't want to suffocate him. I had to do something. I couldn't let this happen.

Ripping off my cotton sweater, I pressed it to his neck. Tried to block the flow of blood. In seconds, blood dripped to the floor, soaked through my sweater.

I slid my hand onto his cheek. "I love you, Ben."

His mouth was open. Trying to speak. His eyes were wide with horror, the whites of his eyes stark, the ribbons of gold in his green eyes no longer glimmering.

I pressed a kiss to his temple. "Hold on. You've got to hold on."

It was useless. A picture of the knife flashed before my eyes again. I should have been quicker. Damn it, if only I'd been quicker.

Ben's eyes suddenly widened, as if with sudden realization and understanding. I hoped he didn't know what was going on, that he didn't know he was dying, that he was oblivious. It would've been better that way.

"Stay with me," I said.

His eyes glazed over, the lids slackening though his eyes stayed open. I didn't know you could watch the life leave someone's eyes.

It was too late.

CHAPTER EIGHTEEN

I held Ben's hand, pressed little kisses to his face, mumbled words of affection while tears streamed down my face. All too late.

The air was sucked out of me. I couldn't breathe, couldn't function, couldn't handle this. It felt like my heart had been ripped out and stomped on and all that was left was a great gaping hole.

Around me, I heard things happening. Lauren was on the phone calling the police and paramedics. Her voice was shaking but she was doing it. There were footsteps as she shuffled to the door and issued instructions, said Mr. Rodriguez had gone crazy, that someone had been knifed, then told two kids to get help.

Who'd have thought Lauren would be so good in a crisis? Maybe practice would do that to a person.

Holding Ben's hand, I looked toward my friend. "It's too late, Lauren. He's gone."

She pressed a hand on her chest and stood there, frozen.

I kept replaying the incident in my head, round and round on a loop. I saw the signs, knew something wasn't right. And every time I was too late. Every time, the rivulet of blood on Ben's neck became a river.

If only I'd got there in time. A sob escaped my lips, then another.

"You can't bring him back," Lauren said, her fingers in her mouth. "I'm sorry."

That's when it hit me, blew me back like a giant wave. "But I can. I have to."

"Nicola…"

I stared at Ben. "I can go back in time. I can change this. I can get rid of the people who gave the order. If it's down to them or you, I can kill them. I'll do it. Whatever it takes, Ben. Then it'll be as if you never died."

He was everything to me. I couldn't go on without him. I wouldn't.

Behind me, Lauren screamed. "Nicola, you're scaring me."

I had to go back to a time before that happened or, better still, much earlier. I couldn't let Ben get so close to death. Nowhere near it.

The mental picture of Mr. Rodriguez slashing Ben's throat pounded in my head, while my heart was being trampled, the pain relentless, like nothing I'd ever felt before. How could something, anything hurt this much?

I don't know what happened next. Don't know how long I stayed hunched over beside Ben's lifeless body holding his hand. Don't know who else was around.

At some point, the room came to life again. Lauren was still there with a female teacher I vaguely recognized and two uniformed cops, both of them tall and burly. Where had they come from?

"What's her name?" one of the police officers asked

quietly. I felt his hand on my shoulder. "Excuse me, Nicola, you can't help him any more."

I glanced up at the officer. "Okay, I just want to kiss him one last time."

"Sorry, you can't."

My eyes were pleading. "A final kiss. It's not too much to ask."

"This is a crime scene, miss."

I tried to lean forward but the man's hand was still there, holding me back.

"One kiss," I said.

"No."

I stood. Saw red. A crime scene. Really? I punched him in the face. Knocked him back. His hand over his nose, he bumped into a desk, stumbled and landed on his butt.

The other cop stepped forward. I smashed him in the gut. My fist sank in deep. He doubled over. Couldn't move.

No way was I going to let anything, or anyone, stand between me and Ben.

"Oh my God." The teacher's voice.

I crouched down, leaned over and pressed my lips against Ben's. Because he was my Ben.

Lauren was still standing there as I got up. She was a sobbing mess. I, too, had a face full of tears.

"Nicola, no." Her voice quavered. "I know what you're going to do."

It struck me as strange that she should know what I was going to do. How could she?

"You're going to kill Mr. Rodriguez," she yelled. "Don't do it! You'll only make things worse."

Maybe I should run after him. Maybe I should want

revenge.

Instead, my whole body ached with need like never before – the desperate need to have Ben back.

I shook my head. "It's not his fault."

"Nicola, you're not making sense."

It made perfect, despicable, horrible sense. They knew exactly how to get to Ben. Through Mr. Rodriguez. He was implanted with a kill chip, programmed to complete a mission.

"That wasn't him," I said. "It was the computer chip."

Lauren screwed up her face. "What?"

"I'm going to fix this."

And I would.

"I can do it, Lauren. I'm the only one."

The woman teacher was frozen to the spot. The two cops were straightening, probably getting ready to take action. They had their eyes on me.

"Nicola, that's crazy talk," Lauren said.

I put my hand out. "I need your keys."

"What?"

"*Now*, Lauren."

She reached into her pocket and passed me her keys. Perhaps she was afraid. Perhaps she wanted me to get away before the police could get to me.

I grabbed my backpack and ran.

I knew exactly what I had to do – go back to a time before Ben had been killed, a time before the school was bombed, back to a time when we still had a chance.

And there was only one way to do that.

I had to return to New Nation in 2120 first.

CHAPTER NINETEEN

A good soldier wouldn't go back to her house to say goodbye to her parents, but I wasn't a good soldier. I was something else. I was also pretty sure I could make it there before the authorities came searching for me. They'd be looking for Mr. Rodriguez first.

Lauren would no doubt tell the police what she'd seen, that Mr. Rodriguez had gone ballistic and slashed Ben's throat. Other witnesses would have seen him running from the scene.

I knew what they didn't because I was aware how clever my superior officers were. They'd found someone Ben trusted – a man who had Kali skills and was good with a knife – and implanted him with a kill chip. The perfect candidate.

The look of horror on the teacher's face as he ran from the room came back to me. He wasn't programmed to kill anyone else, only Ben. He'd realized what he'd done and had run away in terror.

I had to get that thought out of my head and focus. One thing at a time. I pushed open the back door into the kitchen. I'd never been so relieved that Mom was home.

I threw my arms around her, held her in a long embrace, and didn't want to let go. She felt so good that I could almost believe things would be all right as long as we stayed like this and didn't move.

"Honey, are you okay?" She broke off the hug, held me at arm's length. "What happened?"

Was I covered in blood? I didn't know and didn't dare look. I was wearing dark jeans and a navy top, and presumably blood stains wouldn't stand out too much.

"I'm fine." I held her gaze, felt bad that I was going to cause her so much concern. "Where's Dad?"

"It's still early. He's not home yet."

"Then give him one of these from me." I wrapped my arms around her and it felt good again and also bad.

She stepped back, held my gaze. "You can give him a hug yourself."

"Sure."

I backed away, my gaze shifting briefly to April who was staring at me as if I was from another planet.

"I'll get started on my homework," I said.

It didn't matter that I wasn't a convincing liar. I'd go up to my room, then let Mom know the truth when I came back downstairs. Not the whole truth. That would be too much for her. The partial truth would have to do.

In my room, I tipped the school things from my backpack and started to think about what I'd need. I changed into clean clothes and shoved a windbreaker into my bag. It'd get cold later tonight.

What would I need in New Nation? I wouldn't be able to take anything with me anyway. No point worrying about that. I grabbed a knife I'd bought last year and placed it at the bottom of my backpack, along with a torch and the swipe card I'd stolen from the lab. My get-out-of-jail-free card.

Dad had a gun that I could take, but I didn't want to kill anyone. Not anyone in Altabena, anyway.

Besides, I didn't understand this obsession people had with guns, as if they solved all their problems. My problems were in a different league.

The other items I needed were in the kitchen so I shot down the stairs, grabbed a bottle of water and a banana and made myself a ham sandwich. I'd need a balanced meal later. I was a soldier again and had to be practical.

First, I had one less-than-practical thing to do, so I headed outside where Mom was sweeping the patio while my grandparents – if you could call them that – sat in the sunshine with a magazine and the newspaper. I'd grown to love Altabena and loved the sunshine. Still, I'd be back. I hoped.

Best to tackle the easiest part first. I shook hands with April and Michael who seemed surprised but returned my handshake.

I leaned closer to April. "Make sure you take care of Mom."

A confused expression on her face, she nodded. Didn't speak.

"Mom, one more hug!" I raced across the patio and drew her into my arms. She held the broom in her other hand but a one-armed hug was still pretty good.

I wouldn't forget about her. I'd bring back the cancer cure for her too. All the more reason to go.

"Must be my lucky day," she said.

"Remember, you've got to give Dad one of those from me."

Her brow furrowed, she gave me a quizzical look. "What's...?"

I straightened, my hands on her shoulders. "I'm going away for a few days."

She opened her mouth to argue but I got in first.

"There's something I have to do. It's important. For me. For all of us."

"Nicola, you can't just up and leave."

She was such a mom that it was breaking my heart. Or it would have been if my heart hadn't already been ripped from my chest. The hole inside me grew a little bigger.

I held her gaze. "Do you trust me?"

Her eyes suddenly welled with tears. Damn it, I was going to have to get away quickly or I'd lose it too.

"I love you and I'll be back." I pressed a quick kiss to her cheek, and left her standing on the patio holding the broom.

I raced through the house, grabbing my backpack on the way, and made a beeline for the car parked out on the street. Mom's car, actually. I had the keys.

My phone rang as I was driving, so I pulled over a few streets away and saw that Lauren had called. I wished there was something I could say to make her feel better. It probably wouldn't be hard to sound more coherent than I had earlier at school, but there was still no reasonable explanation I could give her. Nothing she could understand, anyway.

Ben had understood. He'd believed in me.

I balled my hand into a fist and pressed it against my top lip to stop myself from crying. Deep breaths, in and out. At least I could still breathe even if my chest felt crushed.

Lauren's call reminded me I should disable the GPS function in my phone, so I did that, switched it off and shoved it into my backpack in case I needed it later.

My next stop was a pharmacy where I picked up some syringes and needles. The young woman serving me hardly even asked any questions.

I drove to the lake and pulled up in a secluded spot at the far end of the parking lot behind some trees. And waited.

Sliding the seat back as far as it could, I put my feet up on the dash and closed my eyes. I couldn't see the swings and the lake from here but I could imagine them. I pictured the picnic Ben had prepared for us and remembered how it had felt when we were snuggled in the giant sleeping bag together. The night air had been crisp on my face but my body had been burning.

This time, as I imagined it, things were different. This time, I let myself go and went all the way with Ben. We were naked, our bodies intertwined, as close as two people can get – except I didn't know what that felt like because I'd never been there. My eyes sprang open.

It was getting dark. It'd be time soon. I reached for the sandwich and bottle of water in my bag and forced myself to eat. I couldn't have wolfed the food down if I'd tried. The banana could wait for later. After all, you never know when you might need a banana.

I waited until nine o'clock.

Then started the engine.

CHAPTER TWENTY

The parking lot outside Geochemical Global Laboratories was empty. That was why I'd waited – to make sure no one was left at the lab when I turned up. Mom's car would stand out if anyone came by, so I had to hope they wouldn't. Only a small risk in the scheme of things.

I slung my backpack over my shoulder and walked down the path to the front door. Though the parking lot was lit, there were only dim lights inside the laboratory and none at the perimeter of the building.

It wasn't that long ago I'd been desperate to rid my body of geopositrons so my superior officers wouldn't be able to trace me. Now, those same tracking molecules were the reason I was here. In fact, I didn't know what I'd do if Reece hadn't stuffed up when he was purging himself of the little suckers.

What would be happening to me now if I didn't have access to geopositrons? Returning to New Nation wouldn't even be an option. Saving Ben wouldn't be a possibility, and I could completely forget about reversing damage at the school and preventing the deaths of all those innocent people.

Funny how going back to my own time was the one thing I never wanted to do and now it was what I wanted most in the world. I needed those geopositrons. I had to hope my superior officers would register that they'd reached a critical mass and then transport me back to New Nation.

One thing I knew for sure – whether they thought it was me or Reece alive in Altabena, they wouldn't let us stay here. They'd bring us back and hold us accountable for our actions one way or another.

Security card at the ready, I held it in front of the tab to the right of the main doors. Nothing. I swiped it more quickly. Waited. I brushed it slowly in front of the tab again. No beep. Nothing.

Kicking the front doors was supposed to make me feel better but didn't. What was the point of stealing the swipe card if the damn thing didn't work? I shoved the stupid card in my back pocket and paced the grassed area at the side of the path.

I had options. There were always options. I could drive the car through the front doors. Maybe not such a good idea given it'd make a phenomenal amount of noise and someone would no doubt call the police. Still, that might not matter if I was quick enough.

There might be a better way. I crept around to the side of the building, keeping my eyes open, just in case. Breaking a window would make a lot less noise than smashing through the front doors with a vehicle. A plan didn't have to be sophisticated for it to work.

It was dark under the shrubbery at the side of the building so I reached for the torch and looked around for something heavy and hard when I spotted a small rockery with ferns growing out of it. Perfect.

I dug around with my bare hands, lifted a large rock and trudged back to the side of the building. I wished Ben were here to help me, then realized that was ironic because if Ben were here, I wouldn't be breaking into the laboratory in the first place.

Using both hands, I slung the rock at the window. It crashed through. I looked around, out of habit more than anything, to see if someone might be coming, then decided I shouldn't waste time. I used one end of my torch to knock out the remaining pieces of glass from the window and clambered inside into an office.

It was quiet. Too quiet. There was no alarm ringing, however I had my own personal alarm.

I made it out of the office into the corridor, jamming the door open with a book from the desk in case I needed to come back this way, then headed for the room where the geopositrons were stored.

The door was locked, no surprises there. I swiped the security card over the tab next to the door, just in case. No luck. I stared at the window that looked into the laboratory and knew what I had to do.

My old favorite rock was exactly where I'd tossed it, on the floor of the office I'd initially broken into. It felt even heavier this time around but I dragged it back down the corridor and felt a second wind as I slung the rock through the window and heard the satisfying smash.

I knocked the remaining shards of glass from the frame and jumped inside. I was getting good at this.

Though the room was dark, there was enough light from the corridor for me to see that the geopositrons were exactly where I'd seen them last time. Two relatively small containers were stored at either end of a long shelf in the room.

Before I even got close, I heard a noise and dropped down behind one of the benches. Footsteps, I could definitely hear footsteps. My heart raced. Maybe I should just grab the two vials and run, barge back down the hallway, beat up anyone in my way.

"Nicola."

Surely that had to be my imagination. Then I heard my name again.

I peeked around the corner of the bench and saw a familiar figure backlit by the lights in the corridor. With that haircut, or lack thereof, it could only be one person.

I got to my feet. "Reece?"

"It's me." He climbed in through the window. "Are you okay?"

"What are you doing here?"

"Looking for you, of course."

Stepping closer, he placed his hands on my shoulders and stared at me as if he couldn't believe I was alive.

I took a step back. "Reece—"

"It wasn't Mr. Rodriguez's fault," he said. "He was implanted with a kill chip. There's no other explanation."

"I know."

One hand on his forehead, he paced the floor in front of me. "At first I thought you were trying to track him down so you could kill him."

"You talked to Lauren?"

He stopped pacing and spread his hands. "It made as much sense as anything."

"How did you know I was here?"

"Those damn geopositrons. I worked it out."

"Then help me."

His mouth fell open. He waited, then nodded.

I shuffled around in my backpack for the needles I'd purchased earlier from the pharmacy.

"What's that?" he asked.

"A syringe," I said.

"You won't need it." I didn't understand, so he added, "Can you remember how we first received the geopositrons when we were kids?"

I wasn't sure I did.

"It was done orally," he said. "I'm sure injecting them would work but you might as well just swallow them. It'll be easier."

I nodded. "Okay."

Reece followed me as I walked to one end of the room, picked up the vial and took off the lid.

"You don't have to do this." His eyebrows went up in the middle and he was pleading to me with his eyes. "There's no going back from this."

I knew what he meant, but going back was exactly what I wanted to do.

"It's time," I said.

The geopositrons were suspended in some sort of plasma, the straw-colored concoction unappealing. I placed the receptacle at my lips and tipped my head back. It didn't taste like anything in particular. I waited. They didn't feel like anything in my stomach either, but they'd do the trick. Hopefully.

Reece strode to the other end of the bench, picked up the second vial and handed it to me. I knocked back the contents again. Maybe the reaction between the geopositrons wouldn't be instantaneous. I had no idea about physics and chemistry and still couldn't feel anything. Maybe it'd take a while for the officers in New Nation to pick up on the signal. Maybe they'd think it was Reece and not me. Only one way to find out.

I felt strangely calm. I should be nervous, frightened, anxious. Not far beneath the surface, I was. I was a lot of things all at once, and one of them was very sure of myself, for the time being anyway.

"What are you going to do when you get back?" Reece asked.

My hands behind my back, I leaned against the bench behind me as if everything was perfectly normal.

"I know who ordered the kill," I said. "It was my two superior officers, generals Willis and Tan. I'm going to eliminate them. I have to."

He nodded. "Revenge?"

I shook my head. Revenge had never seemed like a good idea to me, too primal, too unsophisticated. Maybe I should be fighting for justice or some higher principle but I wasn't so sophisticated myself.

"I just want Ben back," I said.

"How can you get him back, Nicola? How?"

"After I return to New Nation, I plan to find a way to get sent back to a time before Ben was killed and before the bomb went off. Then, it'll be as if those things never happened. It's the only way."

One of the problems Ben and I had in Altabena was that generals Willis and Tan were in a position where they could always try something else – like implanting a kill chip in someone's brain or blowing up the school. If those two men were dead, they wouldn't be able to order those two events to happen. They wouldn't be able to order anything.

"I know those two generals," Reece said. "Or I knew them once. It's not going to be easy."

"I have another contact, my mentor, Lucien. He might help."

"Captain Everett?"

That was exactly who I meant. Reece had been sent back here a year before me, so that meant Lucien had been involved in this plan long before my official role in it. He'd known exactly what was going on the whole time.

Could I trust him? Would I have a choice?

"We should go," I said.

Out in the hallway, we headed for the office I'd broken into earlier. Outside the door, we heard a piece of glass shatter inside the room and stopped. It could've been the wind. Then we heard low voices. The beam of a torch shone through the open door. That wasn't the wind.

"We've got to make a run for it," I whispered.

Reece didn't need to be asked twice. We raced down the hallway and reached a closed door. I jabbed the green release button on the wall and we ran toward the front doors of the building. We had to hope we could get out more quickly than the cops who'd been at the side of the building. They'd have to race around the corner to get to the front whereas we were heading in a straight line.

I was thankful we could get out, thankful for fire safety laws that meant people couldn't be locked inside a building.

Reece got to the release button and banged it. Banged again. So slow. How could it take this long? The doors slid open and we ran out. He grabbed my arm and yanked me in the opposite direction away from the parking lot and the cops.

In the distance, men were yelling at us. Police or security guards, I wasn't sure which, and wasn't going to waste time finding out.

We ran down the street, around the corner, then ducked into someone's yard to hide at the side of their house. Crouched quietly, we waited. There was a small amount of traffic and a few people walked past. Nothing seemed out of the ordinary and if the police were searching for intruders, they must be looking in the other direction.

"They'll know it was me," I said quietly. "My car is still in the parking lot."

Reece's eyes twinkled. "Mine isn't."

He told me how he'd seen my car parked outside the lab, then parked a few streets away before coming back to find me. He was a better criminal than I'd thought, much better than me.

As we headed for his car, a police vehicle pulled up ahead of us on the other side of the road and two officers got out to speak to an older couple walking their dog. We kept walking. My heart rate went up a notch.

"Pretend you're my girlfriend." Reece put his arm around me.

We strode past the police car, still on the opposite side of the road. The cops looked at us, then back at the lady who was speaking to them and pointing down the street. I don't know what she was telling them or what she'd seen but I was happy for her to keep the police occupied.

Reece's car wasn't far. We drove back to his place in silence, then headed straight for his basement. I tossed my backpack onto the carpet and dropped down into a beanbag. Reece went to the fridge and came back with two beers.

"No thanks," I said.

He stared at me as if to say I had to be kidding.

"Don't let me stand in your way." I pulled the bottle of water out of my bag.

He put one of the beers back in the fridge and dragged a beanbag closer to me.

Eventually I said, "I don't even know if this'll work."

He lifted the long neck to his lips. "Beer works better."

"That's not what I meant."

"You're in with a good chance. If it's what you want."

I knew what I didn't want. What I couldn't bear. A world without Ben.

We sat together in silence. Though Reece was probably as lost in his own thoughts as me, I was grateful for the company. There weren't many people left who understood my situation. No one, in fact. I'd blurted out a heap of things to Lauren earlier. She must've thought I was a raving lunatic, which was fair enough because I had been raving and probably did sound like a lunatic. Poor Lauren.

The swish of the fridge door opening grabbed my attention.

"Sure you don't want one?" Reece asked.

I threw my hands up. "Why have beer when you can have geopositrons?" Reece gave me another dirty look, so I apologized for the lame joke.

He sat back down. "Nicola, there's something I forgot to say earlier. I'm sorry. About Ben, about everything."

What did you say when someone gave you their commiserations? How would I ever get used to this?

I should've been used to it. We'd had fifteen hundred deaths at the school, lives over in an instant, and in a very short time those of us who'd survived had been through a lifetime of commiserating.

But this was different.

Every time I stopped and thought about Ben, the hole in my chest got a little bigger. A giant gaping wound. That was why I didn't stop, why I couldn't stop until the job was done.

"I'm sorry too," I said. "Sorry I came here in the first place. If I hadn't, maybe none of this would've happened."

"That's a load of crap, Nicola. If they hadn't sent you, they'd have sent someone else and then that person would've followed orders and got the job done."

"Thanks. You're making me feel much better."

He ignored my sarcasm. "There's something else I wanted to ask. How come you didn't think of this earlier?"

"Think of what?"

"The school got bombed. All those people died. You didn't think about using the geopositrons to get back to New Nation then. The idea only came to you after Ben was killed."

I looked down at the water bottle I was cradling between my hands. Reece had a point. Maybe I should have thought of this earlier.

"They're your geopositrons," I said. "You didn't think of it either."

"I'm not like you," Nicola. "I'm lazy."

"There's no such thing as a lazy soldier."

"I haven't been a soldier for a long time. That's another difference between the two of us."

All those lives lost in the school bombing had been an enormous tragedy but at that point, I hadn't lost my family or my closest friends. I hadn't lost my *best* friend.

How could one death have ripped my heart out when I'd already tolerated hundreds of deaths? How could the human mind work that way? Except it wasn't my mind I was using.

Not long ago, I'd tried to deny I had emotions. In New Nation, we took drugs to suppress our feelings and were taught that emotions were a sign of weakness, a blight that was afflicted upon us, something to be fought. Now, those very emotions were driving me.

I felt a strange sensation on my arm, a pinprick, small but definitely there. The hair on the back of my neck stood on end. I stared at Reece and he stared right back.

"What?" he asked.

I pulled up my sleeve, looked at my arm and brushed my hand over my forearm a few times. I could feel it. It was there. My heart raced.

Slowly, I peeled the PR device from my arm. It stiffened immediately into a hard, flat object. Reece's eyes widened. He knew exactly what this was. This was how we communicated with each other in the future.

I checked the messages. There were none. This was the equivalent of phoning someone up and then not speaking.

Reece leaned closer. "What did they say?"

"Nothing."

Things I knew: my superior officers were aware of a presence and my exact location; they were in touch; they'd want me back if only so I could answer for my disobedience.

I hadn't been sure this would work. Now I knew. Time for my message:

PR device received. Send me back now.

Reece grabbed my arm, which made me smile. As if that would restrain me or stop me being transported in time.

"Be careful, Nicola," he said. "This is dangerous."

"I know."

"You're thinking with your heart. That's the part that's most dangerous of all. You have to delve deep. You have to be a soldier again. Don't let this be for nothing."

"I'll succeed." I had to believe in myself. There was no other way. "And when I do, you won't even know it."

Reece nodded slowly.

If I managed to go back in time, the school bombing and the kill chip in Mr. Rodriguez's brain would be wiped out. Those events would never happen and Reece would be magnificently oblivious. And maybe that was the best way to be.

We sat together in more of that companionable silence while I wondered how long it would take and what they were doing that was taking so long in New Nation. I didn't want this silence. I wanted to go back. Now.

My head started throbbing, so I leaned forward and rubbed my temples. Nausea rolled in my stomach. Pain mounted in my head and I pressed my eyes shut.

Reece leaned across, rubbed my back, said something to me.

Suddenly there was lightening in my head.

I opened my eyes. There was no Reece.

There was something else instead.

CHAPTER TWENTY-ONE

I know this room. I've been here before.

It had worked. I couldn't believe it and yet I could. I was sitting in the chair in the transportation room, the same chair I'd sat in before, and I was naked, just like before too. Only my body had been transported, not my clothes.

My head still ached but the bulk of the pain had been lifted like a great weight taken from my shoulders. Such a relief. I'd made it.

And such a worry too, because of the magnitude of the task ahead.

"Nicola, is that really you?"

The voice was so familiar, so soothing. Lucien's voice.

I looked around. Couldn't focus properly. I remembered this from my previous time travel experiences, the way the trip sucked the energy out of me and left me disorientated.

"I thought I'd never see you again."

Lucien's voice came out of nowhere like a sound floating through a fog. That's what my head felt like. A fog.

I was sitting up straight, my hands on the arms of the chair, when I felt a hand covering mine and looked down. I stared at the long fingers, followed the line up the arm to the shoulder to which it was attached, then looked up and saw Lucien's face, the same olive skin, the same receding hairline and shaved head. Thank goodness it was him and not someone else.

His warm brown eyes were etched with concern. "I thought you were dead."

"I'm not dead." As the words came out of my mouth, I wondered if my brain was functioning properly. My words sounded dumb, even to me.

"I was expecting Reece. It was his signal we picked up, not yours." Lucien reached for some items of clothing from the floor. "Get dressed. I got clothes ready for Reece. These'll have to do."

Nudity wasn't a big deal in New Nation but I'd been away a long time and wanted to get dressed as quickly as possible. I put on the army issue pants, pulling the belt tightly around my waist, then buttoned the shirt. I was swimming in these clothes. I pulled on socks, then slid my feet into oversized boots in which I was going to have trouble walking.

Lucien paced the floor, deep in thought and clearly concerned. I'd thrust myself upon him with no warning, something that hadn't occurred to me before.

A door opened and a tall, skinny young man around my age stepped inside. His skin was so pale that he must not get outside much, not that New Nation abounded with sunshine. He looked rather nondescript with short brown hair and an expression that didn't give anything away. His mouth fell open as he looked me up and down, then he shifted his gaze to Lucien and walked up to him.

"There's been a change in plans," Lucien said, then turned to me. "Nicola, meet Nathan Tyrell."

The young man reached across to shake my hand in a businesslike fashion. "Nicola Gray?"

I nodded. "And who, exactly, are you, Nathan Tyrell?"

"We don't have time, Nicola," Lucien said. "I don't need to tell you what they'll do if they find you here." He turned to Nathan. "Find some clothes for her, non-army, in a suitable size. And a PR. Also a small backpack. Put a bottle of water, some food and supplies in there."

"Certainly, Lucien," he said. Very obliging.

"Meet us in my office."

Nathan turned and left. Lucien grabbed my arm and we waited for a few seconds before leaving.

"Keep your head down," he muttered.

Though my eyes were lowered, I strode at his side trying to appear confident, which was hard to do in oversized boots. The corridors were familiar and not in a way that was reassuring. We passed other personnel who seemed too engrossed in what they were doing to pay attention to me.

It felt like an eternity until we slipped inside Lucien's office. I breathed a sigh of relief as he pressed the door closed behind him.

My head was clearer than before but my legs felt weak so I slumped down on the spare chair in his office.

There was a strange sense of otherworldliness about being somewhere that was at once so familiar and so foreign. Lucien's office was immaculate to the point of being clinical. A drab metal cabinet that held a glass section displaying military awards dominated the room.

Charcoal-colored carpet lined the floor and the walls were white. The window behind his desk looked out onto a gray sky. Nothing had changed.

Lucien leaned against the desk, his arms crossed. "I wasn't prepared for this, Nicola."

I was starting to think that neither was I.

"I was amazed when we picked up a reading on Reece," Lucien said. "Is he there?"

"Who?" I asked.

If no one knew Reece was still alive, then no one would go looking for him. There was no need for me to put him in any more danger.

"The geopositrons in your system came from another soldier," Lucien said. "How did you get hold of them?"

Sticking largely to the truth, I explained the news story about the discovery of GPS molecules that got agitated when they reached a critical mass and also how I'd broken into the laboratory.

"Before that, you found a way to stay, didn't you?" Lucien asked.

I didn't answer.

"Why, Nicola?" Lucien asked. "Why come back?"

I dropped my head into my hands, unsure if I could trust Lucien. He was the one who'd sent me back in time on the mission in the first place. He was also all I had.

He placed a hand on my shoulder. "I know. You're still recovering from your trip."

His touch felt reassuring. In all the time I'd known him, Lucien had never reached out to me physically in this way. This wasn't how we did things in New Nation.

"It's better if generals Tan and Willis keep believing you're dead," he said. "If they think for one minute that you purged yourself of your own geopositrons, that you stayed in Altabena by choice, that you disobeyed orders, the consequences will be final."

If the generals thought those things, they'd be right. And I'd be dead.

He squeezed my shoulder so hard it hurt. "You should've stayed away."

There were lots of things that shouldn't have happened. The school bombing should never have taken place. Mr. Rodriguez should never have been implanted with a kill chip and Ben should never have been knifed to death. Yet of all the things that should or shouldn't have happened, my presence here was the only thing that was right.

I glanced down at his hand. "Please stop doing that."

He let it drop.

"Who's Nathan?" I asked.

"He's a genius."

"What sort of genius?"

"An expert in technology and physics. He has been working on time travel programming for years."

So he'd been in this role when I was preparing to be sent on my mission, yet I'd never been aware of him. He knew Lucien well, probably better than me.

A knock at the door made Lucien turn. He opened the door a few inches and peered out, then pulled it open to let Nathan in. He dumped a carry-all at my feet, and unzipped it so I could see the PR and clothes inside.

I slapped the device onto my arm, then picked up a gray tee shirt. Nathan gave me a quizzical look as I turned my back to him to put it on. Behind me, the two of them were speaking in hushed tones while I dressed in black cargo pants and pulled a gray windbreaker over the tee shirt. I sat down to lace up a pair of black boots, thinking how much I missed my Converse sneakers already.

Another knock at the door startled Lucien.

"Get behind the desk," he said to me.

He and Nathan were in my way so I jumped over the desk and hid inside the foot well. I'd been in worse places.

The door clicked opened.

"General Tan, what a pleasure," Lucien said. I hoped his enthusiasm didn't sound as fake to the general as it did to me.

"Ah, Nathan, I see you're here too," Tan said.

His voice had an air of authority, one of the things I remembered most about him. The other general, Willis, was bigger physically. Tan was smaller and more wiry but made up for his lack of physical assets in other ways.

"Have you prepared your report for next week's strategy meeting?" he asked.

"Not yet, sir," Lucien said. "There hasn't been significant progress."

"You, Nathan," Tan said in a condescending tone. "Are there no developments to report?"

"We've made enormous jumps in technology in the past," Nathan said. "After that, improvements are only in small increments. That's generally the way these things work, sir."

I didn't hear anything, followed by the shuffle of footsteps on the carpet as someone headed to the window that was behind the desk and also behind me. The back of General Tan's legs and boots came into view. He was staring outside, though the scenery was bland to say the least. If he looked down, he'd see me. My heart rate jumped so much I struggled to keep very still.

"There's no need to hurry." He turned from the window. "We've got all the time in the world, haven't we, Nathan? You're the expert."

"I can see how you would say that, sir," he replied.

Lucien let out a short laugh. "The general was making a joke, Nathan."

"Oh, certainly, sir. Very amusing."

The general left the window, much to my relief. I knew the drill when generals were around. Everyone was respectful and obedient. Right now the room was probably filled with stilted smiles.

"I'll leave you to it," General Tan said. "But first, what's that bag doing in your office? The room looks like a mess."

"Nathan was putting away some equipment when I sidelined him," Lucien said.

"Very well, then," Tan said. "Good day."

The door clicked closed behind him and Lucien told me to come out.

"Damn it, Nicola," he said. "The safest thing would be to send you back to Altabena. For you, for all of us." He turned to Nathan. "Can we do it?"

The young man gave a curt shake of his head. "The routine maintenance I was doing was interrupted and now the system will need time to regenerate."

I wasn't safe here and that put Lucien in a precarious position. I also wasn't going back. Not yet. And not to exactly the same time zone.

"Makes no difference," I said. "Whether I'm here or in Altabena, they can track me through my geopositrons, the same way you did."

"Reece's geopositrons, not yours." Lucien shook his head, despair in his voice. "What have you done, Nicola?"

Nathan's expression remained even, as if he was completely unperturbed by our discussions and my presence. I'd always been obedient but Nathan's attitude came across as something in a different league.

"First things first, we need to keep you safe," Lucien said. Then to Nathan, "Can you take her to stay with your family?"

"Certainly, sir," he replied.

With Nathan's family? I had a family here in the sense that there were biological parents who'd given birth to me and my brother, but I was raised in a government home with professional staff who looked after us. Everyone was.

Still, I needed somewhere safe to stay and I didn't particularly care where it was. I needed time for myself, time to think and work out a plan of my own.

"Where is that?" I asked.

Lucien stared at me, his lips thin.

"I'll need to prepare supplies and other items for my parents," Nathan said. "Would that be allowed?"

"Yes, Nathan," Lucien replied.

"Excuse me," I said.

"The items I'm thinking of aren't standard issue."

Lucien nodded. "Whatever you need."

"Hang on." I stepped between the two of them. "Where are we going exactly?"

Lucien held my gaze. "The Badlands."

He had to be kidding.

The look on his face told me he wasn't.

CHAPTER TWENTY-TWO

My head down, I strode through the military compound with Nathan along the corridors and past the rooms that had once been my home. At the time, they'd been the only place I'd known. It hadn't seemed so bad then.

The rest of the compound wasn't as recently renovated as Lucien's office. The concrete in the hallways was polished smooth from years of foot traffic and the walls that had once been white were scuffed a pale gray. I hadn't seen a single window since we'd left Lucien's office.

I felt something akin to claustrophobia, something that made me want to get out of there. I wondered if there was a name for this particular phobia.

Nathan pushed open the main exit door and held it open for me while I strode through, the air outside hitting me like a tidal wave. The atmosphere was so thick with humidity it was like wading through soup. A light drizzle was falling, more like damp air than actual precipitation. I staggered and stopped.

Nathan pulled me over to one side of the path and took the backpack from my shoulders.

"Deep breaths," he said.

Of this stagnant air? I wasn't sure that was such a good idea.

"Just give me a minute," I said.

He nodded.

When I first arrived in Altabena, I'd been taken aback by the beautiful weather and pretty suburban streets. Now I was back in the only place I'd known for seventeen years of my life and I couldn't believe how dreary it was. Dark clouds hung low in the sky, almost permanently from what I remembered. They matched the gray buildings and concrete paths so there was no respite. My world had become an ocean of gray.

"Where are we headed?" I asked.

"C Dock," he said. "It's immediately beside the compound walls."

It wasn't too far. We walked along broad paths past the training stadiums and the climbing wall where soldiers were being drilled. One young woman was being reprimanded and then dropped to the ground to do push-ups. It brought back memories.

As we reached the crest of a small hill, I saw pods in the distance on the track that surrounded the military facility. They looked kind of cute compared to the huge vehicles people used in Altabena. Shaped like bubbles, they generally seated between two and four people and were an efficient and safe means of transport.

Traffic accidents were a thing of the past and the problem of congestion was reduced because everything was computer controlled. There weren't many pods in the compound because we were encouraged to walk or jog everywhere. They were mainly used in the cities, not that I'd spent a lot of time in any of our cities. Not that there were many of them left, either.

A large group of soldiers came out of the stadium, blocking the walkway. Some were dressed in army uniforms, others dressed like me, and all of them were chatting and smiling. I remembered that too, the way I used to feel pumped after a riveting lecture or training session.

Nathan pulled me over to one side. As he did so, a passing runner misjudged the distance and smashed into my shoulder, pushing me off the path.

"Sorry," the jogger said.

He looked me in the eye and I realized exactly how dangerous this was. Just as well he wasn't someone who knew me or the consequences didn't bear thinking about.

I waved it off as if it were nothing. "No problem."

We kept walking. C Dock was a major hub for pods above ground and also below ground for other transportation. At the main station, masses of people were moving in all directions, and they all seemed to know exactly where they were going. It reminded me of an old movie I'd seen that showed Grand Central Station during peak hour.

"Where are we going?" I asked Nathan.

He motioned for me to join him. "Downstairs."

Dust and grit filled the air and covered the platform. Nathan pulled me closer onto a long ground pod. Designed for shifting large numbers of people, it was a lot like a bus, only the ride was quieter and smoother. These were the first of the driverless vehicles, the forerunner to the pods that flew through the air. Old technology, yes, but still efficient.

We passed soldiers and civilians, and found a seat at

the rear. Minutes later the ground pod took off.

I looked at Nathan sitting up straight in the seat beside me. "Were you raised in the Badlands?"

He nodded.

"No one gets out of the Badlands. What happened to you?"

He looked ahead, silent.

I didn't bother hiding my impatience. "You don't say much, do you?"

"On the contrary," he said. "This is an excellent opportunity for us to talk."

It wasn't 'talk' I was after, so much as 'answers'.

"What was it like?" he asked. "The past, that is."

I wasn't about to discuss my feelings about family and relationships and personal freedom. Nathan might have a family in the Badlands but he wasn't overwhelming me with his emotions and insight, and I wasn't about to illuminate him.

"It was old fashioned," I said.

"Actually, I meant your physiological reactions and responses. Was the experience draining and disorientating?"

"Yes," I said. "Probably more so the first time than coming back here."

"Interesting." He nodded. "I've been observing you and you seem fairly coherent."

My eyes wide, I glared. "Thanks."

"That would be sarcasm. An interesting response. Can you tell me about your other experiences after you arrived in Altabena. I'm aware that society is very different from ours. Was your social functioning adequate?"

"Not at first," I said. "I stuck out like a sore thumb.

Everything I said or did was wrong."

I was about to tell him how it took me a long time to get used to having parents and a family, then stopped myself. Nathan had grown up with those things, apparently.

"Did you acclimatize to that environment?" he asked.

"Yeah, I fit in eventually." Or at least I thought I did.

Nathan nodded. "Interesting use of the word 'yeah.'"

Strangely, he reminded me of myself when I'd first arrived in Altabena, only I had a feeling Nathan didn't fit in here either. Either he'd truly embraced the no-emotions culture of New Nation or he was borderline autistic.

"Did you ever wonder about the technology?" he asked.

I stared at him. "You're full of questions."

"That's correct. It's not every day I meet someone who has been such an instrumental part of our development and traveled through time."

"I'm one of a kind."

"Not quite. Weren't you intrigued by the technology and the possibilities?"

I shrugged. "Not my area of expertise, I'm afraid. I'm a soldier. I was ordered on a mission."

He appeared to consider this. "That's very much in line with the way we function here."

"Yep, we're functioning beautifully here."

"That would be more sarcasm. This is fascinating for me."

I raised my eyebrows. "Really?"

"I'm extremely knowledgeable on the subject of time travel and now I have the evidence before my eyes. It was different before. Last year when we sent you there and brought you back, albeit briefly, it didn't seem tangible, certainly not to me. It's different now I can speak to you personally. I understood the physics behind the process and knew it must've been successful, yet only now is it becoming concrete."

"It worked, all right. I'm living proof."

"I would never have been brave enough to go myself, not even for the benefit of scientific research."

"I wasn't brave," I said. "I was obedient."

"Were you aware that a soldier was sent to Altabena before you?"

I decided to play it dumb. "Is that what Lucien was saying earlier? That the geopositrons I located had belonged to someone else?"

Nathan kept looking right through me. "His name was Reece Withers. For the record, you're braver than I could ever be."

Perhaps, but Nathan was smarter than me. I turned to look at the passing scenery, if you could call it that.

"Also for the record," he said. "I can confirm I'm smarter than you."

Could he read my mind? We'd always been told that people in the Badlands had telepathic abilities. It made the hair on the back of my neck stand on end. I was glad I was staring out of the window so my face didn't give me away.

We were passing through a forested area that had been burnt out, presumably by a fire, though it was hard to imagine the sun shining brightly enough to set off sparks. Tree trunks were blackened and where the forest would once have appeared impenetrable, I could now see far into it. Leaves were growing back on the trees and patches of undergrowth were green with new ferns and other small plants.

Regeneration. It was possible. Anything was possible.

I glanced back at Nathan, wondering if he could really be from the Badlands when he didn't have the blackened eyeballs of the people there. Instead his irises were brown, the whites of his eyes particularly stark. He didn't appear to have any physical deformities either, which was one of the main reasons people from the Badlands had been segregated in the first place.

"Lucien said your family was in the Badlands," I said. "How did you ever leave?"

"On a ground pod, much like this one," he said.

"You don't want to tell me?"

"I was young. Only twelve. They wanted me to be part of the scientific program so it was easy getting out. For me, anyway. Getting in is the hard bit."

That wasn't what I wanted to hear. Perhaps my face gave me away.

"They'll do a scan as you try to pass through the gates," he said. "It's unlikely Reece's geopositrons were ever approved for entry into the Badlands. You'll have to hope they were neutralized so they don't set off the alarms."

"You didn't mention that before."

"You're brave, remember?"

Screw bravery. I'd choose security over bravery any day.

It occurred to me that perhaps Lucien was trying to get rid of me and that it suited him for this to happen hundreds of miles away. Then again, he could've found a way to get rid of me quickly and efficiently while I was still at the military base if that was what he wanted.

"Surely you're not permitted to visit your family?" I asked.

"Of course not."

In New Nation, we owed our full allegiance to our country and the government. Families were an outdated thing of the past.

"So how can you go back to the Badlands?" I asked.

"I'm not," he said. "I'm getting off at Barrington Base."

"Excuse me?"

"After that, you're on your own."

Which was not what I wanted to hear.

CHAPTER TWENTY-THREE

"Are you crazy?" I asked.

Nathan shook his head. "Not at all. It's quite straightforward. You'll stay on the ground pod. I'll get off at Barrington and purchase some supplies before going back. That way there will be nothing suspicious about my behavior or whereabouts. You will go on to the Badlands where there will no doubt be a regiment patrolling near the gates."

"And either they allow me through the gates or they don't?"

"That part is out of my hands. I have, however, drawn a map and written instructions to help you find my family where you will have a safe place to stay. It's in the carry-all. There are also some items for my parents. Please remember to give them the chip in the outside zip pocket. I've included a hand-written note introducing you to them. They'll take care of you."

Gifts? Personal messages? It made me wonder about Nathan because in New Nation we didn't show affection for our families.

"What's going on?" I asked. "Do you have feelings for

them?"

The hint of a smile on his lips. "It's not what you think. I worked out the function of the vitamin supplements and stopped taking them long ago, but my brain is wired differently from yours. This is as emotional as I get toward my family or anyone else."

I held his gaze. "Don't you want to see them?"

"That's not possible."

"You made the impossible happen and sent me back in time, then brought me back again. Yet you think it's impossible to see your own family?"

This was the girl from Altabena talking. There's no way that the Nicola who'd been an obedient soldier would speak this way.

"You're forgetting that my movements can be traced and found out," he said. "After that, both my family and myself would be punished."

"Of course."

I was being recalcitrant and should have thought this through. I'd have to start thinking on my feet more quickly.

"There are other ways, however," he said.

"Other ways?"

His eyes lit up, something I hadn't seen before. "I've found a way of hacking into the mainframe to alter location records when necessary."

"So why don't you do that?"

"The process can only be done after the effect which means there's an element of risk. My location could be discovered before I had the opportunity to alter the records and there would be repercussions. In this case, your presence complicates the situation, and the risk outweighs the benefit."

"So it's not worth it?"

"Correct. My focus on time travel analysis has also led me to an unexpected personal conclusion. We can now transport bodies and objects through time, however this does nothing to extend human life. Our time is still limited and I would rather spend my time fruitfully, in the pursuit of scientific knowledge."

I wasn't sure if I was annoyed or illuminated. We pulled up at the station.

"This is your stop, Mr. Fruitful," I said.

Nathan stood. "Good luck, Nicola."

"You too, Nathan."

I liked the guy despite the fact he was slightly weird. Or maybe because of it.

He got off the pod and others got on, mostly soldiers though there were some civilians, many of them chatting to their friends. No one spoke to me, which was just as well.

I leaned back in my seat. Three hundred kilometers down, three hundred more to go, and too much time on my hands. Time to think. Time to feel.

I'd failed Ben. Lost him. Lost part of myself. I pressed my eyes shut, holding back the tears, as the hole in my chest grew bigger. My breath stuck in my throat, panic rising from my stomach.

Could I go on without Ben? Could I do this? One thing was for sure. If I let myself wallow in grief and pain, I wouldn't be able to do what I had to do.

The window. A distraction. We passed through an abandoned city on a bumpy freeway overpass without another vehicle in sight. At ground level, the ancient buildings had been sprayed with equally ancient graffiti and the windows smashed, the sort of behavior that would not be tolerated now. Grass and weeds grew at the top of buildings and in cracks in the masonry. These were huge buildings where people had once lived and worked and gone to school. All empty.

This was all down to the virus. It had swept across the country in 2041, killing three quarters of the population and throwing the country into chaos. Where once overcrowding had been a problem, suddenly feeding the remaining people became paramount, and that was when the Bartley government consolidated its power. The people needed someone to take control and Bartley did exactly that.

Ahead of me a hunk of concrete came loose and slid off the side of a building. I turned as we passed and watched the great chunk hit the ground, dust and debris flying through the air. Which made me wonder about the state of the bridge on which we were traveling. Better not to think about some things.

The pod passed through meadows which then gave way to forest that looked a lot like the landscape that surrounded Altabena, complete with squirrels and other wildlife. The sun even came out for a while. The weather wasn't all bad in New Nation. It just felt like it.

The terrain became hillier with less greenery and more red dirt. We were getting closer. I'd been to the area surrounding the Badlands on training camps in the past. The pod grew quiet.

I lifted the bag Nathan had given me onto the seat and rifled through it. The letter of introduction for his parents was there, hand-written exactly as he'd said. There was another letter too, for his mom. I folded it and put it back.

I had to hand it to Nathan. He'd packed spare clothes, a pocket knife, torch, army rations, water bottle, everything I'd need. Along with several kilograms of chocolate – and not just any chocolate. This was of the highest quality. I'd only ever tasted it once when I received my bravery award though I was sure our officers consumed more than their fair share of it while the rest of us ate the substandard stuff.

It made me smile. Nathan had asked Lucien about supplies that weren't 'standard issue' and now I knew what he'd been referring to. This was a gift for his family.

Eventually the pod reached the end of the line and I shuffled out, along with the rest of the passengers. Unlike C Dock, this wasn't a buzzing hub so I made sure I exited with everyone else, sticking to the rear of the small crowd. So far, so good.

A light drizzle was falling outside the station, nothing to be concerned about. If there was anything to worry about, it lay straight ahead. I'd seen pictures and knew what the Badlands looked like. I'd never been this close.

The concrete walls surrounding the Badlands stretched for miles to either side. They'd been built decades ago and were decaying but would stay upright for many years to come, a symbol of the government's power.

As I strode toward the open gates ahead, others who'd got off the train headed for the offices that were dotted on the side of the road. The crowd was thinning and so was my cover.

A dozen soldiers were stationed outside the gates in full military gear and weaponry though they didn't seem to be serving any function. Their presence appeared to be mainly ceremonial. No one had come out while I'd been watching but several people had entered the gates and none had been pulled aside.

Glancing up, I saw two small black boxes on either side of the gates, in case I'd had any doubt our geopositrons wouldn't be read as soon as we tried to walk through the gates. The soldiers didn't need to check ID here. I knew exactly what would happen to any personnel who weren't authorized to walk through those gates.

My heart rate rose. I kept my stride even and walked straight in, expecting the worst. Nothing happened. No alarms, no shots fired, no soldiers giving chase. I didn't know what was going on with Reece's geopositrons but I was grateful.

Inside the gates, there was an open plaza. Open and empty. Not a good place to hang around so I veered left, following Nathan's directions. The first thing I did was put on the sunglasses he'd packed for me.

As I wandered along the street, it seemed to be mostly older people who been afflicted with deformities, who were missing limbs or who had strange growths. The virus had caused deformities and then there was a genetic component so the problems were passed down, though they were probably slowly being bred out.

Still, most people looked reasonably healthy except for the one thing that shocked me the most, their blackened eyes. Though I'd seen pictures and footage of their eyeball tattoos, it was different seeing them in real life.

I was surrounded. Here, I was the freak. Hence, the sunglasses.

This part of the Badlands was a dilapidated city with decaying buildings and narrow streets. I couldn't get over the number of beggars. In my seventeen years in New Nation I'd never seen a beggar. Didn't think they existed.

The government took care of us or at least that's what we were always told. Clearly they didn't take care of everyone, or perhaps these people didn't count.

I found the town square where I had to turn right. People had gathered around a concrete fountain that may once have had water in it. Market stalls sold hot food, the smell of barbecued meat wafting through the air. A group of old people watched as two young men moved giant chess pieces on a checkerboard pavement, then laughed at a joke.

The surroundings were dire but the mood was light and relaxed. How did that work? This village atmosphere wasn't at all what I was expecting.

As I headed off, the road became narrowed and steeper and the crowd thinned. I could almost have imagined I was on a cobblestoned street in a medieval city, except the dilapidated buildings on either side of me were much newer than that.

At the top of the hill, tables from a café on the corner spilled out onto the street, all of them full. It was almost romantic, except for the burnt out, windowless warehouse across the road.

I stopped near the café to check the map. A short rest couldn't hurt, after all. It wasn't that the walk was physically exhausting, more that my strange surroundings were taking their toll on me.

A middle-aged woman who was clearing a table looked across at me as she loaded dirty cups into a large plastic bucket. Leaving the bucket on a chair, she headed toward me. Her clothes, a gray tee shirt and black pants, didn't look that different from mine except hers were faded and thin. She had olive skin and brown hair and would've looked perfectly normal if not for the eyeball tattoos.

"Do you need a hand?" she asked.

"I'm fine."

She put her hands on her hips. "The sunglasses don't fool me for a minute."

I shrugged, looked away, and she left. A minute later, she returned with a glass of cold water.

I took it from her. "Thanks."

"You looked like you needed a drink."

The cold water hit the spot. I wondered if this could be down to the woman's telepathic abilities.

"Is it far to the monument?" I asked.

"Not far but the lanes and alleys can be tricky if you don't know your way around."

"Don't suppose there'll be any signs."

She laughed. "You suppose right."

Nathan had explained to me earlier that everyone knew their way around the Badlands so they didn't bother with signage. Besides, signs cost money. I'd worked that out.

The woman nodded up the hill. "My father's finishing up now. He can show you the way if you like."

I decided to trust my gut. Despite the eyeball tattoos, the woman had a friendly face and a warm smile.

"Thanks." I handed her my empty glass and she went back inside, coming out minutes later with a man who bore absolutely no resemblance to her. His body appeared in reasonable shape for an old man but he must've been born when the virus was in full swing. And it showed. Thick gray hair covered his huge, asymmetrical head, the skin on his face red and unsightly. One eye was forced shut thanks to growths on the side of his face. The other eye bore a black tattoo – in case it wasn't obvious he was from the Badlands.

"I'm Matthias," he said. "Let's get going."

He headed up the hill before I could argue, so I said goodbye to his daughter and rushed to catch up with him. He was surprisingly agile for an old guy with a huge head.

"So you're headed for the monument?" he asked.

"Yes," I said as we walked up the hill.

"Looking for anyone in particular?"

"No."

He grunted as we turned a corner. I hated to admit it, but it was easier to keep walking than to look at his disfigured face.

After a while, he said, "It's straight down here, then to the right."

We stepped into a narrow lane, more of an alley really. Something didn't feel right. Behind us, the street was noisy which only emphasized how quiet the alley was.

"Is there another way to get there?" I asked.

"Yes, but it takes longer."

He raced ahead unexpectedly and it took me a few moments to catch up with him. I was about to tell him I might take the long way when two men stepped out of a doorway in front of us while another appeared to our rear. Ripped jeans, dirty tee shirts, scruffy hair. Cornered.

One of the men sneered. "What have we here?"

I stepped forward. "Get out of my way."

"Give me your bag."

"No."

"Your PR device," he yelled. "Hand it over."

He'd spotted me as an outsider in an instant.

Matthias stepped between me and the man. "Now just a—"

Whack! A punch in the gut left the old man doubled over and his assailant grinning. Not for long.

I saw the other guy edging toward me so I slammed in a side kick, heard him scream in pain, and kept heading for the guy who'd hurt Matthias.

He threw a big, wide punch. My favorite kind, so easy to block. I stepped closer and slammed in an elbow. He yelled in pain, staggered back, then turned and followed his friend who was already half-way up the alley.

Behind us, the third man had run away. Meanwhile, I stood there, stunned and hoping the old guy was okay.

Matthias put his hand on my shoulder. "Nice work."

I picked up my bag. "Let's get out of here."

I'd just learnt two things. That I should've trusted my gut sooner. And I was not a victim. I was never going to be a victim.

To be honest, I was still slightly shaken but I felt powerful at the same time. When we got to the end of the alley, we turned right onto a street lined with old buildings. My blood was still pumping after the fight.

We reached the monument, or at least I assumed the statue of a soldier in the middle of the street was the monument.

"It's not usually like that around here," Matthias said. "Those men, I mean. I walk down that alley ten times a day and nothing has ever happened."

I stopped by the side of the street. "Thanks for showing me the way."

"Who are you looking for?" I didn't answer so he

added, "You must be looking for someone. Why else would you be here?"

Matthias didn't seem so bad. I could trust him that much.

"Do you know the Tyrell family?" I asked.

He nodded. "This way." When we reached a nondescript building much like the others around it, he said, "They're on the third floor."

After he left, I realized he didn't even know my name.

CHAPTER TWENTY-FOUR

There were four apartments on the third floor and none had names on the doors so I figured it was pot luck.

I knocked on the first door. Nothing. Which made me wonder what I'd do if Nathan's family wasn't home. I was in a strange place and didn't have a Plan B.

I got lucky at the next apartment. As soon as the woman pulled open the door, I knew she had to be Nathan's mother. The same face shape, same pale skin and black hair, only where Nathan's expression was blank, she came across as thoughtful.

One big difference. She had the eyeball tattoos.

"I'm Nicola, a friend of Nathan's." I handed her the introductory letter he'd written.

Though reluctant, she took the letter and started reading, lifting her gaze from time to time to make sure I was still there. It amazed me that her eyes could be so expressive despite the blackened sclera.

She checked the hallway, then pulled me inside, closing the door behind us. Two children, a boy and a girl, sat at a table with books and papers spread across it. Homework perhaps. They looked up, gave a quick smile and continued with what they were doing. Their eyes were wide, the whites of their eyes crisp.

The kitchen was immediately behind the table at which the kids sat; a sofa was shoved just inside the door, and that appeared to be it. Family photos had been hung on the walls, including those of a very young Nathan, and there were kids' drawing stuck on the fridge. Despite the cramped conditions, it felt homely, unlike the place I'd grown up.

The woman placed her hands on my shoulders. "How is Nathan? Have you seen him?"

"He's doing very well," I said. "He came with me as far as Barrington."

Her hands dropped, her whole face, in fact. "He came so close?"

Clearly, I'd said the wrong thing. "He would've come if he could. I'm sure of it."

"Nathan was always special." Pride in her voice, she walked to the other side of the table between the two children and nuzzled between them. "You two munchkins are special too. Even when you're naughty."

Her motherly affection caught me off guard. We didn't have any of that in New Nation or at least not as far as I'd known.

Still, I had to be careful what I said. Careful what thoughts went through my head for that matter.

"What am I thinking?" she said. "I'm Rachel and this is Sarah and Theodore."

The kids said hello. Rachel ushered me toward a seat at the table and reached for my bag.

"Hold on." I lowered the bag onto a chair and unzipped it. "Nathan sent some things for you."

I pulled out the bars of chocolate, placing them on the table in what seemed like a never-ending procession. The children's eyes lit up and they started jumping in their seats, literally.

Rachel grinned. "Oh, Nathan."

She unwrapped a bar, broke it into pieces and extended it to me. "Guests first."

Something seemed strange about her hands though I couldn't tell exactly what.

"No thanks." I could have all the chocolate I wanted when I got back to Altabena. I had to think positive.

The kids devoured the chocolate while Rachel savored a few pieces and chatted to me at the table.

"How rude of me." She got up and came back with some cheese and bread which suddenly made me feel hungry.

"There's more." I handed her the chip from the outside zip pocket of my bag, leaving me free to eat while she was otherwise occupied.

As Rachel placed a laptop on the table, I looked more closely at her hands. Tried not to stare at the extra fingers that protruded on either side of her pinkies. Maybe that was a good problem to have if you lived here.

Though made of plithium, the laptop looked like it was about a hundred years old, a relic from another era. The children were quiet as she inserted the chip and Nathan's face appeared on the screen.

"Hello Mother, Father." Nathan waved, his face as expressionless as ever. "Sarah and Theo, I hope you're behaving and doing well at school."

I tried not to listen to this message to his family. The words were formal and stilted, exactly like Nathan, yet it was also clear he had feelings for his family.

Rachel's eyes welled with tears that she wiped away before the children noticed. She whipped the laptop away and said she was starting on dinner. She whipped the chocolate away too, despite the complaints from the kids.

Dinner was chicken with a side salad, simple and delicious. They had fresh food here so there must be markets and farms nearby. I helped with the cleaning up while Sarah and Theodore disappeared into the bathroom and came back to watch a program on the computer. The episode of the TV series they were watching was older than the laptop but they didn't seem to notice.

As they went to bed, Rachel closed the door behind them. There were only two doors and one of them led to the bathroom so that meant they must all share the same bedroom. I hoped it wasn't as cramped as the living room.

Rachel sat beside me on the sofa. "Nicola, what is it that you're doing here?"

"It's complicated."

"Is it better if I don't know?"

I nodded.

My instinct was to trust Nathan's mother. She was helping me for no other reason than that her son had asked her to. Yet I was still torn by the things we'd all been told about the people in the Badlands. But Rachel didn't appear to have any telepathic abilities. If she did, there was no way she'd have let me in her house. She also didn't appear to be inflicting any emotions on me, another thing we'd been told the people from the Badlands did.

Rachel smiled, her eyes crinkling at the sides. "Then you have to tell me about Nathan, what he's working on, how he's doing. Tell me everything."

She sounded greedy and I couldn't blame her. My mom would be the same if she was in this situation. Hell, maybe my mom *was* in the same situation – except she didn't know I was safe, didn't know where I'd gone and was probably worried I wouldn't be back. With a second round of cancer, Mom already had enough to cope with. More than enough. If only I could help her.

I stared at Rachel, a mother who needed reassurance. "Nathan is very well respected, his work highly valued."

"Is he happy?"

"Seems to be. I gather his research is important to him. He's working on the latest technology, things that are so advanced they're beyond my understanding. A leader in the field."

She was beaming. "He's so gifted. Right from the start, I knew he was different."

I raised my eyebrows. "He's different all right."

She covered my hand with hers. "I'm grateful for that. It's a saving grace. He doesn't feel things the same way the rest of us do and in New Nation, that's a good thing. Then there's his intelligence. It's a gift to him in so many ways."

"Is that how he got out of here?"

She nodded. "He was chosen. That doesn't happen to many people, not from here."

"He doesn't have the eyeball tattoos," I said.

"No, we get them when we're thirteen. We have to. He left just before. I was grateful for that too."

We have to. I'd always known that people in the Badlands had eyeball tattoos. I'd never thought they were compulsory.

"Sarah and Theodore both seem healthy," I said. "You do too."

Rachel held her hands ups and wiggled her fingers, all of them. "The effects of the virus are fading with each generation. My grandfather was terribly deformed, my father much less so."

Did that mean that one day these people would be integrated into New Nation society? Would they want to be? This place was so different from the military compound where I'd grown up and the quarters where my biological parents lived. In many ways, it was better. The Badlands weren't bad. Just poor.

There were other Badlands dotted around the country too, more places like this one, more people segregated from the rest of us because they were different. And not even all that different.

"Nathan sent you here," Rachel said. "He must trust you."

I nodded. "He's also very obedient."

"Good. Hopefully that way, he'll live a long time."

"Can I ask about Nathan's father?"

"He's working on one of the construction projects."

"What projects?"

"You don't know?" I shook my head and she continued. "Rebuilding the cities, roads and infrastructure ready for expansion of the population. Recently, there's been a big push to get more construction finished. He comes home when he can but he doesn't have any choice in the matter."

"Why's that?"

"It's forced labor." She looked at me as if I was an idiot and maybe I was.

The whole time I'd grown up in New Nation, I'd never heard anything like this. If Bartley's government was using slave labor from the Badlands to rebuild the cities, he certainly wasn't promoting the fact. Quite an oversight.

Rachel stood, grabbed some sheets and blankets from a cupboard and handed them to me. "You'll be sleeping on the sofa. I hope you don't mind."

I took the items from her. "This will be perfect."

"At least you'll have some privacy. I have to get up early to go to work."

"What do you do?" I asked.

"I'm a cleaner at the local hospital."

My mind started ticking over. I knew exactly what I'd be able to find at a hospital. Perhaps I had a reason to stay in the Badlands a little longer after all. I was tempted to ask Rachel about it now, but she was tired and on her way to bed. It'd wait until tomorrow.

"Goodnight, Nicola," she said.

I made my bed and lay on the sofa in the dark with my eyes open. I had so much to think about that I couldn't imagine how I was ever going to get to sleep. Tomorrow, I might get one step closer to getting what I wanted, what I needed, what I had to take back with me.

The more I thought about it, the more I hated the lies we'd all been told, the more I hated New Nation and the government. It was all the more reason for me to get home. In fact, I had the greatest reason of all. Ben.

I closed my eyes, wrapped my arms around myself and dug my fingers into my upper arms. I pictured Ben's dashing grin, remembered how good it had felt when he held me.

And hoped the hole in my heart would go away.

CHAPTER TWENTY-FIVE

Rachel strode ahead of me down the same alley where Matthias and I had been attacked yesterday. Perhaps the old man was right and this place wasn't as dangerous as it seemed. Sarah and Theodore were at home getting ready for school while their mother was on her way to work. With me.

"Rachel," I said. "I'm not going away."

She stopped and turned. "You should."

"Please, you've got to help me."

"I wouldn't be helping you at all if it wasn't for Nathan. I can't help you, Nicola."

Rachel had been so warm and friendly last night – the polar opposite of her son – and now she was showing a different side of her personality, understandably so.

I'd asked her for a favor, a big one. As a cleaner at the local hospital, she had access to storage rooms and other places. She could get me into the hospital where I could locate the cancer cure I needed so desperately. I was never going to get this close to the vaccine and I wasn't leaving without it.

"I'm not asking you to steal the C-vac," I said. "I'll do

199

that myself."

"Makes no difference," She shook her head. "I can't do it."

I gripped her shoulders. "You can't get rid of me. I'll follow you."

"I'll lose my job, Nicola."

"We won't get caught."

"It's more complicated than you think."

"Then explain it to me."

I let my hands drop as Rachel spoke. "We only have C-vac in small quantities."

"I only need a small amount."

The cure worked by passing into the blood stream and targeting only the cancerous cells. It would pass through one tumor and keep going through to the next one. Your body never got rid of the cure. It simply kept circulating through your system. If there was a smaller amount, it took longer to work its way around the body but it always did the business.

"Nicola, you don't understand how things work here," Rachel said. "There's not enough of the cure to go around. People die all the time because of it."

I stood firm. "I only need one measure."

"Whether I give it to you or whether you take it makes no difference. It's still one life here in the Badlands that's not being saved. One person who dies. Don't think because I'm only a cleaner at the hospital that I don't care."

She turned to leave but I blocked her way. "Rachel, what would you do to protect your children?"

Her brow furrowed. "What's that got to do with anything?"

"You love your children. You love Nathan so much that you let him go. That must've been one of the hardest things you've ever done." Her lips formed a thin line. I'd hit the spot, which was all the encouragement I needed. "Is there anything you *wouldn't* do to save your children if they were in danger?"

"No." Her eyes narrowed. "Nicola, you can't do this. You can't take advantage of me or my family or the hospitality we've shown you. And you can't steal the C-vac."

"It's for my mother," I said. "She'll die without it."

Rachel stepped back. "That can't be right. Everyone in New Nation gets health care. It's only us in the Badlands who miss out."

"She's not in New Nation," I said.

Another pause. "You're military, aren't you?"

"Yes."

"So why do you even care about your mother? You weren't raised by her. You probably haven't seen her for years."

"She doesn't live here. She lives so far away you wouldn't believe it. And I have to get the C-vac for her or…or I can't bear to think about it. It's the only way. I won't have another chance."

She squeezed her eyes shut in frustration. "Oh….shit!"

That was shit in a good way. That was shit-she's-going-to-help-me. It had to be. Sure enough, she gave a gentle nod of her head.

"Thank you," I said quietly.

"You can't go like that." She pointed at my clothes which marked me as an outsider. My apparel was too new, too military looking, even though it was casual. "Come with me."

Back at the apartment, Rachel gave me some of her clothes to wear – still pants and a shirt, but well worn so I wouldn't stand out.

"There's something else." She ushered me into the bathroom, a cramped dank space.

I pointed to the small glass jar in her hands. "What's that?"

"Eye drops. They'll only last a few hours."

"For what?"

A muscle in her jaw flinched. "The kids needed their eyes blackened for a school ceremony. It nearly killed me. At least now I can put the drops to good use."

Tilting my head back, I let her deliver small droplets to my eyes and felt liquid spill down my cheeks.

"Quick," Rachel said. "Wash your face or it'll stain."

I did so, shocked when I lifted my head to look in the mirror. I looked like a freak, which was exactly what this was supposed to look like.

Rachel kissed her children goodbye while I got out quickly so I didn't have to explain anything to them. We headed back down the alley and out onto the street where the monument was. I made a mental note of every turn in case we got separated or something else happened. It wasn't easy, though. The term 'rabbit warren' came to mind.

The foyer of the hospital reminded me a lot of C Dock with masses of people moving in all directions. There were a couple of wheelchairs that whizzed past and one guy on crutches who people skirted around. A reception desk was at the far end.

Rachel grabbed my arm and steered me down a broad

corridor with beds lining the walls. Patients moaned. They chatted to their visitors. This was normal.

The smell of disinfectant hung in the air and the hospital appeared to be reasonably clean. Meanwhile the walls were scuffed and linoleum on the floor had worn right through in places.

At the end of the corridor, we passed an obese man struggling with two nurses as one of them gave him an injection that immediately calmed him down. Meanwhile, after much walking, Rachel and I ended up in a storage room at the back of the hospital where she shoved a cloth into my hand and wheeled out a trolley of cleaning equipment.

"Where are the medicines and drugs kept?" I asked.

"First we clean the bathrooms," she said. "Then I'll show you."

Cleaning the toilets wasn't below me so that was exactly what I did.

After I finished, Rachel said, "The drugs are stored around the corner. I have access to the room for cleaning but not to the locked cabinets. I'll let you in, then you're on your own."

"Where can I find you after that?"

"You can't." She shoved a key into my hand as we walked. "That's for the apartment, so you can get back in."

"Thank you," I said.

"Don't get caught." She stopped. "This is it."

Rachel placed her hand on a plaque beside a closed door. A hand recognition system. A latch unclicked and the door swung open. I slipped inside, closing the door behind me.

One wall was covered in metal cabinets, all of them

locked, which was hardly surprising. I was surprised, however, to see keyholes, an old fashioned but effective security measure. I jammed my fingers around the edges of the cabinet door and tried to lever them away. That didn't work so I tried kicking them in. No success there either. The cabinets must be made of a plithium alloy. Practically indestructible.

I took a deep breath, slipped to one side of the door so that when it opened, I'd be hidden behind it. I waited. Tried to focus, visualizing in my head what I'd have to do. After a while, I heard the click of a latch and the gentle swish of the door.

A male nurse with dark green scrubs and a shaved head was humming to himself, his head down, his eyes on the set of keys in his hands. Just my luck he was a big guy. As in huge.

He didn't notice when I nudged the door closed. I wished there was another way but there wasn't.

The keys were still jangling in his hands as I slid one arm across his neck, my other hand on the small of his back to get him off balance. He gasped. I had his chin in the bent V of my arm, my hand locked on my own shoulder as I squeezed tightly to choke him out.

Just as well I had the element of surprise because this guy was strong. I kept dragging him around and he knocked into the walls. I kept squeezing. The keys slipped from his fingers and he crumpled to the floor, unconscious. The sleeper hold had done the trick.

Grabbing the keys, I shoved one into a cabinet door. It didn't fit so I tried the next one. Then again. That door opened and I shuffled through the medicines. The C-vac wasn't there so I used the same key on the next door.

I saw it. Individual packages, clearly labeled. A treasure if I'd ever seen one. I shoved one packet into my pants pocket and turned to the door. The enormous nurse was blocking it, so I grabbed him under the arms and dragged him to the side. He moaned. Time to get away. I closed the door behind me as I left. Told myself someone would find the guy. He'd be fine.

No one gave me a second look as I strode down the corridor, trying to remember if the next turn was a left or a right. It still freaked me out to see blackened eyes around me, then I remembered my own had been temporarily dyed.

I kept walking purposefully. The worst thing I could do was look lost even though that's exactly what I was. Any other time, I'd have asked for directions but this wasn't any other time, so I kept going. I strode past yet another corridor lined with beds when a loud snore cut through the air like a foghorn. I turned to see the obese man who'd been struggling with the nurses, now asleep. My savior. I walked straight past him, through the front foyer and out of the door.

The sun had come out, shining on the flagstones outside the hospital. I took that as a good sign and headed back the way I'd come. The apartment was empty when I got there. The children must've gone to school ages ago. And I was alone.

I slumped down at the kitchen table, my head in my hands. I didn't like being alone. Didn't like waiting. My stomach was heavy and it felt like I had spiders crawling under my skin. I scratched my arms. Dug my fingers right in.

The scene flashed before my eyes. Mr. Rodriguez had

the knife, the blade glinting. I was too slow. Fast forward to Ben slumped against the desk, his face pale, his neck a river of red. Too late. I was too late.

His eyes glimmered with realization. I saw his pain. And felt my own heart being ripped out. Felt the great, gaping hole in my chest. Couldn't breathe, couldn't function, couldn't go on this way.

This was what happened when I stopped. This was the reason I could never stop. I had to keep going.

Deep breaths, I told myself. This must be a physiological reaction to the stress. A long breath in through my nose. A slow breath out through my mouth.

I didn't like being human. It had been easier when I'd been obedient and had suppressed my emotions like everyone else in New Nation.

The apartment was small, claustrophobic. How could people live this way? What was I doing sitting around? What was I doing here at all?

It was no good hiding here in the Badlands when my targets were back at the military compound. I was a soldier again. I had to inflict damage.

I barely noticed when Rachel came home and started speaking, mostly because I was already talking to myself. My mind was going a hundred miles an hour, my feet stomping the floor, my head pounding.

Rachel put her hand on my forehead. "You're burning up."

A fever was the least of my problems. I kept mumbling as she placed a glass of water in my hand and I knocked back the tablets she gave me. The next thing I knew I was reclining on the sofa and she was taking off my boots. Voices in my head were speaking quietly so I had to concentrate to hear what they were saying. Then the voices got louder, louder until they were screaming at me and I covered my ears.

I felt a hand on my chest, pushing me back to lie down. There were words, gentle this time. "You need to sleep, Nicola."

I closed my eyes. Lights flashed inside my eyelids. The sparks were dwindling, growing faint, disappearing. I was floating. There was a lightness in my chest and I let sleep come to me.

By the time I woke up, the children were back from school. I should've been well rested but felt drained instead, though I managed to say hello to Sarah and Theodore. An achievement.

Rachel had her back to me, stirring a pot on the stove.

I walked up to her. "I'll give your clothes back now. Then I'll be on my way."

She raised her eyebrows. "Don't be silly. Have a bath and put on fresh clothes, then you can eat. You can leave tomorrow. One more night won't make any difference."

It was the same advice my mother would've given. And it made sense.

My head got clearer with the passing hours and food and people to talk to. By the time the children went to bed, I felt normal again. Rachel tried to tell me I wasn't allowed to help her clean up but I ignored her, grabbing a dish towel instead.

She glanced up from the sink. "Did you get what you wanted today?"

This morning felt like such a long time ago. "Yes."

"I thought so. I heard there was a break-in, and knew it had to have been you."

"Tomorrow, I have to go," I said.

"I know."

I only hoped I'd be able to walk through those gates without attracting attention or setting off alarms. I had to hope Reece's geopositrons would do the trick.

"What would happen if you tried to leave?" I asked her.

"The soldiers can spot us in an instant because of our eyes," she said. "They'd kill us without a second thought. They don't really even need the huge walls around us. We're not going anywhere."

Sounded like history repeating itself. "It's a bit like Hitler's concentration camps where the people he hated were herded together."

Rachel nodded. "You could say that."

"So why hasn't the Bartley government eliminated the lot of you?"

"Because he needs the labor force. We're cheap. Look at the conditions we live in."

It made sense. The virus had killed most of the people and now that the population was being rebuilt, they needed buildings and roads and places for people to live.

Rachel placed the last plate in the drainer and dried her hands. "Bartley would like to exterminate us, of that I'm sure. He tried before but didn't have enough of his cronies behind him in congress and he couldn't do it single-handed."

"Hitler managed," I said.

"Even Hitler got caught out eventually. Bartley plans to be around for a long time. I don't think too much about what happens outside, though. This is my home. I've got my husband and my children."

"Nathan, too. He's doing well."

Rachel smiled. "There's something I want you to give him from me."

Throwing her arms around me, she held me tight. I still had the dish towel in my hands but I returned the hug.

Eventually she held me at arms' length. "He'll pretend he doesn't like it, so you'll have to tell him he has to accept it. A hug is the only gift I can give him."

"You brought him up," I said. "Made him who he is."

"No, Nathan was always…Nathan." She took the dish towel from my hands and tossed it onto the bench. "Goodnight, Nicola, and good luck."

I knew I'd made the right decision to stay one more night. The hardest part was yet to come.

Now I had to kill generals Tan and Willis.

CHAPTER TWENTY-SIX

I had my bag in my hands, the C-vac in my back pocket and my wits about me as I walked through the gates that marked the boundary of the Badlands. I didn't look back as I passed the geopositron readers mounted on the gates. No alarms, no soldiers running toward me, no unusual behavior.

The key was to look confident so I kept up my pace and headed straight ahead for the station. There were fewer people around this time, which was a worry. It was much easier to get lost in a crowd and I didn't want to attract any attention.

I was constantly glancing around to monitor my surroundings, then I saw a familiar face, not a friendly face, but one which was imprinted on my mind. My mouth fell open.

It was my brother, Cain. A shiver went up my spine.

He was in full military uniform, having a heated discussion with two civilians who were hanging off his every word. When an armed soldier spoke, people listened.

Our eyes were the same shade of blue, except it wasn't possible mine could be so cold and unforgiving. I'd always

210

been obedient, but not like him. I'd once thought we had something in common since we were both in the military, until he set me straight and told me I was nothing to him.

I took long strides but felt as if I was walking in slow motion. My brother lifted his gaze, glanced around, looked right through me as if I wasn't even there. I'd never been so grateful not to be noticed.

He shifted his gaze back to the two civilians. I could breathe again and upped my pace to get to the station as quickly as possible. The area was buzzing with activity so I presumed another ground pod had arrived. My head down, I scooted down the stairs to see the pod waiting, jumped on and found a seat at the back by the far window.

My heart was racing. Seeing my brother had thrown me though it shouldn't have. For one thing, I should've been prepared for anything and, for another, I knew he was often on missions patrolling the Badlands. Supposedly dangerous missions. I had my doubts about that now.

I glanced through the window on the other side of the aisle, the one that looked out onto the platform. Cain was striding along, scanning the faces around him, trying to look into the pod, looking for someone. Looking for me.

The doors closed and the pod started moving. I couldn't see my brother any more but he must still be on the platform. I let out a breath I didn't know I'd been holding in. That had been too close for my liking.

Leaning back in my seat, I peeled the PR device from my arm and sent Lucien a message since I didn't think my reappearance would be a pleasant surprise for him. It took him a while to reply. He told me to turn back and that I was putting myself in danger. I ignored him.

I didn't relax until we got to the halfway point at

Barrington and the pod started moving again. A few people had got on and off, soldiers included, but none were looking to arrest me. Cain hadn't reported me. Perhaps he hadn't recognized me after all.

The New Nation authorities believed I was dead, something which my brother would presumably have been told at some stage. My biological parents had probably been told the same thing.

I wondered how that would have felt for them, or if they'd felt anything at all. Though I'd met them on several occasions, I barely knew them and they didn't know me any better. Like everyone else in New Nation, I'd been raised in a government facility then switched to the military because of my natural abilities in that area. I'd been a good soldier. And a non-existent daughter. It was better they thought me dead.

C Dock was just as busy as it had been two days ago when I'd been with Nathan. Being in a crowd made me feel safe, or as safe as I was ever going to feel under the circumstances. I'd contacted Lucien minutes earlier, telling him to meet me in his office.

A pinprick on my arm. It had to be Lucien.

I pulled over to one side of the path and peeled the PR device off my skin to check the message. Sure enough, Lucien was telling me to meet him in the teleport room. I could work out why.

I slapped the PR back on my arm where it melded into my skin, then picked up my bag and stalked away. It was easy to look like I knew where I was going when I did.

It was good being nobody in New Nation. I didn't exist here. My geopositrons – or Reece's geopositrons – gave me access and I could walk unnoticed throughout the compound. Still, I couldn't stay here forever and didn't want to. It was only a matter of time until I was found out.

For obvious reasons, few people were allowed in to the teleport room. Reece had been sent back before me so I was confident he had access. I placed my fingers on the door handle. The geopositron reading would be instant. The door opened. If anyone checked the records, they'd think Reece had been in the room.

Lucien was leaning against a wall, his arms crossed. Brightening as soon as he saw me, he ushered me into the room. I stopped short of the transport chair placed in the middle. I wasn't ready to sit there, not yet.

"Nathan's on his way here," he said. "He knows the technology better than anyone else. He can send you back right away."

I looked him in the eye. "I'm not going back."

"It's the safest place, Nicola, the safest time. You can't stay here."

I needed Lucien's help in so many ways – to find a safe place for me to stay, to let me get through to the generals so I could eliminate them, and to send me back to exactly the right time. I couldn't do this on my own.

"Do you know what they did back in Altabena?" I asked.

Lucien raised his eyebrows. "You mean the school?"

I nodded.

"Yes," he said.

"Blowing up the buildings was one thing. I don't care about buildings. There were fifteen hundred people in there who died, most of them students who had their whole lives ahead of them. *Had*. Past tense."

Matter of fact, he said, "I knew about the plan before

it was enacted, and the bomb, of course."

No doubt he knew about everything. The generals wanted to kill Ben and they didn't care how they did it.

I looked Lucien in the eye. "I should've been there too. I should be dead."

Damn it, did he have to look so calm, so controlled, so casual?

"I couldn't stop Tan and Willis," he said. "Neither of us could. They insisted the loss of life would be worth it."

I raised my eyebrows. "Us?"

When I'd been in the military, Lucien had been my superior officer, my mentor and teacher. There had been no 'us'.

"Nathan has done a lot of research into the technology behind the molecular bomb," Lucien said. "It's physics. That's his specialty, or one of them."

My blood boiled. I bit my lip and turned away, pacing to the wall and back. Better I didn't say anything. Better I didn't show my emotions.

If I was going to get back to Altabena, I needed Nathan whether I liked it or not. Could I trust the young man who'd developed the bomb that blew up the school?

Lucien spread his hands. "Nathan's different from us. He has a strong sense of fairness."

"Killing hundreds of people is a strange way of showing it."

"He cares about science and technology. That's what he understands best. He doesn't want to overthrow the Bartley government or the generals or anyone else."

Tightlipped, I stared at Lucien.

"You're angry," he said. "You've changed."

I had feelings. I was human. I wasn't taking the

emotion suppressing drugs I'd taken every day of my life in New Nation, the same drugs Lucien and everyone else here, with the possible exception of Nathan, was taking.

Time to get my act together. "Generals Tan and Willis planned to get rid of Bartley. They wanted the perfect crime and you were in on it with them."

The generals' plan had been to get rid of Ben, prevent the development of the virus, and therefore stop Bartley's rise to ultimate power. And no one would even know they'd done it. If that was what they wanted, the generals hadn't succeeded. They were wrong about Ben creating the virus. They had to be. Couldn't they see that? Would they even care?

"Tan and Willis have gone crazy," Lucien said. "They're worse than Bartley. It's impossible to work out what they'll do next, what plan they'll come up with, how many people will die."

"I know what they did next. To Ben."

My breath caught in my throat, the hole in my chest jagged and raw as I said his name. I held back a sob and turned away. No way could I let Lucien see how personal this was.

"You're still much better off in Altabena than you are here," he said. "In Altabena, you have a chance."

Lucien was wrong about one critical thing.

Without Ben, I didn't have a chance.

I looked up at my old mentor. "I do want to go back to Altabena, Lucien, but not to the same time I came from."

Lucien's mouth twisted. "What do you mean?"

"I want to go back to the time before things went bad, before the school was bombed, before Ben was killed."

His expression softened. "Fine. We can do that, but it won't stop those events happening. We can't control what the generals do."

Make or break time. I wasn't sure if I could trust Lucien, only that I had to.

"That's where you're wrong." My eyes narrowed. "I can prevent those events from occurring – if I eliminate the generals first."

His eyes widened, his olive skin suddenly pale.

CHAPTER TWENTY-SEVEN

Lucien stared at me. "Have you gone mad?"

Perhaps I had.

"The generals are megalomaniacs." My heart pounding, I took a deep breath. "They're the ones who've gone mad. They'll keep sending bombs or assassins back to the past. They won't stop. And they'll always succeed."

His brow furrowed, Lucien stamped his foot, something I'd never seen before. For him, this was an abundance of passion.

"Kill them?" He threw his hands up. "How? When? Do you really think it'll be that easy?"

"If it was easy, someone would've done it by now."

He jabbed his finger in the air. "You're supposed to have a plan, a precise military schedule of operations, not a vague idea."

"We can develop a plan. I've been away. I don't know their movements. You do."

"We?"

I held his gaze. "Yes, we. You've bent the rules, Lucien. They'll kill you too if they suspect you've strayed even slightly."

Disappointment glimmered in his eyes. "You would betray me?"

I shook my head. "There is nothing they could do to make me talk, Lucien. If I have nothing else, I have my honor. I am loyal."

"You are not so obedient as you used to be. You've learnt to think for yourself. They won't have that. You can't stay."

I had to think on my feet. "Here in New Nation, the generals have the upper hand and always will. They can do whatever they like, and back in Altabena I can only react. The only thing I can be sure of is that they'll do something worse every time."

He nodded.

"It's only a matter of time until they get to you too," I said.

Lucien's shoulders slumped. He turned away.

"Maybe we do want the same thing after all." His back was to me but I needed to see his face. My hand on his shoulder, I pulled him toward me.

He held my gaze. "The world would be a better place without them."

I raised my eyebrows. "Then we agree?"

A curt shake of his head. "It's still better for you to go back to Altabena now. Nathan's on his way. He can send you."

Nathan again? I was sick of hearing about him.

I stepped back. "I'm not going."

"Yes, you are. I can take care of things here while you're gone."

That wasn't good enough. "I can help. I can kill the generals. They're murderers."

"Is that what you want to be too?"

I'd killed before. To save a roomful of schoolchildren. That had been different. I wasn't a murderer. Yet.

Lucien's words stung but that was nothing compared to the hole in my heart or the reason I was here. Besides, I could tell he wanted me to be safe, which was what I wanted too, only not like this.

"I'm not going back until the job is done," I said.

His eyes narrowed. "I'll make you go."

"You'll have to kill me first."

He pushed me. The pain in my shoulder was nothing compared to the shock. Lucien had never laid a hand on me before, not like this. This wasn't a training drill where we got knocked around.

"You heard me," I said.

He shunted me again, so hard my back hit the wall. He wanted me to hit him back, wanted me to give him a reason.

If there was one thing I knew, it was that sometimes it was more powerful not to fight.

Lucien raised his fist. With my back to the wall, this would hurt like hell and I was ready to take it.

His face dropped. His hand too. "I can't hit you, Nicola. I can't hurt you."

I looked up at him through hooded eyes. "Maybe you already did."

"You're like a daughter to me."

Maybe I wanted to hurt him a little too. "Then why send me on a perilous time travel mission in the first place?"

I'd been content when I'd lived here before, if only because I hadn't known any better. Now I understood so much more about life and friendship and family in all its wonder and all its pain. There was no going back.

"I gave you the greatest gift of all." He stared into my eyes. "I gave you life, a *new* life in Altabena."

Lucien put his hands on my shoulders and squeezed them before letting them drop. From him, this was the highest affection and it made me feel strangely warm on the inside.

He'd also given me a mom and a dad in Altabena but he couldn't know how much they meant to me. I'd had years with Lucien and only five months with Jan and Philip Gray yet they meant everything to me. That world was everything to me. And unless I could change the past, that'd be a world without Ben.

I was supposed to return the sentiment and say Lucien was like a father to me but I couldn't. I was having doubts.

The sound of the door swishing open made me look up. I turned, hoping I hadn't been caught out, but it was only Nathan. Very few people would have access to this room so I didn't need to worry about anyone else coming in.

He stepped closer. "I was advised of your return."

I remembered his mother's message, her gift to him. I might not trust Nathan but his mother had been good to me and deserved better.

"Nathan, put your arms out."

He stared at me blankly, perhaps even more blankly than usual. "Pardon?"

I spread my arms so he could see what was coming as I embraced him. He stood bolt upright like a manikin.

"Nathan, that was from your mother," I said. "She told me to give you a big hug from her."

The hint of a smile on his lips made me wonder whether his mother was right and there was more to him than met the eye.

"That is very like her." He threw his arms around me loosely with a movement that would hardly be called a hug in Altabena.

After a few moments, Lucien asked, "What was that all about?"

"I have no idea, sir." Nathan then turned to me. "You have a package of some sort in your rear pocket."

"Yes." I pulled out the C-vac, wondering if I should put it in a safe place.

"You stole it," he said. "You must have."

"Your mother helped me."

"That's not true. This will save the life of one person in the Badlands and you've taken that away from them."

Though he was reacting, his tone was so even, his voice so matter of fact. It was like talking to a robot.

"Your mother got me into the hospital and the room where they store the drugs," I said.

Nathan snatched the package from my hands with such speed it left me stunned. And I'd thought he was like a robot. The first rule of combat – never underestimate your opponent. I'd done exactly that.

Rushing at him wouldn't work. Better to battle with his mind.

"Your mother said you were special," I said. "And that she couldn't say that in front of Sarah and Theodore."

Nathan blinked, back to being a robot.

"She was disappointed you'd gone to Barrington, got so close, then turned back," I added. "But above all, she wants you to be safe. There's someone I want to be safe too. That's why I took the C-vac and also why she helped me do it."

His eyes narrowed. He didn't believe me.

The door swished open. Voices cut through the air, voices I recognized. Nathan shoved the C-vac into his back pocket.

Then I saw them standing in the doorway.

Generals Tan and Willis.

CHAPTER TWENTY-EIGHT

They hadn't changed a bit since I'd last seem them whereas I was a completely different person. Willis was tall with red hair and a ruddy complexion while Tan was smaller but meaner. What he lacked in size, he made up for in other ways.

The two men surveyed the room, looking from one of us to the other. They didn't appear crazy at the moment. No, they seemed controlled.

General Willis closed the door behind them and folded his arms. "This is a surprise."

He didn't look surprised. I opened my mouth to speak. Nothing came out which was just as well because I needed a story, a good one, something so convincing it'd save my life.

Lucien didn't say anything either. I knew his style. He would tread carefully and refuse to fall into the trap of explaining himself too soon.

Willis stared at Lucien. "We were about to issue a communication, then decided it would be prudent to speak to you first, Captain Everett. Turns out we were right about that."

Lucien raised his eyebrows. "What communication, sir?"

"There was a sighting of the corporal." He flicked his eyes toward me. "To think we had doubted its veracity. It seemed so unlikely and yet here we all are."

My brother had reported me. It couldn't have been anyone else. Lucien didn't say anything and Nathan wouldn't speak until spoken to. A wise move.

Willis stepped closer to Lucien, chest to chest, like a boxer in a stare down. "Let's cut to the chase. Tell us what's going on."

"I wish I knew, sir. I'm still trying to put together the pieces."

"Start talking."

"We brought her back – brought someone back – but we didn't know it was Corporal Gray until she arrived."

Willis stepped back, his hands behind his back. "You didn't know?"

"We had a fix on some geopositrons, Corporal Reece Withers' geopositrons to be precise."

"He died over a year ago."

"I believe so, sir. After we got the reading, we set up the transport and this is the result."

Willis turned to me. "What happened to Reece Withers?"

It was better if they still thought he was dead. "Who, sir?"

"You're telling me you didn't know him?"

"That's correct, sir."

Willis started pacing, his hands still behind his back. "First things first, Corporal. What happened to *your* geopositrons? That's what I'd like to know."

"I was in a car accident not long after I went back to Altabena," I said, amazed at the words coming out of my mouth. "I suffered mammoth blood loss, spent months in hospital, didn't even know where I was most of the time. I'd been expecting to be transported back, then found I was stuck in that place. Marooned."

Stick to the facts. Keep the talking to a minimum. I had to be careful or I'd give myself away.

"What about your PR device?" Willis asked.

"I was unconscious and delirious in hospital. I have no idea what happened to it."

"You had two PR devices, Corporal. Are you telling me they were both rendered useless?"

"I only know that they were gone, sir."

He remembered. Either he was quick on his feet or he'd had lots of time to think about this. One of the PR devices had incriminating evidence about Ben on it, information that would have helped the generals trace Ben and make their job easier. When I'd been transported back to Altabena a second time, I had secreted that device away with me. There was also a more advanced PR device that the authorities then transported to me to enable communications. I'd destroyed both of them.

"So many mysteries, Corporal." Willis stood in front of me. "Then there's the new mystery of how you were somehow imbued with someone else's geopositrons. Those of a dead young man, in fact."

I explained how a new scientific phenomena possessing the same properties as geopositrons had been discovered and how I broke into the laboratory to steal them. That was the easy part of the story because I could stick largely to the truth.

While I was talking, I maintained eye contact, kept him preoccupied and peeled the PR from my arm. I had to get rid of the device, otherwise it'd be traced back to Lucien. Besides, the PR had tracking systems so they'd always be able to find me. Maybe they would anyway. Maybe I was doomed. Still, I had to try. Behind me, Lucien took the device from my fingers.

Willis started pacing again. If he thought it would make me nervous, he was right. Meanwhile General Tan stood there like a statue, not a single muscle moving, so controlled and rigid it sent a shiver up my spine.

"That's a very interesting story." Willis turned to General Tan. "Don't you think so? Isn't it amazing?"

Tan didn't flinch. It was as if he hadn't heard.

Willis turned to me. "We sent you back to complete a mission and instead we didn't hear from you again. Now you turn up with someone else's geopositrons. Like magic!"

He laughed. Tan didn't crack a smile, however Willis didn't let that stand in his way.

"Any other tricks in your repertoire?" He laughed again.

"I came back the first chance I had," I said. "That's why I located and ingested the geopositrons."

"You came back with an attitude," he snapped.

"I came back alive!"

Grinning, he spread his arms. "You prove my point."

Silence. Anything I said would incriminate me. The general let me stew, as he stared from me to Lucien, then settled his gaze on Nathan.

"Is it true that you found a reading on the geopositrons, arranged the transportation and then discovered it was Corporal Gray instead?"

"Yes sir," Nathan said.

Perhaps there was hope for me after all. If they didn't believe me, maybe they'd believe their loyal subject.

Willis said, "Nathan, please leave the room and never speak about any of this again. Do you understand?"

"Yes, sir."

And just like that, Nathan left, the cancer vaccine still in his back pocket. I had the horrible feeling I'd never see him or my C-vac again. I felt myself sinking but couldn't let my feelings show. I straightened. These men could never know how far I'd strayed.

General Tan finally spoke. "Do you think we care that you returned to New Nation as soon as you could?"

My heart rate rose. It was hard to breathe. "Excuse me, sir?"

Smooth olive skin was stretched across Tan's sharp cheekbones, his dark eyes expressionless. "You can make all the excuses you like. The fact remains you were sent to complete a mission and you failed."

Every nerve ending in my body was on edge. "Sir."

"You've let down yourself and your country, and you're not going to get away with it." His eyes narrowed, the brown irises now almost imperceptible. "In fact, you're not going to get away."

In the background, Willis was on his PR device, ordering officers to attend immediately.

Try to think straight, Nicola. Stop panicking. Don't let the generals win.

Could I convince them I was innocent? Would they take Lucien's word for it? Did I have another option?

Fear gripped me like a vise. I wanted choices but had

none.

I raised my voice. "General Willis, you sent me on a mission to kill Ben Tanner so there would be no virus and no Bartley in ultimate control. You wanted me to help you bring down the government, both of you."

Willis stepped closer. "That was your mission and you didn't succeed."

"You tricked me."

"I repeat. You failed."

One last chance. I feinted a punch as if ready to hit Willis in the head. He lifted his hands, a natural reaction. Instead I went low and rammed into him. His back smashed into Tan, both of them knocked off balance. *Incapacitate and run.* I had to get away.

Suddenly, hands on my shoulders pulled me back and threw me against the teleport chair. Four soldiers surrounded me, their laser pistols raised. One move and I'd be dead.

The chair I'd refused only minutes earlier didn't seem like such a bad idea now. So close and yet so far. If only it was still an option.

Desperation dripped from me, my heart pounding, head spinning.

"Take her away!" General Willis yelled.

One of the soldiers cuffed me. Two grabbed me. I didn't resist. No point. No point wondering how they'd got in either. A voice command from Willis, perhaps.

I glanced at Lucien, not saying a word because there wasn't a word that would help. Perspiration beaded on his brow.

"You know what'll happen to you," General Tan said, a gleeful glimmer in his eye. It was the only time I'd seen him betray a hint of emotion.

The soldiers shoved me through the doorway. I knew what lay ahead.

Execution.

CHAPTER TWENTY-NINE

In my wildest dreams I wasn't expecting a trial, fair or otherwise. That wasn't how things worked here, not when the crime was treason and two well-respected generals had instigated the charge.

Despite this, I was so naïve. I was expecting something as civilized as jail until the time came for my execution. No such luck.

Instead, I was confined in a metal box too small even for a child. My hands and feet bound, I was in the fetal position with the walls of the box squeezing me in. My muscles had cramped up long ago.

The box wasn't the only thing crushing me. Despair pressed down on me, sank deep into my bones, sapped away at my will, or what there was left of it.

I couldn't work out why the box was tilted on its side, perhaps to make me more uncomfortable or perhaps there was another reason. There were large holes for air so at least I could breathe, even if it didn't feel like it. Bars dug into my back at the top of the box which meant I had sufficient light at least, even if I couldn't turn around.

They'd stripped me naked but that didn't worry me

nearly as much as other possible consequences. I'd heard of cold cells, one of a suite of 'advanced interrogation techniques' used by the government, not that the idea had ever worried me before. I'd never given it much thought and had certainly never thought it could happen to me.

I'd been here for hours or maybe longer and my bladder was full. Set to explode, in fact. My bowels had been rumbling too and that was what I was most afraid of. Releasing the bowels was a natural response to fear. Part of the fight or flight reflex, it was one of the things that often happened when you were scared.

Stick to the facts, Nicola. Forget about your feelings. It was easier to factor in my biology than my fear. I clenched my buttocks, held it in, waited until that particular bodily need subsided, concentrated on only that one thing. It was okay.

My stomach rumbled for a different reason – hunger. As well as having no clue how long I'd been here, I had no idea when I'd last eaten, only that it was long ago. And maybe that wasn't so important given they'd be executing me soon.

I wondered when 'soon' would happen. How often did they hold the executions? Weekly? Monthly? It had been so long since I'd lived in New Nation that the only part I remembered with certainty was that the authorities waited until there was an adequate number of executions so they could be done at once for the sake of efficiency. Because clearly the efficient use of resources was a much higher priority than that of respect for humanity.

My mind wandered. I had all the time in the world to consider these factors. I had all the time in the world and I had none.

I heard a deep grunt. Someone else was here. The sound of a door swishing open cut through the air followed by the shuffle of footsteps. A bolt of fear shot through me.

"Who's there?" I asked.

Another grunt.

"Can you get me out of here? Please help me."

Nothing. The soldier must be standing there, staring at the box.

I could've begged – would've had no problem begging if it would do any good – but this man wasn't in charge and would do only what he was instructed by his superiors. Instead I maintained the little dignity I had left.

Long minutes passed without a sound. I waited. Was this a game to him?

"What do you want?" I asked.

The shuffle of footsteps was closer this time. I tensed up. A hand appeared in front of my face, a straw perched between the fingers. He shoved the straw in and I bent my neck, straining to get my lips around the straw. I sucked in cool fresh water or it may have been stale tepid water. Who was I to judge? It was magnificent.

Above my head, there was a small creak like that of a door opening and a gentle sound I couldn't work out. Something round and white rolled down between two sides of the box past my face but I didn't have enough room to move to catch it. It was sliding down and must've hit the bottom of the box.

Was that an egg? How could I get to it?

Now I knew why the box was tilted at an angle – so they could slide food down where I couldn't reach it.

The soldier on the other side laughed. I wanted to

scream and yell but refused to give him the satisfaction. Despite my desperation to find out if it really was an egg, I wouldn't let him watch me struggle. I could wait. After all, I had all the time in the world.

I don't know how long he stood there watching me until finally I heard his footsteps and the swish of the door as he left. Such a relief.

My head was pressed against the top of the box. My legs were curled up, my feet scrunched up under me. I twisted and turned, skin scraping against the box, as I tried to reach the white thing that had been dropped into the box. If my hands weren't bound, I could've stuck one hand between my legs and grabbed it. Instead I had to deal with the frustration.

Never give up, Nicola. I kept struggling, kept twisting, grunting as I did so. Suddenly, my hands slipped through. I didn't even know how, then I realized the confinement box had probably been built for a man, and I was smaller and slimmer than the average male.

I was not average. And I would do this.

The item was easy to find, as it had rolled into the bottom corner, but it was slimy and hard to grasp. Eventually I got hold of it and then began the task of bringing it back up through my legs. I pressed my knees against the sides of the box as much as I could, struggled and twisted again, and all at once my hand got through.

I looked down at my lap. It was a boiled egg. They'd given me a boiled egg to taunt me because they didn't think I'd be able to reach it. Well, I'd shown them. They'd even peeled it, which seemed strangely considerate and out of character, not that I cared either way.

My first bite was small and tentative. Tasted like egg

white. I took another small bite and saw the edge of the yolk. Yep, definitely a hard-boiled egg. Hard-boiled like me, a thought that made me smile.

Who'd have thought a boiled egg could be so exciting, such a victory? I reveled in the satisfaction as I savored the egg.

Then I felt the first small rumble in my bowels, felt my bladder ready to explode, my personal dignity about to evaporate. A small trickle of urine escaped me. I tried to hold it in. Squeezed my eyes shut. I tried so hard and I'd held on for so long, but I was human with human bodily needs I could only fight for so long.

I clenched my buttocks. It didn't work. Horrified, I defecated and urinated in the box, hunched in the fetal position in my own excrement. It was a relief. Also a nightmare.

My eyes were already closed as I started crying. The box was so small it hurt to sob.

I'd never felt so alone.

*   *   *

Time passed. A day, two days, a week, who knew? Time had ceased to have any meaning for me.

Though my body was useless to me in this state, my mind was in full working order or at least I thought it was. At first I'd been sure someone would come to interrogate me. I went through my story in my head, the same story I'd given to the generals, the one I would stick to no matter what. No way would I betray Lucien.

I was being tortured, that was pretty obvious, and presumably the point of that was so they could get information of some sort from me. So why had no one come to interrogate me? Perhaps the torture was just for fun.

It was certainly torture for someone as physically active as myself – an accomplished martial artist and ex-soldier – to be locked in a box. That was the point, though. It wouldn't be punishment if it was fun.

This struck me as so silly that I chuckled, the shrill sound of my laughter taking me aback. How long had it been since I'd heard the sound of my voice? Of anyone's voice?

"Hi, Nicola." I could still speak, an achievement in itself.

We all had three basic human needs – shelter, water and food. I wasn't sure if the confinement box counted as shelter. The soldier had returned to give me water. I'd been taught that people could survive up to two months without food, even if that wasn't a theory I particularly wanted to test.

I was thinking too much. I didn't have lots of other options.

The soldier came into the room again. The creak of a latch above my head got me excited. It would be more food, another egg, maybe something else. I saw a blur of white. With no room to move, I had no way of catching the egg as it slid out of sight.

I heard a small plop sound as it hit the bottom. My heart sank. The egg had landed in a pool of my own urine laced with my very own poo.

That was why they'd peeled the egg – not to make it easier to eat, but to taunt me.

No, they couldn't do this to me. They couldn't. I had nothing left.

A sob escaped my lips. And another. I heard the

soldier shuffling away.

"Get back here and fight like a man."

I got the words out, then the sobs and convulsions took over. Scrunched up in a ball, I was breathing hard, my heart racing, tears streaming down my face. I screamed and yelled, for all the good it would do. Then I was choking, unable to breathe.

Time passed, lots of time, the one thing I had in abundance until they took that away from me as well.

I'd endured hunger on training simulation camps before but it had never been like this, never been so intense and consuming. I thought about the egg smeared with my own excrement. I thought long and hard. And let it sit there.

I dreamed of chocolate cake and the sandwiches Ben had made with love and remembered the fizz of champagne, the warmth of his body and the feeling of togetherness. The hole in my heart was huge but I tried to fill it with memories, tried to pretend I was somewhere else and that Ben was with me. I may have fallen asleep from time to time. I couldn't be sure and didn't think it mattered as long as my daydreams took me to a better place.

At some point I became aware of the low hum of white noise in the background and wondered what was going on. Fresh air hit my face. I could breathe again. The air hit my back too, where it was pressed against the bars that lined one side of the box.

Then I realized it wasn't fresh air. This was air-conditioning set somewhere near freezing point. They were turning my confinement box into a cold cell, yet another one of their 'enhanced interrogation techniques'.

I started shivering almost immediately. My palms were sweaty, my breath short again, my toes sitting in my own excrement. What was the freezing point of urine? Did it matter?

White noise was also used for torture. Screw them. I focused on the gentle hum in the background. *Focus.* That was the key. Get in the zone, Nicola, the survival zone.

No matter what, I was still a soldier. I did training drills in my head, went through my martial arts moves, remembered the feeling of power that training gave me. Physically, I was confined in a box, but in my head, I was punching and kicking and powering my way through life.

I pictured generals Tan and Willis and imagined beating them. In one dream – was it a dream? – Willis had been beaten to a pulp and was lying in the fetal position on the floor. I could stomp on his head and crush his skull beneath my boot.

Except I couldn't, not even in my dream.

Suddenly, I was back in Altabena and flooded with feelings of warmth. My parents were hugging me and I was pretending I didn't like it. I was lying by Ben's side. He was pulling my tee shirt over my head and I was unbuttoning his shirt. I was burning up for him, couldn't get enough of him. Placing my head on his chest, I listened to his heartbeat. He was so warm, so alive. He was all I wanted. Lauren was there too, laughing with us as we drank mocktails by the pool and ate her home-made wood-fired pizza.

Maybe I was delirious.

Maybe I passed out.

Maybe I'd passed out many times before.

*   *   *

My eyes sprung open. I was lying down, stretched out on something that felt like a bed. The room was white. Even in my weakened state, I was aware that sensory deprivation in a white room was another form of torture, but this didn't feel like torture compared to what I'd been through.

I sat up in bed, realized I was naked. Again.

Bruises had formed where my body had been pressed against the walls of the box. My muscles were sore as I stretched my arms and legs. Sore was an understatement. Pain thundered through my body and I reveled in every moment of it because I could move. I was human again.

A chair beside the bed had a pile of gray clothes folded on it. I shuffled my butt forward onto the edge of the bed, wondering if I'd be able to stand after all this time, how much time, I didn't know. My legs were weak but I could do it. I stood on my own two feet.

I was filthy and could smell myself. The room had a shower and toilet so I did what had to be done and stepped into a shower stall that had actual soap, shampoo and warm water. I scrubbed away the indignity of what I'd been through. Couldn't believe how good it felt to feel clean again.

After that, I pulled on a pair of gray panties. Underwear had never felt so good. I pulled on the rest of the clothes – a pair of sweats, a tee shirt and sneakers – and felt even more human than before.

My eyes went to the door. I tried the handle first. Locked, of course. I kicked the door though I knew it was useless, then turned my back to it and saw what I should've seen in the first place.

A tray of food and a bottle of water were sitting on a table by the wall. I pulled the chair up, unwrapped a toasted sandwich that was no longer warm. The first mouthful got stuck in my throat so I had a sip of water and kept eating. There were also two pieces of roast chicken, a hunk of cheese and a fruit salad. I left the best for last. I'd been given the same sort of chocolate that officers ate in New Nation, not the substandard stuff I'd been told was a treat when I was growing up.

The chocolate was rich and slightly bitter which, strangely enough, summed up my situation. I knew what this was. My last meal. I knew why they'd given me a bed and clean clothing – because executions were public and the authorities didn't want me to look like a tortured prisoner.

This wasn't for me. It was for them, so they didn't look bad.

After the meal, I walked around the room. Walking seemed like such an achievement. There was something else I wanted to try. Even as I got down to the floor, I was weak and unsure if I could do it. I got into press up position and did what felt like my first ever push-up. Yes, I could do it! I did a few more, then some stretches and a few squats and lunges, limbering up as if for a training session, except this wasn't training and I was exhausted within seconds.

Needing a rest, I sat down on the edge of the bed. It'd take time for my body to repair itself after the ordeal I'd been through. My mind might need some repairing too.

The door to my cell opened and a soldier stepped inside, tossed two items across the floor and left without a word. I stared at the hand and leg shackles and wondered if he thought I'd put them on myself without putting up any resistance.

I stood and stretched my arms up – because I could – and sat back down again. I could wait. I was good at waiting.

After a while, the same soldier burst through the door bringing three others with him, all of them with laser pistols in their hands. Four against one, was that even close to being a fair fight?

He pointed to the shackles. "Put them on."

I got up and walked across, considering my options. I could refuse to put the shackles on and they'd beat or shoot me and I'd still end up shackled. Or I could put the shackles on. Not a lot of choice.

Didn't they want to interrogate me first? It didn't make sense.

I nudged the shackles with my foot. "Isn't there something you want to say to me? Something you want to ask?"

The man's face was a blank wall. No response.

One of the soldiers kicked me, knocked me back against the table. "Put them on."

I might be able to fool him but I couldn't fool myself. My throat tight, it was hard to breathe but 'breathe' was what I wanted to do. More than anything I wanted to live.

And it made no difference.

Did I have a scrap of dignity left? I forced myself to bend over and did as I was told.

Sometimes the authorities taunted prisoners with mock executions. I'd heard the stories. A prisoner would be tortured, then prepared for execution at which point he'd confess and say anything to save his life.

I knew what the comfortable bed, the last meal, the plain gray clothes, the shackles and the next steps were for.

This was no mock execution.

The authorities didn't want me to talk.

They were going to kill me.

CHAPTER THIRTY

I'd been a hero once. Now I was a traitor standing in a dock in the facilitation room. I'd never been here before because I'd never wanted to see a public execution. I'd do anything not to be here now either.

Five men stood beside me, their shoulders hunched, heads bowed. All of us had our feet and hands shackled, not because the authorities thought we might run away but because it was humiliating. And it was.

I straightened and looked around. This was like nothing I'd ever seen in New Nation before. The room was wood paneled and filled with people sitting on antique-style leather seats that gave the place a sense of history and legitimacy. I scanned the room to see Lucien and Nathan sitting in the front row. Lucien held my gaze. Strangely, the sorrow in his eyes gave me some solace.

Generals Willis and Tan sat at the opposite end. My eyes glazed over them and landed on my brother sitting behind them, his face blank and expressionless. Was he here to gloat? Was this fun for him?

The facilitator had pride of place on a throne – sorry, seat – at the front behind her grand station where she was flanked by two guards. An older woman, she had her hair pulled back in a bun and wore a highly decorated military uniform.

She started speaking. The man beside me began sobbing as soon as she said his name. The facilitator's words were a drone as she continued with her speech. I felt faint, swaying on the spot, so I took deep breaths but still her words didn't make sense.

This was it. I'd failed. Ben was dead. He'd never come back and I'd never see him again. It felt as if giant hands were ripping apart the hole in my heart, making it bigger, causing me more pain, except my loss couldn't be any bigger.

I'd thought I could do it. Thought I could save him.

Meanwhile my parents in Altabena could only come to one conclusion – that I'd run away and left them. I'd let them down too. They'd spend the rest of their lives wondering what had happened to me. They deserved better.

Even Lauren deserved a better friend than me. I'd abandoned them all.

Had I made the wrong decision? Had I been fooling myself that I had even the smallest chance of success?

At least if I'd stayed in Altabena, my life would've gone on, albeit without Ben, and I wouldn't have caused so much grief for my friends and family at a time when everyone was already dealing with huge losses.

The facilitator was still talking or at least I thought she was. She said my name so I turned to look at her and tried to concentrate on the words. I caught a few: traitor, defector, renegade.

She held my gaze. "Do you have any last words?"

Though I felt as if I was choking, I forced the words out. "Generals Tan and Willis are the traitors. Not me. I can prove it."

The facilitator gave me a look that said you've got to be kidding. After all, how many other prisoners proclaimed their innocence? How many times had she heard this before?

Last words...If I had any last words, I was taking those men down with me.

"Lucien, play the recording." Meanwhile, I hoped like hell Lucien had used my PR device to record what Willis had said.

Then I heard my voice. "You sent me on a mission to kill Ben Tanner so there would be no virus and no Bartley in ultimate control. You wanted me to help you bring down the government, both of you."

General Willis's voice. "That was your mission and you didn't succeed."

"You tricked me."

"I repeat. You failed."

Silence in the room, then the facilitator said, "Play it again."

General Willis stood, flecks of foam forming at the corners of his mouth as he shouted and protested.

"Be quiet, sir," the facilitator said. "Voice recognition makes this easy to confirm."

Willis placed a hand on Tan's shoulder. "Tell them this is ridiculous."

Tan didn't move.

"I've heard enough." The facilitator slammed her gavel on the desk and turned to me. "You are a soldier. Is what you said true?"

"Yes," I said. "I was obeying orders." Which was true. That was what I'd done at first.

She motioned to the soldiers stationed at the side of the room. "Take generals Tan and Willis away and lock them up. The next time I see them, they will be on that dock."

At this, Willis stood, gesticulating wildly while proclaiming his innocence. Tan pulled his shoulders back, his chest heaving with deep breaths.

The facilitator said, "If you move, I will have you lasered right now."

The two men stood stock still. I was in a state of shock as four soldiers approached and manhandled the generals, a soldier on either side of each man. My eyes followed them as they left the room. The breath may have left my body with them.

I couldn't believe it, except I could. Anyone who threatened the New Nation government would be disposed of. The generals might be interrogated and tortured first. That was a distinct possibility whereas a trial was not.

And me? Was I still a threat? Despair gripped me.

The facilitator motioned to a nearby soldier. "Please escort her from the room."

Relief flooded through me as the guard came closer and bent over to remove the shackles.

"Do that later, please," the facilitator said.

I stiffened. Perhaps she wasn't convinced of my innocence after all. If so, there was a good chance I'd be sent back to be tortured again, only this time it would be followed by an interrogation.

The solider took my arm and helped me down from

the dock. Another came and joined me, and the two men led me out along the front of the room, past the facilitator on one side, and Lucien and Nathan on the other.

My eyes were glued to Lucien's, pleading with him not to leave me alone. I was so close to being free again, yet so unsure. I couldn't come this close to have it all taken away from me. My legs weak, my whole body shaking, I wasn't sure I even had enough left in me to fight.

"Where are we going?" I asked as we walked.

No answer.

I tried again. "Are you allowed to remove my shackles yet?"

More silence.

This time I nudged him with my shoulder. "Can you talk to me, please?"

We kept walking around a corner and down a corridor until eventually we stopped. I held my shackled hands out to the first soldier, the one who'd considered removing them earlier.

"Please," I said.

He removed the shackles from my hands and ankles, the other soldier watching intently as if he thought I might try something.

"Thank you." I got the words out though I was choking up.

He nodded in response while the other man edged the door open.

"You have to wait in there," he said.

Finally, one of them had spoken. I stepped inside and saw generals Tan and Willis standing at the other end of the room.

"No!" I turned.

246

REGENERATION

The door was already shut.

CHAPTER THIRTY-ONE

Two of them and one of me. Blood rushed through my veins, pumping to my muscles. My pupils dilated, my field of vision narrowing. I hadn't come this far to have success ripped from under my feet.

The guards must have been in on it or perhaps one of the generals had used his PR device to send a message.

That was then and this was now.

I strode across the room, hoped my desperation didn't show. "You're going to be executed. You know that don't you? They'll never let you live."

"Ha!" Willis snorted. "Thanks to you."

"Why bring me here?"

"I think you can work it out," he said.

I spread my arms. "You don't even have a weapon."

"We don't need one."

Bam! His fist landed on my cheek bone. I lifted my hands too late. I'd been in shock before but that punch had knocked some sense into me. I didn't even care if I had no chance of winning. I'd go down fighting.

Willis threw another punch. I slipped out of the way and threw an overhand right that landed in the middle of his face. Heard the crunch as it landed.

Shit, there were two of them. I had to get Willis between me and Tan or I'd have no chance. I slipped my hands around the back of Willis' neck and dragged his head down, spun him around so he was effectively a barrier.

He was too strong for me and straightened. Pulled me in close, ready to pummel me. He was a highly trained soldier too. Both of them were.

The door swung open. A distraction. I slammed an elbow into his face.

It was Lucien and Nathan. I didn't know how they'd got in and didn't care. Willis rushed at the door. Lucien kicked it shut.

That was when I noticed the laser pistols in their hands, Lucien's pointed at Tan, Nathan's at Willis. A laser was the perfect weapon in an enclosed space like this. It was every bit as effective as a regular gun, only without the problem of bullets ricocheting if you missed. Not that Lucien would miss.

Willis stepped back, his hands out. "Nathan, put the pistol down. You're not trained for this."

Nathan, blank and expressionless at the best of times, didn't say anything. He walked across the room behind Lucien to stand beside me. General Tan stood at the rear, his shoulders back, his face hardened as if he was going to let us fight it out.

"This is treason," Willis yelled.

Finally Nathan spoke. "If you think I have committed treason, you are indeed confused and incorrect."

"Nathan, you won't kill me," Willis said.

"No, I won't." Nathan kept the pistol pointed in

Willis's direction as he pressed the gun into my hands. "*She will.*"

Willis' face dropped, his eyes on me now, pleading. "You're making a mistake. Lucien has misled and lied to you. If you stop and listen, we can find a way."

What way would that be? More torture? Did he think I'd forgotten, that I was stupid? I didn't speak. The look on my face must have said it all.

"I'm unarmed, Nicola." Willis stepped closer, his hands out. "If you take back what happened in the facilitation room, we can come up with an explanation and find a way out of this."

I held the weapon high. "One more step and I'll shoot."

Sweat trickled from my brow down the side of my face. I'd never killed before, not like this. I wanted Willis dead, wanted both of them dead. He'd ordered Ben's death for god's sake and thought nothing of obliterating hundreds of lives by blowing up the school.

I had more than enough reason to kill these men. Willis and Tan would murder me in an instant if they had the chance, and if I made it back to Altabena, they'd find a way of finishing me the way they'd finished fifteen hundred other lives.

Willis shuffled forward, his eyebrows raised in the middle in an effort to appear conciliatory.

I should pull the trigger. Point blank range. One shot would be fatal. The laser would rip through skin and bone and cartilage, slice open flesh and organs, and the wound would expand.

"This isn't the way," Willis said. "You're a good person. You don't have it in you."

He was right. I wasn't a murderer.

Willis' upper lip curled to a sneer and he laughed. "You can't kill me."

"But *I* can." Lucien squeezed the trigger. The laser sliced straight through Willis' heart with not even enough time for him to reach to cover his chest. He dropped to the ground. Lucien sent another beam into the man's head, then shifted his arms to aim at Tan.

The general didn't flinch. "Do it."

Lucien squeezed the trigger. A beam through the chest and one through the head and it was all over as he crumpled to the floor.

I stared at the two dead bodies, relieved and shocked at the same time. As much as I wanted the two men dead, this was still horrible and it was probably most difficult of all for Lucien. Death was hard enough to take, I knew that. Murder was harder. It wasn't glamorous or manly. It was final and I felt sick to my stomach even though I knew there had been no other way. I was grateful too. I'd always be grateful to Lucien.

He reached for my arm. "We have to hurry, Nicola."

"To the transportation room?" I asked.

"Back to Altabena. It's the only place you'll be safe."

Would Lucien and Nathan be safe? I was leaving an enormous mess behind and they'd have a lot of explaining to do.

The two of them put their pistols back in their holsters as we strode out of the room and down what seemed like endless corridors. Lucien seemed to know where we were going, which was just as well because I sure as hell didn't.

As soon as we stepped outside, the glare was blinding. It had rained, nothing unusual, and the sun had come out and was reflecting against the clouds overhead and the puddles on the ground.

I knew where we were though, as we headed to the other side of the military compound. One foot in front of the other. It was the only way to do this. Running would look suspicious and attract attention and that was the last thing we wanted.

"How did you know things would pan out that way?" I asked.

"We didn't," Lucien said. "Not for sure."

"And generals Tan and Willis…" there was a hitch in my voice "…how did you know they'd be at the facilitation?"

"That was the one thing of which I had absolutely no doubt." Lucien added, "We're nearly there."

We weren't. Fifteen minutes felt like fifteen years until we finally reached the right building. Despite the soldiers around us, for once I didn't feel threatened and wasn't worried about being recognized. I was on my way home.

We turned a corner and entered a quieter part of the facility where the teleport room was located.

"Nathan, can you do this?" I asked. "Can you really send me back?"

His lips curled to a confident smile as he walked. "I've already programmed the coordinates and merely need to do some last-minute checks. I am very good at my job."

And I was glad of it.

Then I saw my brother heading straight for us like a steam train. Did he suspect? What could the generals have said to him?

Lucien raised his pistol. "Stop right there."

Cain kept coming. Lucien fired at his feet.

My brother looked down and stopped but didn't raise his hands. "I worked it out. You're going back to kill Ben Tanner."

"No, that's not it!" I said.

"You can't. That's treason. You can't do anything to sabotage the government."

He was my brother but he didn't know me. He'd never known me. He was a loyal subject, raised by the government, indoctrinated by the regime and loyal to a fault. Like I had been.

Cain stared at me, then shifted his gaze to Lucien. "I won't let you near the transportation room."

Lucien shot a beam through my brother. I gasped. As I watched him drop to the floor, I felt something I couldn't quite describe. I didn't have a lot of feeling for this brother who'd never wanted me, yet it still hurt. The hole in my chest grew a little bigger. And I didn't have time to deal with it.

"This is very bad," Nathan said.

"We have to go." Lucien waved for us to follow and we did.

Outside the transportation room, he placed his hand on the recognition plate and the door opened. We were in.

I stared at the chair in the middle of the room. The arms still bore the moon-shaped imprints of my fingernails or perhaps someone else's. I didn't know how many people – or drones, for that matter – had been sent back before or after me.

I turned to Lucien, ready to hug him. I was going home and he was the one giving me this chance. Perhaps he saw the affection in my face and guessed what I was about to do or perhaps he had no clue. Either way, he ushered me to the chair, his hand in the small of my back.

"It's time, Nicola." Urgency in his voice but no emotion. He'd said I was like a daughter to him. Wouldn't a father be overwhelmed with feeling when giving his child the ultimate farewell?

I had greater concerns. "One more thing. I'm not going back without the C-vac."

Fire in his eyes. "The chair, Nicola!"

"It's okay, Lucien." Nathan pulled the packaging from his pocket. "I came prepared."

Eyes wide, I stared. I could've hugged Nathan too, except that hadn't gone down so well the first time. What had changed his mind about the C-vac? Maybe thinking about his own mother had done it.

I reached for the package in his hand.

"No," he said. "Don't worry about the vaccine. I'll send that exactly one minute after your arrival in a separate teleport. I already told you I've taken all factors into consideration."

It made sense. Transporting human matter was a complex process so inorganic items were always sent separately. Like clothing. I was going to have to think things through better if I was going to survive.

"Thank you, Nathan," I said. "I could kiss you."

He held his hand out. "Please don't."

Lucien pointed to the chair. "There's no time."

I sat down, gripping the arms of the chair.

"Good luck, Nicola."

They were the last words he said as he left through the other door in the room, the one that led to the systems panel.

"Thank you for everything," I yelled, unsure whether

Lucien could hear me.

Nathan held my gaze. "I'll send you back to a time before Ben Tanner's death and before the school was blown up. As you wished."

Nathan was chattier now than I'd ever seen him before. He seemed to be in his element.

Knocking at the door sounded like thunder. The teleport room had restricted access but it was only a matter of time before the person outside got in. Or people. Or a whole army for all I knew.

"I presume you have a plan for preventing the disasters that are to come?" Nathan asked.

"You mean the school being blown up?"

"Yes."

I wondered what he was talking about. "The generals are dead. They can't blow up the school or kill Ben, not now."

"Not now, Nicola, not after they've already done it."

More banging came from outside the door.

"Nathan, you're the time travel expert," I said. "You'd better explain this to me right now."

"It's quite simple. Generals Tan and Willis have already blown up Altabena High School and placed a kill chip inside the science teacher's brain. That's in the past. You will now be sent back to a time before that happened, however those things will still happen."

My eyes were wide. Surely he could see the terror in my face. Surely this couldn't be happening.

"Are you serious?" I asked.

"I don't joke, Nicola."

My head dropped into my hands. How could I have been so naïve? I'd thought I had it straight in my head and that being sent back in time would solve everything.

"I don't joke around either, Nathan," I said. "Send me back."

He left the room.

More banging outside.

It wouldn't be long now.

CHAPTER THIRTY-TWO

I was lying in the fetal position, my arms wrapped tightly around my head. Pain blasted through my head, made it feel as if it was going to split open, pain so severe I couldn't move. Then, as suddenly as it had come, the pain lifted.

The fetal position. I was naked again. Terror cut through me. My eyes squeezed shut, I was back in the confinement box – except I wasn't. I could move after all. A miracle. I opened my eyes into slits and groped the ground trying to work out where I was. The concrete floor below me was cold and unforgiving but a hell of a lot better than that damn box.

Stretching my limbs, I sat up, looked around and worked out I was in the locker room at the martial arts arena. Not so bad. Locker rooms had clothes and I'd need some of those.

I stood up, tentatively at first because my legs felt weak. I didn't have time for weakness, so I tried several lockers, all of them locked. Spotting a dirty pair of red Converse sneakers lying around, I slipped them on and tied the laces. They weren't exactly boots that were made for kicking but they'd have to do. I didn't think how crazy I'd look if anyone walked in right now — naked except for a pair of sneakers. I front-kicked a locker, once, twice, three times did the trick.

The lock hadn't given way, so I grabbed the crumpled top corner of the locker door and pulled it open. With no time to be fussy, I found a stained white tee shirt, slipped it over my head and pulled on a pair of khaki cargo shorts that had seen better days. It was all for a good cause.

The C-vac flashed in my mind. It was supposed to be transported immediately after I was. My eyes went straight to the spot on the floor where I'd landed and I couldn't believe it. The package was right there.

I went grabbed it, a big smile on my face as I shoved it into a pocket of my pants.

"Thank you, Nathan," I said.

Leaving the broken locker behind me, I strode around the corner and past the lockers on the other side toward the door. Two girls in tennis outfits strolled into the room, blond ponytails swinging as they stopped and looked me up and down.

Tennis? Honestly, what a waste of time. They sidled past me without a word.

"Excuse me," I said. "What time is it?"

"Hang on," one of the girls glanced back at me, then placed her racket on a bench. She opened her locker and rummaged through it to look at the time on her phone. Didn't anyone wear a watch nowadays? Eventually she said, "11.35."

The other girl headed for the back of the room where she started undoing her laces.

"Shit." The word slipped out of my mouth.

Nathan had sent me back to the correct time and place, all right – with 25 minutes to spare. I was about to panic except I didn't have time for that.

I shook my head in disbelief. "Thanks *a lot*, Nathan." Hoped he could hear my sarcasm. I'd asked him to take me back to a time before the bomb and he'd taken that quite literally.

The girl at the back of the room straightened. "Are you okay?"

No, I was absolutely not okay. Ben was okay, though. I pictured his winning grin and my heart swelled to explosion point. Ben…the reason I was here. He'd be on the bus on his way back from the science excursion at Geochemical Global. Safe for now.

I stormed out of the locker room, past the martial arts arena and down a corridor lined with classrooms. I could run through the school, yelling there was a bomb. And everyone would think I was crazy. No one would pay attention.

Stop and think for a moment, Nicola. I had to get fifteen hundred people out of here and fast.

If there was a serious bomb threat, the school would be evacuated. We'd had at least one drill while I'd been at Altabena High where we'd all left the school grounds in an orderly fashion and gathered on the oval, a safe distance from all the buildings.

Therefore, I had to be a serious bomb threat. First things first, I needed a phone. Damn it, where was a phone booth when you needed one? I wasn't sure I'd even seen one the whole time I'd been in Altabena. Which only left me one option.

A guy younger than me walked past, headphones

plugged in, his bag slung over one shoulder. The perfect candidate. I turned and followed, confident he wouldn't hear the gentle squeak of my sneakers as I caught up to him.

My pulse was skyrocketing. *Focus, Nicola.*

I got him from behind, my arm around the front of his neck in a rear naked choke before he knew what was going on. He struggled but I kept squeezing and dragged him back so he couldn't get his balance.

Lights out. His knees buckled and I went down with him, the two of us falling in a heap. I pulled out his ear buds and followed the white cords to the phone in his pocket. Too easy.

I grabbed the phone and ran. Behind me, I heard a distressed voice say, "Oh my god," and knew someone had found the guy. Just as well.

Outside, I was panting as I dropped down onto a bench and stared at the time on the face of the phone. 11:38am. Three minutes gone.

I dialed 911 and got through to the police. I put on a deep voice, partly to disguise my own and partly to sound more threatening, and told the woman at the other end that a bomb at Altabena High School was going to explode at exactly noon.

She asked a couple of questions and seemed calm. Too calm for my liking. She didn't believe me. I had to make her believe me.

"You'd better get those kids out of there or that fucker is going to blow," I said, then hung up. I was trying to sound tough and had no idea how a criminal in this situation would talk.

My heart was pounding. I couldn't fail. Couldn't let all

these lives be lost.

The phone still in my hand, I looked up the number for the school and called it, then pressed zero to get put through to reception. Each second felt like an hour. Finally someone picked up.

I put on the deep voice again, told her there was a bomb planted in the middle of the school and that it was going to explode at exactly noon. Panic in her voice, the receptionist at the other end was falling apart and had trouble putting together a sentence.

"Evacuate the school," I said. "Get everybody out of there."

Which probably wasn't what your average bomber would say but it was the best I could do under pressure.

I checked the time. 11:42am. If only time could stand still while the school was evacuated. I took deep breaths to calm myself. I couldn't let panic take over.

The next time I looked at the phone in my hand, it was 11:43am. No sirens, no one moving, no evacuation taking place. What was taking so long?

Time to take control. I got up, knocked on the door of the first classroom I came to and walked straight in. At the front of the room, the woman teacher turned to look at me and frowned at the interruption.

"Excuse me," I said. "Ms. Di Giorgio has asked me to go from class to class. A bomb has been planted in the school. We have to evacuate immediately."

A murmur rose from the room and I realized there was no way I could make it to every classroom in time, not on my own.

"I need ten students from here to go from class to class and spread the word," I said.

The teacher stood. "Now look here. If there was a bomb–"

Sirens cut through the air, such a magnificent sound, such a relief.

I backed out of the room, heard an announcement being made through the intercom system, but didn't stay to listen. Outside the classroom, I looked at my phone. 11:46. Would fourteen minutes be enough to evacuate fifteen hundred people? I hoped so.

I ran down the corridor while it was still empty and headed toward the front of the school. Students were pouring out of classrooms and heading toward the oval. They weren't moving fast and certainly didn't seem agitated. Probably thought it was a hoax. Still, that was better than mass hysteria.

Walking down the front path away from the school, I remembered my first day here, meeting Lauren, finding Ben, remembered what a supreme dork I'd been when I arrived. It was amazing I could've been a highly trained soldier and yet so clueless.

I felt a twinge of regret at the memories I was leaving behind. I couldn't save the school but I could save the people and that was infinitely more important.

It'd be hard to explain my actions and how I'd warned one class about the bomb before the sirens had gone off. I didn't care. Erratic behavior was better than dead behavior. I'd have to come up with a story, though.

Crossing the road, I strode further up the street to where the bus would soon be pulling up with Ben and the others. I shoved my hands in my pockets and watched the oval filling with people. At the far end, students – hundreds of them – were being led onto the oval away from the school. The further, the better as far as I was concerned.

I looked up the street and saw the school bus coming, so I stepped back to give it plenty of room. This was what I'd been waiting for. Ben.

He was one of the first off the bus. My heart exploded as soon as I laid eyes on him, living and breathing and walking toward me. I ran to his arms, threw myself at him, covered his face with little kisses.

Eventually he held me at arms' length and looked into my eyes. Ben was looking into my eyes. He was alive. A picture of his face as he lay dying flashed before me, made my heart jump to my throat. For a second I was back there in that black place watching the light leave his eyes.

I blinked through the tears. Choked on the lump in my throat. My greatest nightmare turned to a dream-come-true. I had Ben back again. There was so much I wanted to tell him but the words wouldn't come out. Where would I start? How could I begin to tell him how much he meant to me?

"I was so worried about you," he said. "Where were you?"

I couldn't stop staring at him. "I've been everywhere and nowhere."

"Nicola, are you okay?"

He wiped the tears from my cheeks, tears I hadn't even realized were there.

"I'm fine," I said. "Ben, listen to me. The school is being evacuated."

He glanced at the oval filled with bodies. "I can see that. Any idea what's going on?

"A bomb. It's going to explode at exactly noon."

"How do you know?"

"I know a lot of things."

The look on his face told me he thought I was a rambling idiot and maybe I was, but I had to make him understand that I knew exactly what was going to happen.

I said, "On the bus, when the driver drove past the school, some yelled 'Just keep going!'"

Ben eyed me suspiciously. "Someone always yells something stupid."

"Then Mr. Rodriguez said we should all walk because it wouldn't kill us."

His eyes narrowed. "We? How do you know this? You weren't on the bus."

"Any minute now, a yellow car is going to drive past and some guys will be hanging out of it, yelling."

A few moments later, that was exactly what happened.

"Did you see them coming?" he asked.

"I've seen it before, Ben. I've been on this science excursion before and the last time I was here, I watched the school blow up with everyone in it."

"What are you talking about?"

Ben eyed me suspiciously and I couldn't blame him, though I could try to console him. Pulling him closer, I put my arm around him, then saw Lauren and called out to her.

"What's with the outfit?" she said, looking me up and down.

I put my other arm around her and held her tight. The ground beneath our feet rumbled, the kids around us becoming suddenly silent.

A giant roar ripped through the air.

The school exploded before our eyes.

CHAPTER THIRTY-THREE

"The school just blew up," Ben said, his reaction much calmer than the first time around. Perhaps my garbled explanation had done the trick and prepared him for the shock.

"Oh my god, oh my god." Lauren's hand flew to her mouth.

For a few moments, no one said or did anything, just stood there stunned and watched a cloud of pale ash rising from where the school had been. Even though I'd been here before in this same spot at this exact time and had already seen this happen, the magnitude hit me all over again.

Then there was a stirring around us. White ash flew up in the air and floated down, slowly covering us. Girls started screaming. Guys were yelling, some sort of general panic taking place.

Screaming had never sounded so good. This was so much better than the first time around when the terror of hundreds of lives lost started setting in.

A police car pulled up behind the bus. At first I was puzzled because it hadn't been here the first time around, then I realized it must've arrived as a result of my phone call about the bomb.

I pulled Lauren and Ben close to me, the three of us wrapping our arms around each other.

Lauren was sobbing, then managed to get some words out. "The school, all those people, all dead."

"The school has been evacuated," I said. "Everyone was on the oval. Didn't you see them when you got here?"

"I can't remember," she mumbled.

"I saw them," Ben said. "On the oval, just like Nicola said."

Then a voice sailed over the noise as Mr. Rodriguez took control, told us to stay where we were and gave instructions for two students to call for police and paramedics.

That was Mr. Rodriguez, always good in a crisis. Mr. Rodriguez…Dread weighed on me like a lead shroud at the thought of what this good man was going to do in a few days' time. I couldn't think straight, couldn't come up with all the answers at once. I'd have to leave that for now. I had to get through today first.

The next thing we had to do was call our parents to let them know we were okay. I had a phone in my pocket but couldn't use it, not when the police would easily be able to trace the threatening calls to this phone. The poor kid who owned the phone was going to be in a hell of a lot of trouble. At least someone had found him immediately after he'd been mugged so that would work in his favor. Meanwhile, I'd have to dump the phone on my way home.

Sirens in the distance came closer. The area would be cordoned off. We wouldn't be allowed to leave. Or maybe we would. Before, there'd been so few survivors – only those of us who'd been on the science excursion – whereas this time the police had fifteen hundred individuals to deal with. It wouldn't be feasible for them to leave that many people on the school oval.

I looked from Lauren to Ben. "We have to call our parents and let them know we're okay."

She nodded and pulled out her phone, stepping away as if to get some privacy. Ben's phone was in his hand too but he was still trying to take stock of the situation.

"Where's your phone?" he asked.

"I don't have it with me," I said.

"Well, that would explain why you weren't answering all morning." He sounded agitated, suspicious even, and rightly so.

I pulled him to the side away from Lauren and the others. "The bomb…it wasn't a normal bomb."

His face clouded over. "Nicola, you couldn't? You didn't have anything to do with this? Tell me…Please, no."

"No, it wasn't me. I knew the bomb was going off so I made a fake threat, except it wasn't fake. It was real, the bomb, that is."

"I didn't think it was you. I thought…"

I had to stop rambling. "People from the future planted that bomb, not me, not anyone here."

His eyes narrowed. "What about that stuff you were saying before? You knew what kids had said on the bus. You knew more than that too."

"If you watch the news tonight, they'll say this was no normal bomb. They'll tell you it has obliterated matter to the molecular level."

"How do you know all this? How can you be so sure?"

"I've been to New Nation – to the future – then I had

them send me back here, back in time where I belong."

The look on his face would've been hilarious if this wasn't so serious.

*   *   *

It was good to be home, better even than I'd imagined because this was the real thing. I was here now and no one was going to get rid of me.

Dad had come home from work as soon as he got word about the school so the whole family was here, my supposed grandparents included. I guess I had to take the good with the bad.

Outside, Dad told me I was the most beautiful wreck he'd ever seen and wanted reassurance that I hadn't been a hero, all things I'd heard before. A strange sense of *déjà vu* came over me. I'd better get used to this.

"Honey, what are you wearing?" Mom asked after she let me go from the world's longest hug. "What happened to your school uniform?"

"A long story," I said. A really long story.

In the living room, Mom ushered me toward the sofa while April objected because I'd get it dirty. This was bordering on *déjà ridiculous* and I couldn't help but laugh. Meanwhile, my parents probably thought I was delirious.

Michael raced to the kitchen to get me some water, which was much appreciated, as was the fact that I had one 'grandparent' who seemed vaguely normal.

I explained what had happened at school, how it had been evacuated and then the bomb had gone off. I'd heard about injuries – a couple of broken bones from people who stumbled in the crowd on the oval in the panic – but, so far, there was no one who was unaccounted for. No deaths, and that was the main thing.

As I was speaking, I wondered if I should fill my voice with emotion and start sobbing because that was what April expected of me, then decided better of it.

This was me, and she could take it or leave it.

Then came the outrage I knew was coming from April. "How can you be so calm? Why aren't you crying? We haven't even seen you shed a tear."

Mom stood, venom in her voice, and she gave her own mother a mouthful and told her not to question me.

I couldn't believe it. This was even better the second time around! Go Mom! She deserved a hug for that. Dad, too. They deserved a lifetime of hugs.

Maybe it wasn't fair but I had one up on April. I knew her so much better than she knew me.

I cleared my throat. "April, people have different responses to stress and disasters. It's part of being human. The main thing is that no one died, not as far as we know, and no one was seriously injured. You can't imagine how bad this would've been if all those students and teachers had died."

"You're so right, honey," Mom said. "And so mature."

I suspect the last part was directed at April more than me. I also had to remember that for those around me, the school bombing was a huge disaster – and it was – whereas, for me, it was a hell of a lot better than what had happened the first time around.

After spending lots of time reassuring my parents that I was fine, I cleaned myself up and had a long soak in a hot tub, which gave me time to think. My parents hadn't yet told me about the resurgence of Mom's cancer. They wouldn't tell me until tomorrow, however tonight I could act.

In the kitchen, Mom was making burritos, one of my favorite dinners. I couldn't remember the last time I'd eaten and couldn't wait to eat.

"Mom, you need to relax," I said. "You're worried about me and you don't give a second thought to yourself."

She opened her mouth to argue, then probably realized she didn't have a leg to stand on.

"Can I do anything in here?" I asked.

"No, just leave the burrito filling simmering."

Much safer than entrusting me with any actual cooking.

My hand on the small of her back, I ushered her into the living room where the others were sitting. "I'll make a round of drinks for everyone, Mom, you look like you need a margarita."

She dropped down onto the sofa beside Dad. "That'd be wonderful."

"Dad, a gin and tonic?"

He nodded and I turned to the old folks.

"G&Ts for us too, thanks," Michael said, leaving April sitting there open mouthed.

In the kitchen, I found the juicer, squeezed a lime and poured Cointreau and tequila into a shaker, then added the special ingredient. The C-vac was in two capsules, so I opened them up and sprinkled the powder into the mix, hoping the alcohol would cover the taste. Luckily the mixture was already a little cloudy with stringy bits from the lime.

The G&Ts were more straightforward and the orange juice I poured myself from the fridge was even quicker still.

Back in the living room, I handed the drinks around from a tray, then sat down and raised my glass. "To happiness, health and long lives."

I saw Mom's jaw flinch at the word 'health' and Dad put his arm around her. The two of them had no idea. This was going to be the world's healthiest margarita.

April sipped her G&T, looking across at me through hooded lids. "You seem to know a lot about cocktails for someone who's underage."

"That's because of her friend, Lauren," Mom snapped back. "She makes mocktails, and Nicola has seen me make a margarita."

"You shouldn't be drinking at your age, you know," April said to me. "I can't believe you're condoning the use of alcohol like this."

I laughed. As if I was going to get drunk. As if that was something my parents should be worried about.

The suspicious look didn't leave April's face. "Are you sure that's orange juice?"

Mom rolled her eyes at her mother, then turned to me. "This is the best margarita I've ever had."

Shame I wouldn't be able to recreate it. "Well, you're the best mom I've ever had."

My comment brought a smile to Mom's face and a scowl to April's. I hid the ripple of sadness swelling inside me – for another mom back in New Nation, the mother I'd never known, not like this, the mother who was lost to me.

"That's not much of a compliment," April said under her breath.

Mom knocked back a big mouthful of margarita. "Loosen up, Momma! That was a joke. In fact, you can loosen up or leave."

My mom was making me proud. I was going to be leaving after dinner myself. For one thing, I didn't want to watch Bartley on the television telling us how he'd find the people who planted the bomb and how this was the time to band together and become more strict so this would never happen again.

And for another thing, I had to see Ben.

CHAPTER THIRTY-FOUR

"Can you go through this with me one more time?"

Ben was sitting cross-legged on his bed opposite me, his brow furrowed as he tried to take it all in. There'd been a time when Ben's father hadn't wanted us alone together in a room with the door closed. We'd come a long way since then.

"So the bomb had nothing to do with the drone, then?" he asked.

"They were sent by the same people," I said. "Separate incidents."

The drone was done and dusted as far as I was concerned, but I had to remember that even if it was ancient history to me, it was relatively recent for Ben.

"I hear what you're saying," he said. "There's a lot to let sink in."

It was a lot and I hadn't even got to the difficult part yet. I explained how I'd got hold of the geopositrons and arranged to come back to Altabena to a time before the bomb went off.

"And your mom," Ben said. "While you were away, you stole some cancer vaccine for her? Wow, you were busy."

"Ben, I need you to believe me."

I stared into his eyes, looking for the Ben who was determined and deep and intelligent. He had to be in there somewhere.

"I'm not making this up," I said. "If I was going to make something up, I'd make it glamorous or funny or something that made me look good. At the very least, I'd make it believable!"

"I'm trying, Nicola," he said. "Truly I am."

I edged closer to him and took his hands into mine. "There's something else I haven't told you yet. In a few days, Mr. Rodriguez is going to take a turn for the worse. He'll be implanted with a kill chip."

Ben's eyes widened. "Is that what I think it is?"

I nodded. "He was programmed to kill you."

Shock in his eyes. "Me?"

"And Mr. Rodriguez succeeded. It wasn't his fault. He was programmed to do it and had no control or choice."

Ben lowered his gaze, staring at our intertwined hands. "Did I...die? Are you telling me I'm going to die?"

"Look at me, Ben." I waited until he met my gaze. "I'm telling you I know exactly when Mr. Rodriguez is going to do it. We can stop him. We have to stop him. I'm not going to let this happen."

I let the silence between us linger.

Eventually he spoke. "That was why you left, wasn't it?"

I nodded.

I left because I love you. The words I couldn't say. I wrapped my arms around him and he hugged me back. Finally, I was getting through to him.

"We have to stop Mr. Rodriguez," I said.

"Is there anything we can do to stop the chip being implanted?" he asked.

"That's out of our hands."

"Can we change the program?"

"Once it's implanted, there's no way of altering the chip, not that I know of. Mr. Rodriguez won't stop until he's completed what he's programmed to do."

I truly hoped Ben didn't ask me if he should kill Mr. Rodriguez before the teacher killed him. Or whether I should do it. Could I kill him in self-defense? Could I kill for Ben? All questions I didn't want answered.

"Can we surgically remove the damn thing?" Ben asked.

"It'll be embedded in his brain. I don't know exactly where."

That was the whole problem. There were so many things I didn't know.

Ben cupped my jaw in his hands and pulled me closer. He pressed his lips against mine and kissed me tenderly while I wondered where on earth this had come from.

Then I realized the kiss had come from his heart. This was my Ben.

He took my hand and we lay together on the bed facing each other. He pushed back some loose strands of hair that had fallen over my face, then took both of my hands into his and held them close to his chest. I'd never felt as close to him as I did at that moment.

"Despite everything," he said. "I'm glad you've told me."

I hadn't been completely honest. It wasn't fair that he'd opened his heart to tell me his innermost thoughts and now he didn't even know about it. I didn't want to have one up on him.

"There's more," I said. "Soon after the school disaster, we needed time together and had a wonderful, intimate evening, just the two of us."

Ben's eyes widened. "We had sex!"

"No," I said calmly. "That's not what I meant."

He grinned that magnificent grin of his. "Just as well. It'd be pretty tragic if we made love and I couldn't even remember."

"You told me something you'd never said before, and you deserve to know what that was." The look on his face told me he had an inkling what I was going to say, so I continued. "You said you were afraid I'd leave you, that I'd get killed, that I'd disappear one day, go back to New Nation. And part of the reason you're afraid is because that's exactly what your mom did. She left you."

Ben's eyes glimmered with emotion. "How could you know?"

"Because everything I've said tonight is the truth. Because you told me."

"Okay, this is freaking me out a bit," Ben said. "I actually opened up and said those things?"

"The champagne may have helped."

"We had champagne?"

I nodded.

"I can't believe I came out with that stuff," he said. "Out loud, I mean."

Which was exactly why I had to come clean about everything now.

I cupped his chin in my hand and pulled him close. "You don't have to be afraid, Ben. I'll always come back."

He kissed me again, softy, tenderly, exactly the way I needed.

I wasn't sure if it had sunk in completely that I had risked my life to go back to New Nation so I could save him. That I loved him so much I'd have done whatever it took. That I was taking the biggest risk of all.

Because I loved him.

CHAPTER THIRTY-FIVE

Reece paced the floor in his basement while Ben and I lounged around on beanbags and tried to pretend this was perfectly normal.

Reece stopped, hands on his hips. "Tell me again about the generals. You're sure they're dead?"

"Very sure. I saw it happen."

Deep in thought, he bit his lower lip.

"You didn't mention this to me last night," Ben said.

"You had a lot to take in," I replied.

"What about Reece?"

"The two of us grew up in the same place. He spent years there as a soldier." Ben had been jealous of Reece before, but he sure as hell had no reason to have those feelings now. "We can't do this on our own, Ben."

"I knew it," Reece said. "As soon as I watched the news and they started talking about destruction on a molecular level." I raised my eyebrows in disbelief, so he added, "Okay, I didn't know the bit about how you'd gone back in time. I was only starting to work things out."

Ben had sunk deep into his beanbag. "So as soon as Nicola started talking, this all seemed logical and believable?"

Reece looked at Ben as if he were an idiot. "Of course I believed her. Why would she make this up? Besides, everything she has said fits perfectly. She wouldn't be able to make up a story that good." Glancing at me, he added, "No offence."

"None taken," I said. "We've got a big problem with Mr. Rodriguez."

Reece dropped down to the sofa. "The question is what are we going to do about it? We can't kill him."

"Lock him up," I said.

"Forever?" Reece asked.

I shrugged. "Got any other ideas?"

"You went to the future," Reece said. "Couldn't you have brought back a scrambler or a deprogramming device?"

"That's it!" Ben tried to lean forward in the beanbag, then gave up and shifted to the floor. "That's the answer. An EMP weapon."

"A weapon?" I said. "That sounds deadly."

"Weapon is a bad word," Ben said. "An electromagnetic pulse device. It creates an instantaneous burst of high power that damages electronic devices. Turns computers to toast."

I felt suddenly hopeful. "Really?"

"Sure. I've read about how they're a potential terrorist weapon, where our computers and electronic devices could end up useless and then there'd be complete chaos. Pretty clever really."

"Are you sure it'll work?"

Ben nodded. "It's pretty simple, really. You need an iron core, a coil of copper wire and a power source. We've just got to make sure the burst of power is a high enough voltage to do the job."

"I can help," Reece offered.

Ben ignored him.

"What about Mr. Rodriguez?" I asked.

"Oh, he'll be fine. That's the beauty of it. Electromagnetic pulses disable electronics but they're completely harmless to humans."

Then maybe Ben would be 'fine' too. He was alive and I wanted to make sure he stayed that way. I threw my arms around him, knocking us both onto the carpet, which was dirty but I didn't care.

"Come on, guys," Reece said. "Give me a break."

I dusted my jeans off and sat back on the beanbag. Ben snuggled up beside me which probably wasn't what Reece wanted.

"What was it like back in New Nation?" Reece asked.

I wasn't sure where to start. "Exactly the same, only different because I was seeing it through new eyes after living here."

The doorbell rang from upstairs, faint but definite.

"Are you expecting anyone?" I asked.

"Yeah, Lauren, Will and Dominique," Reece said.

I screwed up my face "What? Like a party? At a time like this."

He stood. "How was I supposed to know?"

I was still annoyed. While Reece went to the door, Ben mumbled bits and pieces about electromagnetic fields and power bursts and I felt more hopeful than I had since I'd got back.

Dominique sauntered into the room. Wearing black jeans and a fitted red sweater, she made the most casual outfit look glamorous.

"Where is everyone?" she asked while the others came down the stairs behind her. "I thought there were going to be more people."

"It's just us," Reece said on his way to the fridge.

Looking down her nose, Dominique sat on the edge of a chair while Lauren and Will took over one end of the sofa. Reece placed beers and cokes on the coffee table.

"Help yourselves," he said.

"I can't drink that stuff," Dominique said. "Not while I'm training."

"I've got just the thing." Reece handed her a bottle of Perrier, earning a smile for his trouble. He seemed pretty pleased at the result as he sat at the other end of the sofa not far from her. Predictably, we talked about school and the bomb. Although Will still had a school to go to, he'd taken the day off to be with Lauren.

"I'm a bit freaked." Dominique bit her lower lip, then added, "It's already interfering with my training. I've got to focus."

Reece went all doe eyed which looked slightly ridiculous under all that hair. "Focus on me."

She screwed up her nose. "What?"

"Focus on being free," he said. "Free of school."

"Not for long." Will put his arm around Lauren. "Soon, we'll be at school together."

"What are you talking about?" Reece asked.

"Seniors from Altabena High are being squeezed into classes with us at Hamilton. Meanwhile juniors are being bussed to other schools and they're setting up makeshift classrooms for the other kids at various places around town."

We were going to Hamilton. My breath caught in my throat. Mr. Rodriguez would be there too, I was sure.

"That'll be fun," Dominique said with maximum sarcasm. "Apparently the martial arts event has been postponed two weeks."

As if I cared. That was the least of my worries. Dominique got up, sauntered toward me, crouched down and tried to get me in a rear naked choke. I saw it coming, slipped out of her grasp and got to my feet, my hands out. She was standing now too, her hands on her hips, head tilted as she considered me.

"I'm going to annihilate anyone who gets in my way." Dominique pointed a finger at me. "I am so going to kick your ass."

"Take it easy," Ben said to her. He'd got up and reached across for my hand.

"I didn't train this hard to be Number Two," she said. "I'm the best and I'm going to come out on top. Total domination."

"Yeah, I know, it's gonna be a war." I rolled my eyes because I'd heard it all before. "Geez, Dominique, you've seen too many pre-fight interviews."

"Is that what you think?"

There was no glimmer of self-doubt in her stance or her eyes, but I knew what lay beneath that exterior. I knew her much better than she thought.

At that moment, I decided to throw the fight and let her win the tournament and martial arts contest. It was no skin off my nose. Besides, I'd already won in every way that mattered. I squeezed Ben's hand as the two of us sank back into the beanbag.

Reece couldn't take his eyes off Dominique. "I admire

a girl with guts and determination."

"Puh-lease!" Will said. "Are you trying to make us all vomit?"

As if to make a point, Dominique slid onto the sofa beside Reece, her long legs butting up against his as she leaned in close. Her expression was smug, her eyes narrowing as she stared at Will. She made me want to hit her, then I remembered my vow and also the damaged Dominique who'd bared her soul to me that day. If I was going to hit her, it could wait.

Will nudged Dominique who in turn bumped into Reece. "Lauren's got some news too."

"Not exactly news," Lauren said. "It's a bit tacky really."

"What is?" I asked.

"Pulse Magazine wants me to write an article – the student who saw the school blow up before her eyes, that sort of thing."

I raised my eyebrows. "Pulse Magazine asked you?"

I could give her a few insights to add to the story, except they'd be too incriminating and unbelievable to anyone who read them.

She shrugged. "I'm worried about other stuff that's going on. I don't want to get busted or called to the principal's office or anything else."

Lauren had to stand up to authority. We all did. I hadn't been supportive the first time around, but things were different now. We didn't have the mammoth loss of life and the government wouldn't succeed in trying to tighten the reins. Not yet anyway. It was too soon.

"You've got to be true to yourself," I said. "Write an honest story. They can't throw you in jail. Can't even expel you because you don't have a school any more. Besides, you can go to the media. Hell, you *are* the media."

Lauren's eyes lit up. "Yeah, I am the media! Except that's such bad grammar. How can I, singular, be the media which is plural?"

I held my fist in the air. "That's my girl, Lauren! Not afraid to be a word nerd in the face of adversity."

"Your mom will be behind you," Will said.

Lauren put on the annoyed face she used when talking about her mother. "She's already involved in another protest. Bartley's calling the school bombing a war on terror but Mom says the government is waging war on the people and that he has no right to get strict and introduce more rules."

"Your mom's right," I said at great risk of cheesing Lauren off even more.

It made me think about my own mom. Dad had panicked and taken her straight to the doctor this morning after she came down with flu-like symptoms. Meanwhile, I'd been secretly pleased because I knew it was only the C-vac doing its business. They hadn't told me about Mom's cancer yet and maybe they'd never need to.

"Hope you don't mind." Ben stood. "I need to get going."

I reached for his hand and he helped me up.

"Me too," I said.

If Ben had to go home and build an EMP weapon, I had to go with him. Wedged into a corner of the sofa with Dominique, Reece looked like he didn't want to move, so we saw ourselves out.

Ben was racing to his car, more determined than I'd seen him in a long time. 'Complacent' was a word from the past.

I grabbed his arm when we reached the car. "I know what's on your mind. What can I do to help?"

"Nothing." He looked at me blankly. "I'm fine."

"Come on, what do you need to build this EMP thing? Is there anything I can get hold of for you, something from the science lab maybe?"

He shook his head. "No drama. I can get everything I need from a hardware store."

"Remember what I said. You can't do this on your own."

"I'm not." He opened the car door for me. "I might need a hand from Lorenzo or Daniel. The theory behind this is pretty simple but I have to get the voltage right, and they're both into science and computing, experts in the field."

"Oh."

He put his arm around me. "You're a different sort of smart. You're Number One when it comes to beating people up and saving lives but science isn't really your thing."

I hated it when he was right.

CHAPTER THIRTY-SIX

It was just the way I remembered it. The end of the day, the same classroom, same kids in the class, same teacher at the front. Mr. Rodriguez was seated behind the desk at the front of the room, as cool as ever with the new pencil thin moustache he was sporting. He didn't look like a killer. He looked like a nice guy, probably because that's what he was.

I thought about the damage he'd caused, the slash of the knife, the blood flow and pushed the image away. This wasn't the time for a flashback. I had to be alert. If the EMP device didn't work, I'd have to take drastic action.

No, that was not going to happen. I wouldn't let it.

Mr. Rodriguez wandered to the back of the class where we were seated and asked if Ben would stay at the end of the lesson. Despite the gentle smile on his face, his left eye was twitching uncontrollably. It had to be the chip, affecting that one small part of his nervous system.

He placed his hand on Ben's shoulder, shifting his gaze to me. *Act natural.* My heart pounded as I smiled right back and the teacher wandered away again.

Only a few more minutes now.

Time would've passed faster if I could concentrate on the reading Mr. Rodriguez had set for us but there was no way that was going to happen when there was an EMP device in my backpack at the foot of my chair. I'd been expecting something that looked like a gun or a bomb. Instead it looked like an iron core with a bunch of copper wire wrapped around it. Which is exactly what it was. It was powered by a not-so-big battery and a huge capacitor that provided a burst of high voltage. I'd have to get close – that was the part that worried me – because this thing only worked short range.

I kept surveying my surroundings, ready to pounce if needed, though I was torn. If something went wrong, would I flick the switch on the EMP device in my bag and hope for the best or throw myself between Ben and the knife?

I'd never been one for hoping for the best. Instead, I was hyper-aware, blood pumping to my muscles, chemicals surging through my body.

Finally, the bell went. While the other kids left, Ben took his time gathering his books and laptop, glancing up at the teacher from time to time.

I made my way to the front of the class, the bag in my hand. Reece came in, not worried about the flow of students leaving the room. He took the backpack. Knew what to do.

We'd talked about this before. I was the bodyguard. I'd protect Ben with my life. I didn't trust Reece to do that. His job was to flick the switch.

"You can get going, Nicola," Mr. Rodriguez said.

I wasn't going anywhere. "I've got a question, sir."

He swatted the back of his neck though there were no

flies in the room. Was that where the chip had been implanted?

"Nicola, this isn't the time," he said. "I need to speak to Ben."

This was the perfect time.

"Now!" I yelled.

Lauren called out to me from the doorway.

I didn't even look. "Wait outside, Lauren."

"Reece, what are you doing here?" Mr. Rodriguez asked without turning to look at him. His eyes were glued to Ben who was slowly making his way to the front of the room.

The teacher's left eye was still twitching like crazy. It made my heart race faster.

The room was quiet now as he said, "It would be better if the rest of you left."

"Ben, go," I said.

The teacher glanced at me, then reached down to his shoe. I didn't catch a glimpse of silver. I didn't need to.

"Reece, now!" I yelled.

No boom, no explosion, no sudden movement. A click or a crackle perhaps and I could've sworn there was a sizzle in the air.

Mr. Rodriguez pulled at the bottom of his trousers as if they'd been creased, then straightened. No knife, not that I could see. He had a dazed look in his eyes, eyes that were still. No twitching.

Ben, Reece and I didn't move. Lauren was probably still standing in the doorway.

The teacher put his hands on his hips. "What are you all doing standing around here?"

His words were so inane it almost felt like an anticlimax. I was still waiting for a bomb or a fireball to go off.

Mr. Rodriguez eyed us suspiciously. "Is something going on?"

This was definitely the teacher we knew, our Mr. Rodriguez, the same man he'd always been.

"No, we were just..." I couldn't come up with anything.

"Leaving," Ben said.

"Good, because I need to..." Mr. Rodriguez looked at his watch. "It's stopped. What's happened to this thing?"

"Let's go." I grabbed my bag.

Ben headed for the door, Reece and I following close behind. Lauren was still standing in the doorway, her eyes glued to the phone in her hand, a look of disgust on her face.

"This thing is toast," she said. "Just a black screen. It was fine a minute ago."

I grabbed her arm, dragging her away. "Come on."

"Hey," Mr. Rodriguez called out. "My phone's not working either. What's going on?"

The three of us dragged Lauren down the hallway, protesting and complaining all the way. We let her shake us off after we got out of the door.

"Nicola, what is wrong with you!" She glared at me. "My phone's out of action. This is a major disaster."

The EMP had worked. It had disabled the kill chip as well as nearby electronic devices. Our phones and laptops would be toast too and I couldn't be happier about it. Lauren might be pissed off but Ben and Reece looked relieved.

I gazed at Lauren, then put my arm around her shoulder while she gave me something resembling a death stare. I reached out to Ben with my other arm and Reece joined us in a group hug.

Disgusted, Lauren pushed us away. "What is with you guys?"

I was grinning. "This is the best disaster ever."

CHAPTER THIRTY-SEVEN

"How did you know this was my favorite?" Mom asked, staring at the cake on the table.

"Chocolate cake is every woman's favorite," Ben said.

I'd stood in this exact same spot at another time, about a hundred years ago, when Ben had baked a cake for my sick mother. It wasn't exactly *déjà vu*. This was *déjà*-slightly-different.

Mom had been sick for several days and was feeling much better as of yesterday. She and Dad hadn't yet told me about her cancer diagnosis but no doubt they would and when they did, I'd be a rock, not the huge mess I'd been last time. Then they could tell me how the cancer was subsiding, a medical miracle, something not even the doctors could explain. And I could pretend to be surprised.

"You've clearly been very well raised," April said to Ben, then winked at me. "I think this one's a keeper."

I was starting to win April over – 'starting' being the operative word. She didn't have to like me but she was beginning to get used to having me around whether she liked it or not.

291

Mom gave Ben an appreciative kiss on the cheek before we left. As he opened the car door for me, I saw a bunch of flowers on the back seat and a single rose on the dashboard and wondered what was going on.

In the car, he passed across the red rose tied with a white ribbon and kissed me. Beaming, I thanked him.

"A rose by any name would smell as sweet," he said.

"That's a beautiful quote," I said though I had no idea what Shakespeare had to do with anything.

"There's something I've wondered," he said. "Is your name really Nicola? Back in New Nation, I mean."

"Yes, I've always been Nicola, always the same person."

He started the engine and pulled away. "Actually, you've changed a lot since you got here."

"For the better, I hope."

"Absolutely."

"So where are we going?" I asked.

He pulled up at a red light. "I'm taking you to meet someone."

"Who?"

"That's what you'll find out, but be prepared. It's not what you think."

We'd had this discussion before and Ben was maintaining his mysterious exterior. I'd told him all about how romantic our champagne picnic had been, and he'd insisted he was not predictable or boring or repetitive. A champagne picnic would definitely not be happening, but something would.

I wasn't sure what to make of it when he pulled up outside the Altabena Cemetery. We'd been here last year for a completely different reason. I could be fairly sure we wouldn't be incinerating a PR device today.

Ben took my hand as we headed up the path and made our way past the gravestones. He had the posy of flowers in his hand and as far as I knew, he'd only had one person in his life pass away. I didn't speak, didn't break the silence. That was Ben's to break if and when the time came.

Eventually we stopped in front of his mother's grave. Heather Tanner. Ben had refused to visit his mother's grave in recent years or at least that's what he'd said.

He let go of my hand and crouched down to place the flowers at the foot of the stone. "It's been a while, Mom. I came to say I forgive you. And that I'm sorry too."

As he stood, I reached out to put my arm around him and he drew me close while we both stood looking down at the grave. He was trembling.

"I love you, Mom." Ben's voice cracked. "And I always will. Goodbye."

We walked away slowly.

"Are you okay?" I asked.

"Better than I have been in a long time, actually. I don't want to hold a grudge any more. I'm tired of being stuck in the past."

"I'm glad, Ben."

"It always felt as if she'd *chosen* to go. Now I don't think she had much of a choice. She was sick. She had depression. Sure, she killed herself but she wouldn't have done that if she'd been healthy."

"Have you been thinking about her a lot lately?" I asked.

He stopped under a maple tree, holding both of my hands in his. "I've been thinking about people who left me. And people who came back."

"I'm here, Ben. I'm not going anywhere."

He flashed that million dollar grin. "If you leave again, can you take me with you?"

I pressed a quick kiss to his lips. "I'm here to stay."

"That's what I like to hear."

"But now you're taking me somewhere, aren't you? That's what you said."

He took my hand and we ambled down the path again.

"You told me about that romantic dinner and the champagne and picnic," he said.

"Yes."

"Well, 'romantic' would be boring and predictable, so we're going to ditch that idea. I'm taking you to Cha Cha Grill."

Now this was a surprise. "We're having burgers?"

"I happen to think burgers are extremely romantic." Putting his arm around me, he pulled me close. "'Romantic' isn't about where you are. It's about how you feel on the inside."

"Well, you make me feel good," I said.

He made me feel a lot of things.

I had Ben back and nothing was going to change that.

INFILTRATION (BOOK 1)

2120: A world ravaged by a devastating virus. Those healthy enough to live in New Nation lead a sanitized, orderly life where everything is tightly guarded by a brutal government. Lives, thoughts, information and emotions are all strictly controlled.

Now: Seventeen-year-old elite soldier Nicola Gray is sent back in time for an important assignment. She alone will stop the virus before it takes over the world – her mission, to gather intelligence, find the cause and stop the threat, whatever it takes.

She is trained to kill.

But the past is not what Nicola is expecting. Overwhelmed by an alien world, she discovers feelings she can't handle and a world with immense personal freedom and people who care for each other. She wants to stay. She wants to live. She wants a lot of things she can't have...

VALIDATION (BOOK 3)

School's out for Nicola Grey but just as the party is about to begin, she is hauled back to the future to brutal New Nation. Suddenly she's hailed as a hero of the people when that's the last thing she wants and this is the last place she wants to be. *How did things go so wrong?*

Nicola is desperate to get back where she belongs – with boyfriend Ben, in the past. But that isn't going to happen, not when millions will die in a world decimated by a deadly virus, her country ruled by a despotic regime. Unless she can stop it.

It's Nicola versus New Nation. She has to change the future and save the world.

PARALLAX ERROR

Coming early 2018

One girl. Two lives. No way back...

Sasha Pierce is the school nerd – bullied, abused and alone.
Alienation takes on a whole new dimension when a global
glitch catapults her into an alternate universe. And into the
body of an elite military bodyguard.

Suddenly she's a ripped, ultra-honed, teenage fighting
machine. Except that inside she is still the same Sasha,
flung into a body and a world she can barely comprehend.
All she wants is to go home and she is ready to risk life
and limb to return. There will be no second chances. This
will be the biggest fight of her life.

ABOUT THE AUTHOR

Susanna Rogers is the author of kick butt books for young adults. She also writes romance and at one point moved to a life of crime – you might be seeing more of that. She loves writing young adult, partly because she's an overgrown teenager and partly because she can write the kick butt heroines she adores. She's also a kickboxer and dreams of empowering girls and guys around the globe to believe in themselves, to take care and follow their own dreams.

Susanna believes in love and kicking ass and a little bit of murder here and there.

She would love to hear from you – susannarogers.com.

If you like her books, please post a review on Amazon or Goodreads. She'd like that a lot.